BLINK

Also by K.L. Slater

Safe With Me

BLINK

K.L. SLATER

bookouture

Published by Bookouture
An imprint of StoryFire Ltd.
23 Sussex Road, Ickenham, UB10 8PN
United Kingdom

www.bookouture.com

ISBN: 978-1-78681-129-5
eBook ISBN: 978-1-78681-122-8

To Mama,
Who never doubted I could do it.

BEFORE

You don't know this, but I watch you. I watch you a lot.

And when you spend a lot of time observing someone, you often wish you could give them advice, tell them where they're going wrong.

Unfortunately, you are the sort of person who always knows best.

The kind of person that carries on your merry way each and every day, oblivious to the danger that is right in front of your very face.

Despite this, I would like very much to share something with you – as you would a friend, if you like. Even though I acknowledge you have no idea that it is possible to feel so much pain . . . yet.

Here is what I would like to tell you; it's a simple thing.

When you first realise your child is gone, you will think it is the worst time.

Very quickly, there will come a sort of seeping feeling, like your very life blood is oozing out and there is nothing, nothing at all, that you can do about it.

You will feel it flowing away and it simply cannot be stopped. But by then, you have stopped caring about yourself.

For you only care about her, your baby.

Forty-eight hours. This is the approximate length of time you will teeter on the edge of madness, still somehow believing it is possible to wish things back to how they were.

You will stay awake for days, until they sedate you, and each time you stir from your drugged slumber, there will be one – just the one, single second – when you open your eyes and think everything is alright again. One single second when you believe it has all been just a terrible figment of your imagination.

And then you will think that *this* must the worst time.

And it is almost exactly this time that hope begins to crumble.

It slides slightly at first and then it gathers momentum and then suddenly hope crashes away from you. If hope is like the softest snow, then the dread that replaces it is the razor-sharp ice that will slash and pare your very soul to ribbons.

And everyone you know, every single person, they all say the exact same thing.

They say, 'Whatever happens, you must *never* lose hope.'

But it is too late for such cautionary words because hope has *already gone*. It has completely gone.

This truly feels like the worst time. But it soon becomes apparent that you are so, so wrong.

For one day very soon, you will wake up to the realisation that the horror has only just begun.

PART I

CHAPTER 1

Present Day

Queen's Medical Centre, Nottingham

Tick tock, tick tock, goes the clock.

It sits neatly on the wall, just at the periphery of my vision.

At the other side of my bed there is a pool of light, a window. I can detect a soft, muted mass there. I think it might be the colour green. It brushes gently against the glass, whispering, when everything else in this small, white room is still and silent.

There are voices, footsteps. I hear them just outside the door.

The two doctors step inside the room and I strain to catch their movements, a blur of white. They come every day at about this time, when the light is a little softer. This is how I know it is the afternoon.

My heart pulses faster. Will this be the time they notice I am still here behind the invisible, soundproof partition that now separates me from the real world?

To them, I am in a *vegetative state*, lying on the narrow bed, eyes wide open, frozen. Still as a corpse.

But inside my head I am standing tall, hammering my splayed fingers and flat palms against the non-existent glass. Screaming to be let out.

Look at me, I yell. *Look at me!*

But they hardly ever do. Look at me, that is. They talk about me, observe me from a distance, but they don't touch me or look me in the eyes.

If they did, a doctor or a nurse might see the slightest flicker of an eyelash, an almost imperceptible tremor of a finger. Dear God, even the cleaner might spot a spark of life if she'd only *look* at me occasionally.

'It's the cruellest thing,' the female doctor says softly, taking a step closer to my bed. 'That she still looks so alive, I mean.'

I am alive, I scream. *I AM alive.*

I summon every ounce of effort and determination I have in me and send it to the hand that lies motionless on top of the pale blue blanket. My left hand. The hand they can see because it is right in front of their unobservant faces.

All I have to do is move a finger, shift my palm. A millimetre of movement, a mere twitch would be enough. If they could only spot it.

Anything that can tell them I am very much still here. Frozen solid, but very much alive. A prisoner, buried inside my own flesh.

'There's nothing left of her, she's just a shell,' the male doctor states quietly. 'It's been that way since the day she had the stroke.'

'I don't envy you,' the woman sighs. 'You'll have to speak to the family soon.'

'There is no family,' he replies. 'We don't know who she is yet.'

The door opens again, and then closes.

The footsteps walk away and the room falls quiet.

Now the only sound that fills the room is the raspy sigh of the ventilator that is keeping me alive. And in between each raspy sigh, there is silence.

I can't breathe without one machine. I can't swallow without another.

Breathe, I tell myself. *This can't be real. It can't be happening.*

But it is. It is happening.
And it's very, very real.

What I can still do is think. And I can remember. Somehow, I can remember the past with a clarity I didn't possess before.

Yet I know instinctively that if I remember too much, too soon, the pain will be too intense and I will close down completely. And then what will happen to my beautiful girl?

Everyone gave up on Evie some time ago. The official police line is that it continues to be an open case and any new information will be investigated, but I know they're not actively pursuing new leads, because they haven't got any.

No evidence, no sightings. Nothing.

For months after it happened, I slavishly read all of the comments people posted underneath the online news reports. They talked as if they had personal knowledge about Evie's 'terrible, neglectful mother' and her 'unhappy home'.

Others openly discussed how Evie could possibly just disappear like that. Everyone an expert.

European paedophile rings, a child serial killer, Romany travellers passing through – all those terrible theories of how and why Evie had gone. I'd heard them all.

Eventually, and without exception, they all wrote Evie off.

Not me. I have chosen to believe that Evie is still alive, that somewhere out there, she is living and breathing. I have to hold on to that.

That's why I must not panic. Even though I cannot move a muscle or utter a sound, there has to be a way for me to help them find her, save her, while I can still remember everything so clearly.

There is only one thing for it: I must think back, right to the very beginning.

Way back, to before it even happened.

CHAPTER 2

Three Years Earlier

Toni

The stark, bare walls of the new house were smooth and cold, like exposed bone. Nothing to flesh them out. The whole place was just a slew of empty packaging, devoid of any content or character at all.

One big smudge of magnolia eggshell. Definitely not mood-inspiring – unless you counted misery and dread.

Yes, it was clean and functional, but I had always loved *colour*.

I'd relished the plentiful space of our old living room with its big bay window, and the feature wall of turquoise and black paisley wallpaper that had taken me over a week to choose; a week living with wallpaper samples taped to the chimney breast and all three of us having a different opinion before agreeing on the same design.

I glanced around the walls, the skirting boards, the tiny hallway and the clutch of minuscule rooms beyond. As if I might have missed the charm of the place the first ten times I'd looked around.

I felt as if my life had been bleached of colour and texture, like my very soul had been daubed an insipid magnolia shade, inside and out.

I turned away and stood at the small window which looked out on the damp patch of scuffed grass. The letting agent had had the audacity to call it a 'front garden'. What a laugh that was.

Weeds choked the slender borders and dandelions sprouted between the paving slabs in awkward, impractical places, buffeted by the cool breeze and swaying like drunken soldiers.

I turned away from the window and looked around the room. Piled up in the corner were a few cardboard boxes and over-stuffed bin bags. The sum total of the last eight years of our lives.

All the good times and the bad times were documented in those bags; sentimental items tangled up together and packed in tightly so nothing moved, so nothing else could slip.

A burst of laughter, bright faces and family times filled my head and then were gone, like the brief flash of an old celluloid film before it finally dies. Perhaps one day I'd manage to unravel it all, smooth out the fine, knotted threads of everything that went wrong. Finally make sense of why the nightmare had happened to *us*.

Maybe then I'd have a chance of sleeping again.

A noise at the door made me start but I turned to see it was only Mum, her face worn and lined, her wiry frame too rigid and tense. Her energy and drive to get things done was enviable, but now it stuck in my side like a blunt needle, constantly reminding me of my own inadequacies.

She frowned at me, seeing the truth with her special mother's X-ray eyes. 'Leave no time for thinking, isn't that what we said?'

She clapped her hands and there I was, ten years old again with Mum demanding I hurry up and get dressed before I miss the school bus.

If only it were that simple, I'd willingly transport myself back there. What I'd give to have another go at life, make some better decisions.

'Fancy a cuppa?'

ided, watching as Mum walked over to the boxes and
the handwritten labels.

I caught sight of my handbag sitting there on the floor, where
I'd left it while I humped in bin bag after bin bag from the boot of
the car. I moved forward and reached past Mum to pick up the bag.

'Just need to check my phone,' I muttered as she turned to
watch me.

I didn't root around for the phone, but stood stock-still, hugging the handbag to my chest like a prize.

Mum looked at me for a long moment.

'What?' I challenged.

She broke her gaze, sighed and pulled open a box, effortlessly
plucking out the kettle and two mugs she'd shrouded in bubble
wrap.

'Tea,' she announced, disappearing back into the kitchen.

I hated deceiving Mum. But then, deceit was probably too
strong a word. What I was doing didn't affect her in the least. It
was more a case of me not telling her every last thing.

After all, at thirty-five years of age, I was more than entitled
to make my own decisions without involving my mother. That's
what I told myself anyway.

It was true I had a lot to thank Mum for.

After months of deliberations and dithering, she had persuaded me to up sticks from Hemel Hempstead and move Evie to
Nottingham, closer to her, to make a fresh start.

I'd always thought it was an overused phrase: *make a fresh
start*. You could say it so quickly and easily, but in reality it took
months to plan and sort everything out. And even then, there
was still masses left to do.

Still, I had already arranged for Evie to start at the local, Of-
sted-rated 'good' school, St Saviour's Primary, at the beginning
of term.

Like Mum said, it was important to keep her educational upheaval to a minimum.

Somehow, I'd muddle through and try to do my best for my daughter. For our now less-than-perfect family.

'Evie is really excited about starting her new school,' Mum called from the kitchen. 'She was chatting to me about it this morning before I dropped her off at playgroup.'

A spike of conscience jabbed me in the guts. I hadn't yet had time to sit down and talk to Evie properly about all the change, what with selling and renting houses and making all the necessary moving arrangements, as well as trying to settle Andrew's medical bills with the insurance company. It had all been a nightmare.

But I was pleased to hear Mum say Evie was excited.

'I've made an appointment to look around the school tomorrow afternoon at two,' I called back to Mum. 'If you fancy it, you could have a run over with us.'

She groaned.

'I've got my osteopathy appointment. I had to cancel it last week, remember, because of collecting your keys?' I received the barb loud and clear. 'I don't think he'd appreciate me doing the same tomorrow, but I do want to know *all* about it when you get back.'

Though Mum was fond of reminding me how much she helped me and Evie out, truthfully, I don't quite know what I'd have done without her. How I'd have got through, after Andrew died.

Eighteen months ago, they'd called him back to Afghanistan for an urgent mission. A 'special operation', his sergeant had called it, attaching status with a few meaningless words as if Andrew ought to be grateful – honoured, even.

He had been both of those things.

I'd wished desperately that this time, by some miracle, he wouldn't want to leave Evie and me. But as soon as I broached the subject, Andrew had said simply, 'It's my duty.'

And I knew that meant the subject was closed.

He didn't know it then, neither did I, but in that single moment he had indelibly sealed his fate. He had sealed all of our fates.

I knew Andrew loved us but he loved his job and his country too. And me and Evie, well, we never really stood a chance from the moment he got called up.

Andrew was already estranged from his remaining family when I met him, due to some terrible family argument from years ago that was still alive and kicking. I'd tried to reach out to his dad and brother after the accident, offering to take Evie, who they'd never met, to Liverpool to visit them. I never received a reply.

After the accident, Mum had helped us financially, even though, since her partner Brian had died three years earlier, she hadn't a great deal of money to spare herself. We'd been through years of hell and worry with Dad's heart problems before his eventual death. Then two years after Dad had died, Mum had met Brian at her local rambling group and we thought she'd found a new shot at happiness. Sadly, within six months, Brian had been diagnosed with terminal cancer and Mum had had to go through it all again.

Sometimes, it was hard to fight the feeling that, basically, life just sucked.

CHAPTER 3

Present Day

Queen's Medical Centre

I stare up at the blank, white ceiling, momentarily absorbed in how the cheap eggshell paint reflects the shards of light that arrow in from the window, turning them into lasers.

It's the same view 24/7, unless somebody or something decides to change it. Yesterday, a black fly crawled across the vast whiteness of the space above me. It stopped directly in my line of sight and proceeded to clean its front legs.

The longer I stared, the closer it seemed to be, magnifying itself until I became convinced I could clearly see its iridescent, compound eyes and its sucking mouthparts.

I was utterly revolted but completely unable to stop looking at the useless thing. Until I remembered that the fly could do more for itself than I can.

There is no fly here today; it must have taken off. Flown to its freedom, bored of my hopelessness.

I search my mind for clues of what happened to me. How I ended up here.

Unlike my body, my memories are alive. I can feel them, hovering in the back of my mind, just waiting to be captured.

* * *

It had been just an ordinary evening at home. I remember watching TV and walking into the kitchen to make a hot drink.

I was probably thinking about the things I needed to do before I could go to bed. Stack the dishwasher, turn off the lamps, organise Evie's clothes for the morning, when the kettle slipped from my hand.

The boiling water splashed onto my arm and I screamed.

Everything sounded so loud. The noise from the TV and the kettle clattering to the floor were like cymbals being repeatedly bashed, close to my ears.

No sheet of blackness fell. There were no flashing lights nor vivid dreams. I didn't float up to the ceiling and look back down on myself.

There was simply a nothingness. A gaping void where I used to be.

I woke up in here.

I'd suffered a stroke, I heard them say as they scribbled on their clipboards. A bad one. Lots of things can happen to a body after a stroke, I'd seen lists on the 'Raising Awareness' posters at the doctors' surgery. The doctors here knew a lot about what strokes could do.

But there is something else, too, something they don't know.

Something else that happened to me, *after the stroke*. Something that trapped me inside myself like a bug in amber.

A tube travels up my nose and down my throat. Feeds me. Another tube in my side takes away the waste.

There are plenty of things I can do for myself, but only inside my head.

Clock on the wall, I can't move at all.

I know I am still alive because I can still make up stupid rhymes, mainly about the clock. I can clearly remember Evie's tinkling laughter, the soft contours of her face.

That's something the machine can't do.

The clock is just about the only thing that changes in here, and most of the time it's the only blurred shape I can see.

My heart is pumping harder, thumping faster. The machine isn't doing that either; the thoughts in my head are making it happen.

Because I'm alive.

I'm alive.

I.

AM.

ALIVE.

I scream out the words again and again but the silence around me remains.

CHAPTER 4

Three Years Earlier

Toni

'Your furniture's arriving at one,' Mum called from the other room. 'You can start unpacking the boxes, if you like.'

I didn't like. I didn't feel like unpacking boxes or doing anything remotely physical at all. I didn't even feel like driving over and picking up Evie from the crummy council-run holiday club in our ten-year-old Fiat Punto. It had been desperate for a new exhaust for over a month but was still putt-putting out clouds of illegal emissions while I tried to find funds.

But I had no choice in the matter.

'I'll go and pick Evie up now,' I called to Mum, snatching up my car keys off the side. I didn't wait for her reply. I suddenly felt like I had to get out of the house, just for a while.

A radio outside, turned up far too loud, blasted crackling pop music out onto the street. I looked around to identify where it was coming from and saw the downstairs window of the house next door was propped open. The offending radio was perched on the sill.

So, we were to have anti-social neighbours to boot. It just kept getting better.

I averted my eyes and headed for the car which, in the absence of any driveway or garage, would have to continue to be parked on the road.

I'd just belted up when a tap on the window gave me a scare. A thin woman with stringy, over-bleached hair and a missing front tooth grinned at me and raised her hand.

I lowered the window slightly as the odour of stale cigarettes filled the car.

'Hello, neighbour.' She grinned, the gap in her front teeth like a magnet to my eyes, although I did make an effort not to stare. 'I'm Sal. Me and my two lads live next door.'

She nodded towards the blaring radio house. I lowered the window a little further.

'Hello.' I smiled, extending my hand awkwardly through the gap. 'Me and my daughter, Evie, just moved in today. I'm just off to pick her up from playgroup.'

Sal ignored my hand so I pulled it back inside.

'Just you and the little 'un, is there? No bloke, like me? Better off without 'em, love, that's what I reckon, what d'ya say?' She spoke via a constant string of rhetorical questions.

'Yep, just me and my daughter,' I confirmed, choosing one to answer.

'My two, Ste and Col, they're all grown up now. I'm not one of those mothers that thinks the sun shines out their backsides, if you get my drift, Toni? They can both be swines at times and if you get any trouble from 'em, then I want you to let me know straight away, right?'

'Trouble?'

'Oh, you know. Lads will be lads, yeah? Always up to their daft tricks and they're noisy little boggers at times. Our Colin's just spent a short time at Her Majesty's pleasure. Spent his nineteenth birthday inside, he did. He's a nuisance at times but I'm glad to have him back. They'll always be our little babies no matter what though, eh, Toni?'

'He's been in *prison*?' I tried to keep my face impassive but I felt the horror of her words settling over it like a fixed mask.

'Course it woren't his fault. Just a little misunderstanding with some youths out in town one night, you know? First sign of trouble round here and the coppers come looking for our Colin. They like having someone to blame, don't they?'

The realisation that I'd dragged my daughter from a respectable neighbourhood to live next to a convicted criminal made me sick to my stomach. I was sick of the stuff Sal was telling me and sick of the smell of smoke that hung around her like an odorous fog.

'Well, I'd best be off,' I muttered hastily before she embarked on another disturbing tale. 'I don't want to be late picking up Evie.'

'OK, love, pop round for a cuppa and a chat once you're settled in.' Sal raised her hand by way of saying goodbye and walked away from the window.

Quickly, I started the engine and pulled away from the kerb before Sal remembered some other worrying detail about one of her sons that she felt compelled to tell me about.

Although Sal and I had zero in common, her invite to pop round for a chat had managed to shake up my memories a little, feel the weight of what life used to be.

I valued my close relationship with Mum, I really did, but I suppose what I missed was having a really good, impartial friend to talk to. I missed the release of unburdening myself, perhaps over a glass of wine, to someone who wouldn't judge me. Someone who understood.

There was nobody like that left in my life. My best friend, Paula, had moved to Spain five years ago, and although we'd Skyped at first, contact had dwindled to a Christmas card each year, in which we'd both write, without fail, 'Must get together soon', in the full knowledge it wouldn't happen.

Then there had been Tara. We used to meet up as a foursome for drinks and meals out when our husbands were home and get a film and a takeaway in when they were working away.

Her husband, Rob Bowen, had been with Andrew on duty that day. He'd died instantly at the scene.

Tara had been four months pregnant at the time of the accident and I heard she'd lost the baby. Our loss should have bonded us together, but instead it seemed to force us apart.

I sent a condolence card in the midst of my own grief, but what good was that? I remember struggling with what to say to her, settling on 'I'm so sorry'. It had felt woefully inadequate.

Needless to say, I wouldn't be 'popping round' next door any time soon. Sal was a nice enough woman but her use of bad language was terrible, and not something I wanted Evie overhearing. And although I believed everyone should be given another chance in life when they'd made a mistake, I didn't like the sound of her older son, Colin, one bit.

I drove up to the large roundabout at the top of Cinderhill Road and joined the queue of cars. There was a steady stream of slow-moving traffic pouring from the M1 into the city centre and I had to wait nearly a full minute before I could drive straight across and onto the Broxtowe Estate.

I passed a large hotel on my left as I crawled around the roundabout. Giant posters announced a sprawling wedding fair that was taking place later in the month and a Take That tribute band that would be performing on the weekend closest to Halloween.

Too late, I realised I was in the wrong lane and tried to manoeuvre the car into the nearside position. The vehicle behind emitted a continuous beep and I glanced in the mirror and raised my hand in apology, just in time to see the driver's face morph into a mask of pure hatred while he mouthed insults at me.

I had to fight a sudden urge to slam on the brakes, forcing him to smash into the back of me, just to inconvenience him. I didn't know where these random maverick thoughts came from. Since Andrew's death, they seemed to just drop into my head like they belonged to someone else.

When I looked down at my hands I saw I was gripping the steering wheel so tight that my knuckles had turned white.

CHAPTER 5

Three Years Earlier

Toni

'They didn't have ANY of the new Lego sets in there, Mummy,' Evie complained as I led her from the crèche and out to the car.

Her blonde curls bounced and shone in the weak rays of the September afternoon sun and her button nose wrinkled, making her look cute, rather than annoyed. The birthmark on her neck seemed illuminated, like a small strawberry. 'AND they tried to make me drink milk. They said it was good for your bones. Is it good for your bones, Mummy?'

Evie enjoyed milk on cereal but couldn't stand it as a drink on its own.

'It is good for your bones because it contains lots of calcium,' I explained, as I steered the Punto back onto Cinderhill Road. 'But you can get calcium from lots of other foods, like yogurt and cheese, so you don't *have* to drink milk if you don't like it.'

Evie nodded solemnly. 'I told them milk maked me poorly, and once, it made me sick on next door's cat. Then they let me have juice, instead.'

I suppressed a snort. She really had been sick over our former neighbour's rare Persian Blue. I don't think they – or the cat – ever properly forgave us.

Back at the house, Evie immediately headed over to her over-sized box of Lego and emptied it out in the middle of the room. I sighed and shook my head.

'Evie, I really don't think this is the time to get—'

'Toni, let her play, love,' Mum overruled me, earning her a sweet smile from Evie. 'We can work around her.'

'Nanny, I need the toilet.' Evie pursed her lips and frowned.

'Come on then,' Mum pandered. 'Nanny will take you.'

Evie was five years old, and perfectly capable of taking herself to the loo. But I swallowed down my irritation. They would only both ignore me if I tried to intervene.

When they left the room, I sat down in one of the fold-up deckchairs we were making do with until the furniture arrived. I looked over at the boxes in the corner again but I didn't make a move to unpack them.

I wasn't ready to say goodbye to all the good times we'd had in the old house, the place in which Andrew and I had poured all our future hopes and dreams, and which was now another family's home.

Not for the first time, I felt an overwhelming urge to run.

Run away from Mum, away from the memory of Andrew and, today, even run away from Evie. Just for a short while.

Regret corkscrewed into my chest. What fools Andrew and I had been, bounding ahead in life like hapless puppies, never thinking to watch out for the tripwire.

I felt the familiar beginnings of a panic attack building inside with no way of assuaging it. I pulled my handbag towards me and peered inside, just to reassure myself everything was still in there, tucked out of sight.

I kept trying to remind myself that I did have choices. Like, I could admit everything to Mum right now and put things right before it all got out of hand.

Yet the thought of asking for help felt like a knot of eels stirring in my stomach.

Deep down, I knew I couldn't do it. Not yet.

More importantly, it would feel like I was overreacting. It wasn't as if things were totally out of control, I was simply relying on a temporary solution for a short time. A crutch.

I knew what I was doing and I promised myself I wouldn't let it slide too far.

I forced myself over to the corner of the room and half-heartedly pulled open the torn cardboard flaps of the box nearest to me. I sighed when I saw the contents: memorabilia of life as it used to be.

Family photographs taken on holiday, at Christmas, a celebratory meal out. A favourite painting of the three of us that Evie had done at nursery. Elaborate greetings cards: *To Daddy, To My Loving Husband, To My Darling Wife.*

I hadn't been able to leave all this stuff behind, despite knowing there was a chronic lack of space in the new house. Part of me still needed it, to look at. So I could remember who we used to be. It was a way to keep hold of the frayed edges of what used to be my life.

I bit down hard on my tongue to bring me to my senses. I had to at least *attempt* to put an optimistic spin on things. This house signified a new start for me and for Evie, it was our new beginning. Like Mum said, I just had to give it all a chance to come right.

'Stay positive and really try to believe it,' I said out loud to myself. 'Everything will work out for the best.' But the words rattled empty and lost in the echoing space that surrounded me.

When Mum and Evie came back downstairs, we sat drinking tea. Things felt calmer, more settled.

Until there was a sharp rap on the door.

Mum and I looked at each other in surprise but Evie didn't even look up, so absorbed was she in assembling her coloured bricks.

'Do you want me to get it?' Mum said.

'No, I'll go.' I hauled myself up and smoothed the escaped wisps of my hurriedly scraped-back pony tail.

I could see right away there was no shadow cast by a caller standing at the opaque glass but I opened the door and prepared myself to smile at the delivery man or postman or whoever it might be that would appear.

But there was nobody there.

I looked down. A beautiful arrangement of lilies sat on the doorstep, one of those expensive, handtied bouquets where the water was self-contained in the big plastic bubble at the bottom. The whole thing was set in a glossy black bag, complete with carry handles.

I stepped over the flowers and out onto the grass, looking up and down the street, but no one appeared to be around.

I picked up the arrangement by the handles but it felt a little unstable, so I held it by the stylish black casing and carried it back inside.

'Look what I found on the doorstep,' I said with a grin, walking into the lounge.

'Ooh, pretty flowers.' Evie jumped up. 'Who sended them, Mummy?'

'I don't know who sent them yet.' I smiled. I set the bouquet down on the floor. 'Have a scout around in the flowers, Evie, see if you can find the little message envelope.'

Mum raised her eyebrow. 'Any idea who they're from?'

'Not a clue.' I watched as Evie carefully parted the blooms, looking for the sender's message. 'Although I did send our new contact details out to my entire address book, so might be any one of them.'

'Well, I can tell you now, that display won't have been cheap,' Mum remarked. 'Those Stargazer lilies are—'

Mum was cut short by Evie's blood-freezing scream.

'Evie, what is it?' I jumped up and ran over to her.

She began slapping her hands together and whimpering and I saw an insect fly up towards the ceiling. I glanced down at the flowers as a wasp emerged. Then another. And another – all heading for Evie's pale, exposed arms and hands.

'Wasps!' I screamed, launching myself at my daughter and using my own arms to cover her head and body. 'They're in the bouquet!'

Evie's screams and Mum's wailing masked the pain I could feel pinching at my arms and shoulders. I smashed my arm to the side to push away the flowers and the whole thing toppled over.

'There's a nest in there,' Mum shrieked. 'Get outside!'

I picked Evie up and dived towards the front door. Mum followed right behind us and slammed the door shut. The three of us spilled out into the street, Evie still screaming and batting at her arms and face.

Mum and I smacked the insects from each other's limbs and I pulled another one from Evie's scalp as it stung at my fingers.

I looked back at the lounge window. Watched as the vicious, striped, tiny bodies hurled themselves against the glass in their mad rage, still desperately trying to reach us. To do us harm.

CHAPTER 6

Three Years Earlier

The Teacher

Harriet Watson emptied the shopping bags onto the worktop and began grouping the tins. She opened the cupboard door and placed them carefully, one by one, on the bottom shelf.

Three tins of baked beans, two tins of chopped tomatoes and four tins of tomato soup. All labels facing outwards and grouped by their contents.

'Those belong on the second shelf.'

Harriet jumped back, dropping the tin of peaches in her hand, watching helplessly as it crashed down onto the worktop, narrowly missing the carton of free-range eggs perched there.

'Mother.' She turned around. 'What are you doing up?'

'This is my house, remember? I can get up any time I want to.'

Harriet narrowed her eyes until her mother's outline came into sharper focus.

'Tinned fruit, rice pudding and custard belong on the *second* shelf,' the old woman said. 'How many times do I have to tell you?'

'Yes. I'm sorry, I wasn't thinking.'

The surface of the worktop felt smooth and cool beneath Harriet's fingers. She picked up the tin of peaches and turned back to the cupboard, sliding it onto the second shelf, into its rightful place. *In front* of the fruit cocktails and *adjacent* to the orange segments.

When she turned back to the doorway, her mother was still standing there, watching.

Harriet noticed she was bare-footed and wearing her lily-of-the-valley embroidered cotton nightdress. The one that hung loosely on her bones, like a filmy shroud.

'You ought to wear your dressing gown and slippers,' Harriet said, reaching for her spectacles that lay abandoned next to the stainless steel sink. She took a few steps forward. 'You'll catch a chill on these floor tiles.'

'Oh, you'd like that, wouldn't you? Pneumonia would be a clever excuse to keep me bed-bound and out of your hair.'

'That's not the case at all, Mother.'

'When is she coming?' The old woman rubbed at the loose fabric that gathered around her frail wrists. 'When will she be here?'

Harriet wanted to reach out and press the cool tips of her fingers into the pale, wrinkled skin on the old woman's forearms. Skin that was once so firm, and decorated with clusters of merging freckles like skeins of spun sugar.

'I told you, Mother,' Harriet sighed. 'I'm working on it.'

Her mother huffed, then turned and hobbled back down the hallway.

'I'll bring you some tea up once I've finished my jobs,' Harriet called, but there was no response.

A minute or two later, she heard the stairlift whirring into action.

She finished arranging the last few tins before standing back to admire the symmetry. Then she sat down at the kitchen table with the enormous bag of her mother's medication that she'd collected on repeat prescription that morning.

Harriet opened all the packets and carefully counted out the correct mix of multi-coloured tablets, dropping each tiny pile of seven pills into the daily sections of the medication box.

As she worked, deep frown lines lined up like tiny soldiers alongside the deep vertical scar that divided her forehead.

It was difficult to imagine how these minuscule, powdery torpedoes could keep a person alive. Twice a day, the old woman flipped open the relevant daily box and tipped the tablets into her palm. She studied each and every pill before tipping them all into her mouth and flushing the whole lot down with water.

It was the drug companies that her mother needed to watch; *they* were the ones who cared more about profits than people.

'Medicine and money mix about as well as education and budgets,' Harriet had commented only the previous evening whilst reading an article about NHS-banned medicines.

Her mother's answer: 'Did you take the salmon fillets out of the freezer?'

Luckily for the children in her care at school, money had never been Harriet's primary motivator in life.

The education system focused on examinations, even for the youngest students. Harriet felt sure that Ofsted inspectors were only interested in test results, not the young people or their lives. She had been through four inspections now and the officers had never cared enough to carry out even a cursory study of exactly how she, personally, had affected the lives of her children.

The inspectors were only interested in the qualified teachers. It was an insult.

Well, more fool them. She had far more power and influence over these children than people realised.

In just under two months, it would be her nineteen-year anniversary as a teaching assistant at St Saviour's Primary School. Nineteen long years of giving her all, of making sacrifices that nobody cared enough about to count or quantify.

As far as Harriet was concerned, she was a proper teacher and that's exactly what she told anyone who asked what she did for a living.

'But you're not a teacher, you're a *teaching assistant*,' her mother was fond of pointing out. 'That's like the difference between a fully qualified doctor and his auxiliary who empties the bedpans.'

She had asked her mother to stop saying that but the request had fallen on deaf ears.

Harriet taught the children in her care. She gave them valuable insight about themselves, insight they wouldn't find anywhere else in a world that pandered to their every whim.

Her mother didn't have a clue. None of them did.

All she wanted to do was help people, couldn't they see that?

But she hadn't got this far by taking unnecessary risks. She picked her children very carefully; she knew exactly what she was looking for.

She pulled the new term's class admission papers towards her and glanced over the names again. Yesterday, Harriet had logged into the pupil database, printed it out and made pencilled notes alongside each child.

This term there was a girl admitted from down south. Single mother, father deceased. They'd just moved into a property on Muriel Crescent. Harriet knew it, just off Cinderhill Road in Bulwell, not a million miles away from her own house.

According to the database, today was their moving-in date, their first proper day in the area. She smiled to herself, wondering how they were settling in.

Harriet turned back to the medicine organiser and snapped the lids firmly closed, pausing to stare briefly out of the kitchen window.

Steel-grey and fluffy white clouds butted up against each other as if they were battling for control. She watched as they scudded across the sky, burying the last bright rays, until not a single glimmer of sun remained.

CHAPTER 7

Present Day

Queen's Medical Centre

Beep, hiss, hiss, hiss, beep.

This is the sound of my life. What's left of it.

I drift in and out of consciousness – not sleep exactly, just nothing. No dreaming, no turning over or shuffling to get comfortable. Just a sheet of darkness that falls without any warning.

Then suddenly I find myself back again, staring at the ceiling and trying to make sense of what has happened to me and when it might go away. When I might move and speak once more. So I can tell them about Evie, tell them what happened and how it was all my fault.

When I am conscious, I try to use every second to remember. Snatches of memory drift by my staring eyes like elusive wisps of cloud. I pluck at them, missing some but pulling others in, so that they turn like small, shimmering snow globes in my mind's eye.

Old memories don't always make a great deal of sense but they sometimes bring me comfort.

Today, the prize won for sifting through hours and hours of thoughts was recalling the softness of Evie's hair, like spun gold that laced around my fingers as I stroked her head during those long nights she would sob herself to sleep. And the smell of her damp skin after a bath, new and fresh, like morning dew.

The door opens, tipping me into the present, and I brace myself. I know the doctors can't just switch me off, but one day, that time will arrive.

Inside I am screaming, thrashing, punching. Anything to let them know I am very much still here. Surely they have some way of knowing, of telling whether someone is alive or dead?

But the room remains perfectly silent and I remain perfectly still. I am trapped in a vacuum that exists between life and death.

I wait for the familiar voices, the medical terminology. The terrifying jargon that barely conceals the fact they are planning to murder me.

Because that's what it would be. If they turn off the machine, they will kill me.

But the familiar voices do not come. Instead, I hear a new voice.

'Hello, I'm looking after you, just for today. I'm doing temporary cover, you see.' A beaming face appears above mine momentarily. She surprises me and my eyes struggle to focus. 'I don't know if you can hear me but I'll carry on as if you can.'

None of the other nurses speak to me and I have never seen any of their faces.

She disappears again and I hear her humming something tuneless, busying around the equipment, taking her readings and making her evaluations.

'It's a nice day outside,' she says. 'Sunny, but not too warm, just how I like it. I'll be going down the allotment for a couple of hours when I finish my shift. Nothing like being in the garden, is there?'

Another memory slips down and I manage to grab it.

From the first day Evie began playing in the garden at the new house, I made it my priority to keep a careful eye on her.

Being so unfamiliar with the estate, I had carried out a bit of a recce on moving-in day, walking around the exterior of the house and through the surrounding streets to get an overview of how secure the small, cramped garden was.

Unfortunately, the answer was *not very*.

The new house was at the end of its row. A four-foot fence surrounded three sides of the grassy back yard with a gate that did not lock. A ragged hedge separated the space from next door.

The gate led directly onto a narrow path that ran the length of the row of houses. This path in turn led onto the busy main road. The joined-on neighbours were a rough-looking family, a wretched looking woman . . . I reached for her name but it was gone . . . with her two grown up sons who seemed to spend their entire day smoking weed, if the smell leaking from the open windows was anything to go by.

There were days I had to ask myself the question, why on earth would anyone in their right mind choose to live here? What kind of mother would put her child at risk like this?

I made a promise to myself there and then that although there was nothing I could do about the decision now, I would do whatever it took to keep Evie safe. I would look after her, no matter what.

The sad thing was that, back then, I really believed that I could.

But in the end, I let Evie down just about as badly as I could have done.

CHAPTER 8

Three Years Earlier

Toni

After all the silent moaning I'd done about Mum's indulgent attitude towards Evie, the tables turned. After the wasp attack, I ended up thanking my lucky stars that she was around.

When we rushed outside, Evie screaming and Mum yelling, plenty of faces appeared at windows but only a lady from across the road came over.

'I'm Nancy,' she said, crouching down in front of Evie. 'I'm a nurse. What happened?'

Mum told her.

'Nasty,' she said, scanning Evie's stung cheeks and then reaching out to inspect her arms.

'No!' Evie pushed her face into the side of my leg and snatched her hands behind her.

'Evie, let the lady see.'

'I don't want to.'

'It's OK.' Nancy smiled at her and then looked up at me. 'Just pop some Savlon on, all the swelling should go down in a few hours. There doesn't look to be any stings left in there, so she should be OK.'

'Thanks so much,' I said. 'You've saved us a trip to the walk-in clinic and probably several hours of waiting.'

'Just keep an eye on those stings,' Nancy added, standing up. 'If they start swelling or get really red and painful, it could be an allergic reaction. Then you'll need to take her in straight away.' She glanced over mine and Mum's angry red stings. 'Same goes for you two.'

We thanked Nancy and moved into the back garden, away from prying eyes.

Unsurprisingly, Evie was inconsolable. She just couldn't seem to settle, even though she'd completely tired herself out sobbing. She sat alternately on my and Mum's knees, half-dropping to sleep one minute and then sitting bolt upright the next with wild eyes that searched every inch of the space around us.

From the garden, Mum phoned her neighbour, Mr Etheridge.

'Mr Etheridge is a retired pest controller,' Mum said. 'He'll know exactly what to do.'

Next, I rang the police. Once we'd been through the name, number and full address rigmarole, the controller asked me what was wrong.

'Someone deliberately placed a nest of wasps in our home,' I said, realising it was going to be a difficult one to explain. 'My daughter has been really badly stung. We all have.'

'Is the offender still on the premises?' the controller asked calmly.

'No, there was never anyone on the premises. The flowers were delivered anonymously.'

'And the wasps came out of the flowers?'

'Yes. When we brought it inside, they flew out of the bouquet and stung my young daughter badly.'

'But you don't actually know that someone deliberately intended to harm you?'

'I know there was half a wasps' nest wedged in the bottom of the bouquet.' I clenched my jaw. 'Someone must've put it in there. Can you just send an officer out, please?'

As the call ended, my heart sank. If the controller's laconic reaction to my call was anything to go by, it would probably be days before the police bothered to visit. If at all.

Mr Etheridge was round within an hour, dressed in full head-to-toe white protective gear. Even his shoes were covered, and he was sporting one of those beekeeper nets on his head. Though he seemed rather unsteady on his feet as he ambled towards us.

'Stand back,' he instructed, his voice raspy. 'I'm going in.'

'Jeez, how old is he?' I whispered to Mum.

'Probably in his early eighties now, but that's not the point,' Mum said crossly. 'He knows what he's doing, Toni, he had his own pest control business for years.'

Mr Etheridge disappeared into the house, closing the door behind him. Fifteen minutes later he emerged again.

'All dead.' He peeled back his protective head covering. 'There were only about a dozen wasps in the room at most.'

He held up a clear plastic bag containing the crumbling remains of the grey, conical nest that had tumbled out of the bouquet. Evie whimpered and turned quickly away, pressing her face into Mum's neck.

'You were lucky, most of them were already dead.' He peered at the nest. 'Where's your wheelie bin, dear?'

I thanked Mr Etheridge and Mum slipped him a twenty-pound note, which he readily accepted. I watched as he surreptitiously pushed a can labelled 'Wasp & Insect Killer' into his rucksack. It was just the regular sort of spray you could buy from any supermarket – and for a hell of a lot cheaper than the twenty quid Mum had just stumped up. But I kept my mouth shut. After all, it had got a very unpleasant job done.

While Mum sat in the back garden with Evie, I swept up the soft, stripy bodies from the windowsill. The room was thick with insect spray so I wedged open the windows.

I stood there for a moment, taking a few breaths of fresh air and surveying the street. Directly opposite stood a neat row of houses, identical to our own.

It occurred to me that from any one of those windows, someone could be watching me right now. Enjoying the sight of me sweeping up the dead insects with satisfaction, congratulating themselves on a job well done.

Coming up with a reason *why* that might be the case was a little trickier. As far as I was aware, nobody here knew us. Perhaps someone nearby just didn't like newcomers – but if that was true, they'd gone to pretty extreme and pricey lengths to show it.

A slight breeze tweaked the crisp, gossamer wings of a couple of the wasps piled on the plastic dustpan and I jumped back, terrified for a second that they weren't quite dead.

Mr Etheridge had bagged up the flowers and tied the top of the bin bag in a knot. I shuddered as I took it outside and dumped it directly into the wheelie bin in the back yard.

'All done,' I said to Evie, loosening the damp strands of hair that tears had pasted to the side of her face. 'You can come back inside now, poppet.'

'No!' She clung tightly onto Mum, burying her head into the top of her shoulder.

'Now listen to me, sweetheart. Mr Etheridge is one of the top exterminators in the country,' Mum tried to reassure Evie. 'All insects and pests are terrified of him. They will never come back in this house now they know he is around.'

Doddery old Mr Etheridge the country's top exterminator? It would be laughable if Evie wasn't so distressed. But remarkably, Mum's claims seemed to actually perk Evie up a little.

'What's an exterbinator?' Evie asked, wide-eyed. 'Is Mr Ethriz like a ghostbuster for wasps?'

'That's exactly what he is,' Mum nodded. 'Mark my words, there'll not be so much as a harmless fly that dares to show its mucky face in this house again.'

Evie would remember such wild promises, but I was grateful to Mum for saying exactly the right things to reassure her for now.

'Let's go and sit in the kitchen and have some juice and biscuits,' Mum soothed. She slid Evie gently from her knee and stood up, clutching her hand.

'Biscuits *before* teatime, Nanny?' Evie threw me a sly look.

'Absolutely.' I winked at her. 'No biscuit rules today, poppet.'

We all walked inside together and I looked up to the sky; the clouds hung low and heavy above us, threatening rain despite the warmth.

I felt grateful the wasp episode was behind us but troubled as to exactly how and why the insects had found their way into our home.

It was a malicious act, it had to be. Wasps don't make fully formed nests in freshly arranged bouquets. Simple as.

A quick, sharp movement registered at the edge of my vision and my head snapped round towards it.

The upstairs curtains of Sal's house next door were slightly open and I could just about make out the silhouette of a person stepping back from the window.

Someone was up there, watching us.

CHAPTER 9

Three Years Earlier

Toni

The next day, I sat at the kitchen table, surrounded by unpaid bills and Andrew's benefit statements.

I'd been tapping away at the calculator for the last thirty minutes, multiplying, dividing and everything else in between, trying in vain to get the income and outgoings figures even remotely similar.

I hadn't told Mum the amount of debt I was in. Partly because I was ashamed, partly because I would never hear the last of it. Andrew and I had relied heavily on credit cards for most of our married life. We'd tried to stop charging things to credit, but you could guarantee, each time we resolved to stop, there was always some emergency that sprang up: a new washing machine needed, a lawnmower repaired, birthday gifts for friends and family . . . the list went on.

Both the MasterCard and the Visa had been maxed out for as far back as I could remember and we could only ever afford to pay the minimum amount each month. We knew we were paying a fortune in interest but that became less important than just surviving until pay day.

When Andrew died, the credit companies wrote to me and said their records showed I was the main cardholder, so despite the fact I'd just lost my husband and our family's main wage earner, they regretfully had to inform me that I was personally responsible for the entire debt.

Eventually, I pushed the calculator away in frustration and reached instead for the *Nottingham Post*, turning to the jobs section.

Working again would bring its own problems, I knew that. Sorting out care for Evie was just for starters, but I had to get us out of this mess somehow.

Back in Hemel, and over a period of about ten years, I'd worked my way up to managing a medium-sized independent estate agency in the centre of town.

It didn't matter where you lived in the UK, you could always be confident of finding property sales and letting agencies. And if you were lucky, one or more might be hiring.

I couldn't help thinking that the logistical problems of getting a job would surely be outweighed if it allowed me to keep financial ruin at bay. And it would be such a relief to have just a little spare to treat Evie now and again and buy one or two nice bits for the house, to make it more of a cosy home.

A familiar, unpleasant fluttering sensation rose up into my chest, my heart seeming to perform an unpleasant little backflip every few beats.

I looked over at my handbag longingly. It still felt a bit early in the day, but I felt sure it wouldn't hurt this once. But just as I started to move towards relief, the doorbell rang.

I sat down again, rooted to the spot. Nobody knew we lived here yet. It was likely to be an opportunist seller, so I decided to ignore it.

The doorbell rang again.

'Mummy, SOMEONE IS AT THE DOOR,' Evie roared above the television in the other room.

The front door opened directly out onto the pavement. Evie had shouted so loudly, the caller would have almost certainly

have heard her. Reluctantly, I ditched my plan to pretend there
was no one home.

I opened the door to a plump, middle-aged woman. She had a
thatch of short, curly brown hair that was shot through with wiry
grey, and pale bespectacled eyes that darted around but didn't
seem to settle on anything.

'Hello?' I said, relieved she didn't look in the least bit official.

'Mrs Cotter? I'm Harriet Watson from St Saviour's Primary
School.' She peered at me over a bulging canvas shopping bag
that she held in both arms. 'Evie is starting in my class next
week.'

The awful state of the Lego-strewn living room next door
flashed into my mind but I pasted a smile on my face and stepped
back from the door.

'What a nice surprise. Please, come in, Mrs Watson.'

'Actually, it's just Miss.' She stepped inside the tiny hallway
and set down the bag. 'I thought I'd drop some work off for Evie,
seeing as I won't be around when you visit the school this afternoon.' She glanced at my tatty leggings and T-shirt. 'I do hope
you don't mind me just turning up like this.'

'Not at all,' I said, holding out my hand. 'I'm Toni, by the
way. Evie's mum.'

Harriet Watson had a deep scar, about four centimetres long,
that divided her pasty forehead into two. Her hair was so tightly
curled, it looked as if she'd modelled each coil individually with
styling wax.

'I've brought mainly worksheets and reading material.' Harriet shook my hand and her fingers, loose and clammy, pressed
against my palm. 'If she can get through some of this, it'll stand
her in good stead for the new term's work. Introduce her to the
sort of things we've been doing in class.'

Evie came running full pelt out of the lounge and crashed
into my side.

'Careful,' I chided, putting an arm around her and hugging her to me, instantly shamed by the fact she was still dressed in her pyjamas. 'This is Evie.'

'Hello, Evie,' Harriet said.

'Hello,' Evie muttered.

'Miss Watson is your new teacher. She's brought you some worksheets to do before you start your new school.'

'And some reading material,' Harriet added.

Evie regarded the bulging bag at my feet.

'What do you say?' I nudged her.

'Thank you.'

I became conscious of the booming television noise emanating from the lounge. Harriet would think I was the kind of mother who allowed her child to sit and watch it all day long like a zombie. Which, I admit, I sort of did, at the moment. But that would change once we got organised.

I realised with a sinking feeling that it was rude to expect Harriet to stand in the poky, cold hallway any longer. I pinched the fabric of my T-shirt away from the damp patch that had already formed at the bottom of my back and felt a welcome kiss of cool air there.

'Please, come through to the living room,' I said loftily, as if we lived in one of those million-pound penthouse apartments on the banks of the River Trent. 'I'm afraid we're not quite settled in here yet.'

She followed Evie and I into the lounge. I strode across the room and snatched up the remote control, switching the screeching volume to mute.

'That's better, I can hear myself think now,' I said brightly.

The whole room smelled of biscuits and warm bodies – and not in a good way.

I stood for a second or two and looked at the room through Harriet's eyes. Barely an inch of carpet was visible in the middle of the room, due to Evie's latest sprawling Lego structure and the piles of multi-coloured bricks that surrounded it.

An old PlayStation that Mum had picked up at a car-boot sale for Evie's birthday sat redundant in front of the television. The numerous wires of its controller snaked and coiled around discarded empty glasses and toast-crumbed plates.

'Evie, come on, let's start to tidy this mess up,' I pleaded.

Somewhere between the doorbell ringing and leading Harriet Watson into the living room, the fluttery sensation in my chest had developed into a full-blown, irregular hammering. I could feel sweat patches pooling in my armpits.

'I'm sorry about the mess.' A silly little laugh escaped my lips as I swept my arm around the room. 'We've only just moved in, you see. I haven't had time to get it sorted out.'

Harriet cleared her throat purposefully. 'Perhaps you could help, young lady?' She glared down at Evie through stark, wire-framed spectacles. 'Instead of making more of a mess for Mummy.'

I felt a sharp spike in my throat and tried to swallow it down. I supposed I ought to feel relieved Miss Watson was trying to support me, but it wasn't her job to chastise Evie in her own home. Particularly after all the upheaval she'd been through.

'That's OK, I'd rather she spent her time playing,' I said crisply.

The teacher said nothing, tight-lipped and disapproving. I felt a sudden need to try to rescue the situation.

I resorted to Mum's failsafe solution to solving the woes of the world.

'Miss Watson, can I offer you a nice cup of tea?' Her face remained stony and I noticed she still hadn't invited me to use her first name. 'I can explain one or two things, if you've got time for a quick chat.'

Harriet gave a curt nod and followed me into the kitchen.

'Please, sit down.' I nodded to the tiny breakfast table and its two flimsy folding chairs.

I made mugs of steaming tea, kicking myself that I hadn't got around to doing a proper food shop yet. I didn't have so much as a shortbread finger to offer Miss Watson and our tea took the last of the milk.

I set the drinks down on the table and was relieved to sense things becoming a little more relaxed between us. We chatted about the onset of autumn and the recent cooler weather.

The tension in my shoulders had just begun to dissolve when I realised, with a start, I'd seated her directly in front of the scattered unpaid bills and benefit statements I'd been perusing earlier.

'I'm so sorry, let me move this.' My face flooded with heat as I swept the papers into an untidy pile, scooping them up into my arms and setting them on the side.

Miss Watson didn't comment. In fact, to my huge relief, she showed no sign of having even noticed the personal papers.

'So,' she said, taking a sip of her tea and setting the mug back down. 'Tell me a little bit about Evie.'

I told her about Evie's love of reading and how she enjoyed building Lego structures for hours on end.

'I try to encourage her because spatial skills are important too, aren't they? I think there's too much emphasis, these days, on academic work.'

Miss Watson sniffed and took another sip of her tea.

I told her how Evie had enjoyed having a good group of friends at her old school, how they'd often taken turns having sleepovers at each other's houses at the weekend.

'When my husband, Andrew, had his accident, everything changed,' I told her. 'It's been so hard for Evie, having to leave her old life behind on top of everything else.'

I wanted to say it had been hard on us both, but I didn't. I wanted Evie's teacher to understand what it meant for her.

'How did it happen?' Harriet asked. 'Your husband's accident?'

I took a breath. I'd learned that the best way to deal with this question, and get through it without breaking down into tears, was to keep things as simple as possible and stick to the unadorned facts.

'Andrew and his team were on a night mission in Afghanistan. Intelligence had provided them with maps but the directions were off. Andrew led his men straight over the edge of a cliff. Two men died, Andrew was one of them.'

Harriet nodded but she made no comment.

'One man died at the scene but they got Andrew to hospital. He had massive head injuries. After a few weeks he was able to come home and we thought he'd make a partial recovery but he suffered a massive blood clot to the brain and died just a few days later.'

She afforded me no appropriate noises of sympathy and somehow I found that a relief. It encouraged me to carry on talking.

'It's been two years now,' I continued. 'My mother encouraged me to move up to Nottingham. It felt like it was time for us to make a clean break.'

For a moment I couldn't speak.

'And here you both are,' Harriet remarked.

'Evie has been through a lot for a child of her age,' I told her. 'Being here feels like the fresh start we've been looking for.'

Harriet looked at me, and for the weirdest second or two, I thought I saw a faint smile playing at the corners of her mouth.

CHAPTER 10

Three Years Earlier

Toni

When our visitor had left, I went back into the kitchen and sat alone at the table for a few minutes.

Harriet Watson was a strange woman. She hadn't really commented sympathetically, as most people tended to do, on my story of how things had gone so terribly wrong.

Yet I'd found that reassuring. I had opened up emotionally, more than I'd ever done to a complete stranger. Her apparent indifference made me feel as if the reasons for holding back had been neatly swept away and, for a short time, that had been somewhat of a relief.

I'd probably said more than I intended to, though. She was Evie's teacher, for goodness' sake. I shouldn't have gone into all the gory details. Too late now.

At least she had a fuller understanding of Evie; you never knew when she might need an extra bit of slack cut for her at school. I was especially worried about the new, blossoming impatience and stubbornness she'd displayed lately.

I took a few deep breaths, suddenly aware of my dry mouth and the heat in my hands. My heart had ceased merely fluttering and was now banging like a drum inside my chest.

I had too much thinking to thank for that.

Reaching for my handbag, I slid out the small bottle with shaking hands. It was half-filled with hard-angled, light blue tablets. Andrew's name was printed in bold type on the neat, white label.

One wouldn't hurt, not after my ordeal this morning.

It wasn't good to get so het up. Wasn't good for me, or for Evie.

Maybe I was being too hard on myself. Plenty of people downed a couple of glasses of wine at night when they were feeling stressed. Nobody seemed to judge you for that; it was something to joke about.

One tablet was fine. One would be OK, just to take the edge off and push my problems a little further back.

Just for today.

CHAPTER 11

Three Years Earlier

Toni

I felt myself being softly shaken then, when I didn't respond, pushed a little more roughly.

I was too deep, I didn't want to surface. I just wanted to be left alone to lie here, on the nice soft, squashy cushions.

'Mummy!' An urgent voice broke through the fog. 'Mummy, I'm hungry.'

I opened my eyes. Blinked. Closed them again.

'Mummy, wake UP! I'm trying to tell you something.'

Evie shook me again, rocking her weight against my arm.

I opened my eyes and frowned against the splitting headache. My daughter's outline flickered slowly into focus.

'Someone knocked on the door,' she said. 'I didn't answer, like you told me, Mummy. I hid.'

'Good girl.' The words sounded clear in my mind but left my dry, cracked lips as a croak.

Evie stood up and walked out of the room.

'Wait,' I tried again but my words were just a garbled mess.

Then Evie came back with a glass of water that sloshed and spilled over my arm. I pushed myself up to a seated position and she shuffled onto the couch next to me and pressed the glass to my lips. I took a deep draught of cool, refreshing water.

'Thanks, sweetheart,' I managed, battling the rush of nausea and heat that hit me once I sat upright. I felt desperate to lie back down and sleep for longer. But I didn't. Instead, I focused on Evie's tear-stained face. 'You've been crying,' I whispered.

'I shouted very LOUD in your ear, Mummy, but you still didn't open your eyes. You didn't wake up.'

My stomach started to cramp when I heard her words.

'I'm sorry.' I slid my arm around her, pulled her close and kissed the top of her warm, silky head. 'I'm so sorry, Evie.'

'I'm hungry. Can I have some toast and then bananas and custard for pudding?'

The thought of dealing with food turned my stomach.

'Give me two minutes to come round a bit, darling,' I told her, smiling. 'Then I'll make you some tea.'

I glanced at my watch. I had been asleep for nearly two hours.

I remembered I'd taken two tablets. *Two.* When I'd promised myself I'd manage with just the one.

What if Evie had scalded herself with the kettle or fallen down the stairs? I had put my daughter, the person I loved most in this world, in danger.

I had to do something.

This had to stop.

It took me a bit longer than a couple of minutes to 'come round', as I'd promised, but Evie didn't complain.

I sat like a zombie, staring at the pile of Lego bricks in the middle of the room, listening to my daughter explaining her latest masterpiece and how it was going to be some kind of ark for homeless animals.

I tried my best to give her the impression I was really listening, but from the way she kept scowling at me and repeating details, stretching the words out slowly, I think she probably guessed I was still out of it.

Finally, I felt up to standing and walked slowly into the kitchen make her toast.

The table was as I'd left it, home to two dirty mugs from Harriet Watson's visit. As I picked up the mugs to transfer them to the sink, I caught sight of the calendar and it hit me.

I'd missed our appointment to look around Evie's new school this afternoon.

I held on to the edge of the worktop and waited until the room stopped spinning. The consequences of taking that extra tablet just kept on coming.

I'd have to ring the school. I could tell them I'd been ill, and surely they'd be able to fit us in another day.

I glanced at the bills and documents I'd hastily piled on the side when Harriet had arrived. The newspaper was still open at the jobs page.

There was so much to do to get this house in order, but I had neither the energy nor the inclination to even make a start.

I saw the flyer just as I was about to close the newspaper and set it aside for the recycling bin. I pulled it out to read it.

Assistant Residential Lettings Agent – part-time
Required ASAP at Gregory's Property Services, a small, independent estate agency in Hucknall town centre.

When I checked their location map, I found the town was just over three miles away from our house here in Bulwell. Even better, it seemed there was a direct bus to Hucknall that I could catch from the stop that was situated just at the edge of the new estate.

That was certainly useful to know, should I have to take the car off the road until I gathered together enough funds to replace the exhaust.

Assistant lettings agent was certainly a bit of a drop from the agency branch manager I used to be, but I really couldn't afford to think like that. 'Beggars can't be choosers,' I could imagine Mum saying.

The advert gave a link for applicants to access the job description and person specification online. I pulled my bulky laptop towards me and piggybacked the 4G connection on my phone.

I'd already emailed the telephone and internet provider twice in the past two days, trying to organise a connection earlier than the engineer's confirmed appointment next month. So far, I'd had no response.

I copied the link into the address bar and the details slowly loaded. The duties of the job were as I'd expected: compiling property details and arranging photographs to be taken; marketing and promoting properties to let; advising clients and helping tenants decide on suitable properties; taking details of any issues that arose with lets that the agency managed on behalf of private landlords.

My heart sank a little, despite my little pep talk about thinking positive. I could do this stuff with my eyes closed.

The spec stated: *Previous experience would be preferred but not essential.*

I was woefully over-qualified, there was no doubt about that. But hopefully they'd be able to see the benefit in hiring someone with so much experience, even if I wasn't getting paid at that level.

I saved the online application form to my desktop and made a note of the closing date, which was only three days away. Looked like I'd spotted it just in time.

I felt stirrings of excitement in my stomach. It felt good to get a sense of control again.

For once, it felt like I was actually moving forward, doing something for me and my daughter instead of remaining stagnant and relying on my dead husband's stolen tablets to function.

CHAPTER 12

Three Years Earlier

DIARY ENTRY

25th August

TIMELINE
Arrival at watch point: 7.30 a.m.

8.21 a.m.	Subjects arrive at new property in silver Fiat Punto: CV06 HLY. Semi-detached town house: 22 Muriel Crescent, Bulwell, Nottingham.
8.46 a.m.	Mother drives child to Little Tigers day nursery, Broxtowe Lane, Nottingham. Grandparent remains in property.
9.02 a.m.	Mother returns. No movement.
11.45 a.m.	Mother drives to day nursery to collect child.
12.01 p.m.	Mother and child return to house.
12.17 p.m.	Furniture arrives.
1.06 p.m.	Bouquet delivered.
1.13 p.m.	Desired response elicited.

Departure from watch point: 1.15 p.m.

GENERAL OBSERVATIONS

- Adults seem downcast and cautious of new surroundings. Child is bright and enthusiastic.
- Neighbourhood is not close-knit, neighbours pay little attention to what is happening around them. Area is low income/unemployed, property security is poor.
- Grandparent lives nearby in Nuthall.
- Awaiting further instruction.

CHAPTER 13

Three Years Earlier

Toni

Spurred on by the thoughts of making a fresh start, I buckled down for the next couple of days, getting lots of boxes and bags unpacked and managing to get most of the stuff downstairs put away, or at least relocated into the correct rooms.

I opened up the final box in the lounge, breathing a silent thank you that I'd finally reached the last one. I was starting to worry just how long the bottom of my back was going to hold up.

'Mummy, there's nowhere in my bedroom to put my soft toys or sort my Lego bricks into colours and shapes.' Evie stood in the doorway, hands on her hips.

'I know, sweetie, just put them in neat piles along your wall for now. We'll be getting some nice new furniture soon.'

Evie huffed her disapproval and bounded back upstairs. Her old room had boasted a full wall of mirrored wardrobes that had held tonnes of stuff.

I started to compile a list of items we desperately needed: two chests of drawers and a wardrobe for Evie's room. All the bedroom furniture had been built in at our old place. We needed a coffee table and rug for the lounge because I'd foolishly managed to ruin both with hot wax by knocking over a burning candle just before we left. New curtains, blinds for the kitchen . . . depressingly, the list went on and on.

I ended up pushing my pen and paper into the cutlery drawer and trying to forget about how I was ever going afford everything.

If I could get the job at the property agency then what we needed would follow, but if not, then I didn't really want to think about it.

I chewed my nails, pulled at my hair and drank endless cups of strong coffee. But at least I didn't go upstairs and reach up to the back of the top shelf of the bathroom cabinet behind the tampons and hair remover.

I was determined to manage without that little brown bottle full of calm, which I knew was a sure-fire road to ruin.

I had to make a stand against popping the pills right now. Otherwise, where would it stop?

My mobile rang. It flashed up with the caller's name and I thought about ignoring it, but I knew that would only result in a key in the lock within the hour.

'Toni, it's me, love.' Mum's voice filled my ear. 'Now, are you absolutely sure you don't want me to come over? I really don't mind.'

'Honestly, Mum, thanks but we're fine. Evie's organising her toys as she wants them in her bedroom and I'm unpacking the last box downstairs now.'

'Well, if you're sure.' She sounded disappointed and I felt a pinch of meanness at my throat.

'Look, we'll pop round to yours for a cuppa later, if you're in?'

'Lovely,' Mum replied in a brighter tone. 'I'll put the kettle on around four then, if that suits you.'

'Perfect, see you later.'

Mum was a massive part of our lives and I loved her to bits, but the move to Nottingham signified a fresh start for us on a number of fronts.

I wanted to look after my daughter and myself, regain some of the self-esteem that had chipped off like cheap nail varnish over the last two years.

Every time I thought about the money Mum had stumped up periodically to help us out, a hot flush crept up into my neck and face.

At thirty-five years old I needed to be able support myself and my daughter. I needed to find the person I used to be, the woman who had plans and goals, and who had built a successful career, juggling all the usual responsibilities – a husband, a home and a child.

It wasn't such a big ask, was it?

Losing Andrew had been a sucker punch to my very core. I knew part of me would never recover, no matter how much time elapsed. No matter what the future held.

Still, I couldn't help thinking that it could have been so very much worse. Evie was young, she would bounce back. I would never let her forget her daddy, of course not, but she deserved the freedom to live her life without sadness and pain.

It wasn't too late for me to give Evie that gift.

I knew the little brown bottle was leading me in the opposite direction to that. Rebuilding our lives, I couldn't afford to keep taking the easy way out.

But as with a lot of things in life, it was far easier to make the observation than it was to actually *do* anything about it.

The brown bottle had so far stopped me dealing with the grief and pain of losing Andrew. It had delayed it until, I told myself, I was in a more stable place to deal with it.

Mum was another crutch I knew I had to wean myself from overusing. It wasn't fair on her, for one thing. I knew she constantly worried about Evie and I, and that she felt obliged to help out in ways she shouldn't have to do.

I thought again about the property agency job and a swell of hope rose inside me. It was the closing date tomorrow, so if I wanted to go ahead, I had to make certain to get my application completed and submitted in good time.

Mum's free childcare was an integral part of me working and I couldn't really get away from that fact, but I'd noticed that Evie's behaviour had worsened since she'd been spending more time with her nanny. Discipline was a word Mum didn't understand when it came to her beloved granddaughter, although she'd never had a problem being strict when I was growing up at home.

Dad had been the soft one, always getting himself into trouble with Mum for winking at me when she was telling me off, or sneaking snacks and comics up to my room when I'd been banished upstairs for insolence or something similar.

But we lost Dad after the second heart attack and Mum became even stricter then.

'It's for your own good, Toni,' she'd lecture me when I complained about having to get a paper round for pocket money, or keep my bedroom ridiculously tidy compared to the state of all my teenage friends' rooms. 'I want you to have a good life, be financially independent and not struggle like I'm doing, now your dad's gone.'

I sighed and walked into the lounge to get the last of the toiletries out of the box. How utterly ironic I'd ended up just the opposite of Mum's vision for me.

But not for much longer, I promised myself.

I was going to make this new start count. And an undeniably important first step in my plan was to get myself a job.

CHAPTER 14

Three Years Earlier

Toni

Mum had Evie over at her house for a couple of hours on Friday morning, so I took the opportunity to finish my job application.

By lunchtime I'd emailed it off, together with the required covering letter.

I made a cheese sandwich and ate it while I watched the news headlines. I heard the letterbox snap, mail falling on the mat. After I'd eaten my lunch I popped into the hall and scooped up the small pile of post, taking it through to the living room. The usual combination of glossy pizza delivery and double-glazing leaflets nestled amongst utility letters addressed to 'The New Tenant/ Owner'.

I spotted a thicker letter than the other items, handwritten. My curiosity was piqued right away. I tore open the pretty lilac envelope to find a 'New Home' card and a letter from my old friend Tara Bowen, whose husband, Rob, had died instantly in the accident with Andrew.

I sat down on the couch and read the letter. It was printed and only took up half an A4 sheet, so it didn't take me very long, but when I'd finished it, my eyes were prickling.

Predictably, Tara was only interested in how Evie and I were doing and how we shouldn't lose contact as friends. She'd always been a very selfless person, doing lots of voluntary work for animal charities on her weekends, even though she'd worked full-time as a veterinary nurse before her life was steamrollered flat, in the same way ours had been.

When I got to the last line of the letter, Tara referred to herself only once to tell me she had been diagnosed with multiple sclerosis. Never one to dramatize her problems, she said it like it was nothing: 'Oh, and I now have a positive diagnosis for MS. At least I know now what's been causing my insomnia.'

I folded up the letter and slid it back into the envelope, and then I sat, watching tiny rainbow spheres dancing on the wall, created by the sunlight filtering through the beautiful crystal vase that Andrew had given me as a gift before he died.

It was easy to get caught up in your own problems, focusing on what was lacking rather than counting your blessings. Reading the last line of Tara's letter put things into sharp perspective. Life had lambasted her yet again, but was she complaining? No.

Thanks to Tara, I felt a sharp resolve. It was time I got my act together and sorted out my life.

At that very moment, in the kitchen, I heard my laptop ping with an incoming email.

Unbelievably, it was from Gregory's Property Services, inviting me to interview at 3 p.m. on Monday afternoon.

I swallowed hard, trying to relieve the dryness in my mouth and throat. Although my stomach was fluttering at the thought of my plans coming together, Evie started her new school on Monday. I'd wanted to take her and pick her up on her first day at least.

My heart rate instantly doubled. At least it felt that way.

Desperate to share my news, I picked up my phone and fired a text off to Mum.

Got interview on Mon for the job I told you about! Be over in 20 mins to pick up Evie x

It was brilliant and completely unexpected; they must have been really impressed with my application to get back within the hour.

But then I suppose it was easy enough to appear competent on paper. What if I flunked the interview? What if they thought I was too experienced, or too old for the role of assistant?

I glanced at my phone but Mum hadn't yet replied to my message.

Despite feeling relieved I'd actually managed to get a shot at securing a job, the whole of my upper body felt tight and tense, every muscle as taut as an overstrung cello.

A few weeks ago, I'd downloaded a relaxation app on my phone that gave breathing exercises and even played mindful music while you did them. I opened it up and sat for a few minutes, trying to keep focused on the narrator's voice. The entire time, the little brown bottle called to me from the bathroom cabinet but I forced myself to ignore it.

When I'd completed the first stage of the relaxation, I felt even more stressed than when I'd started.

I grabbed my keys and left the house before the pull to go upstairs grew too strong.

I didn't trust myself anywhere near those tablets.

'I think you're rushing into things with this new job.' Mum jumped straight in, as soon as I walked into her kitchen. My heart sagged in my chest; I didn't feel up to an argument. 'Your priority should be to get the house comfortable and properly organised and to get Evie settled into school.'

'I need extra cash to get the house looking right,' I tried to reason with her. 'And it's only part-time hours, I'll still be able to take Evie to school every morning.'

'I don't want to go to a crèche, Mummy,' Evie whined, wrapping her little arms around my neck. 'Nanny said I shouldn't have to.'

'What have you been telling her?' I quickly bit down on my tongue but the unspoken words burned in my mouth like acid.

'I haven't been telling her anything,' Mum replied calmly. 'I just said that Mummy might have to go to work and if so—'

'You should have let me tell her in my own time.' I tried to stop, but in the end I just had to spit the words out. 'I am her mother.'

'Oh yes, we know that, don't we?' Mum said shortly. 'We know that you're her *mother*.'

I heard the subtext as clearly as if she'd shouted the words at me. *You're her ineffective, unreliable mother who can't function without my help.*

It was yet another reason I had to get my life back on track.

I bit down my retort and looked away from her challenging stare. I couldn't afford for Mum to retreat into one of her silent protests. I'd known them to last for days before.

And as much as it stuck in my craw, I needed her.

CHAPTER 15

Three Years Earlier

Toni

In the early hours of Sunday morning, I woke up with a jolt.

I thought I'd heard something outside but now I wasn't sure. It's hard to tell exactly what you heard when you snap awake in an instant. After holding my breath for several seconds and staring into the thinning darkness as my eyes adjusted, I heard nothing more.

That didn't stop my heart from pumping and my hands from sweating.

My bedroom overlooked the street. I slipped out of bed and padded over to the window. The streetlights illuminated the line of new mews-style houses across the street that mirrored ours. They stood identically uniform and cramped, bathing in the pools of sodium orange light, like a real-life toy town.

There was nobody around. It was 3 a.m. Blinds were down, curtains were closed. There was no movement at all and I felt like I was the only person who couldn't sleep. I came to the conclusion that I must have dreamt the noise.

My legs felt restless, in need of a stretch.

I crept out onto the landing and looked in on Evie. She slept peacefully, the whisper of her breath reaching me at the door. I stood for a moment just gazing into space, the strangeness of the new house still prickling at me.

Back in my room, I sat down on the edge of my bed and looked around. I could feel the springs jabbing at the backs of my thighs through the cheap mattress. All my meagre worldly goods were pathetically on display. Black bin bags full of clothes that now hung too loose on me lined the wall at the bottom of the bed. My shoes were piled up in the corner, a couple of coats and a hat draped on top, so that the whole thing resembled Guy Fawkes on a bonfire. Another corner housed a heap of mismatched, greying underwear.

I'd made a start but there was still so much to do. Getting the house organised felt like the craggy shadow of a mountain looming over me.

I climbed back into bed and tried in vain to sleep, but hours later I was still tossing and turning.

Aching.

Hurting.

Since Andrew died, my entire skin felt raw. I had been turned inside out like an old, discarded sock, no longer of use to anyone.

There were times it felt as if I was just killing time until my husband came back. At the old house, I would often pretend he was just away working and would be walking through the door in a couple of days.

The tablets helped me do that. They took the pain, encased it in a thick wad of cotton wool and packed it down, deep inside, where it stopped being a problem for a short time. The painful reality would be held at arm's length for another long day.

I stood up and headed for the bathroom. It was no use trying to fight it.

Tonight, I was going to need a little help.

CHAPTER 16

Three Years Earlier

Evie

She had tried to wake her mummy again and again but she just wouldn't get up, even though it was way past waking-up time. Evie could tell this by the way the sun was shining in through Mummy's thin, floral curtains.

In the end, Evie went downstairs on her own.

When they lived in their last house, Mummy had had a job and got dressed early each morning. Her eyes had been brighter then and hardly ever half-closed-sleepy in the daytime.

That had all changed when Daddy went away to be with the angels.

Mummy didn't have a job anymore and she never used her sparkly eyeshadow now or sprayed on the perfume Evie liked, the one that smelled like a mixture of bubble gum and flowers.

As soon as she got downstairs, Evie got scared that the wasps might be back. She was too afraid to go into the sitting room without Mummy doing her daily wasp check, so she went into the kitchen instead.

The floor felt cold on her feet and there was no TV in here to watch CBeebies on. Evie stood on a chair and pulled the cereal box from the cupboard. There were still no clean dishes, so she wrapped her blankie around her and sat at the table, pulling

Frosted Shreddies straight from the packet and popping them into her mouth.

It was lots of fun, pretending to be a grown-up. You could eat cake and biscuits for breakfast and, if you wanted, you didn't even have to put milk on your cereal, or eat it with a spoon.

Evie took Flopsy Bunny off the table and sat him on the chair beside her.

'Don't start,' she scolded him. 'You'll do as I say. You don't want to upset me, do you?'

Flopsy ignored her. He never cried like Evie sometimes did, when her Mummy got cross.

Evie knew he didn't like it here in the kitchen because he wanted to watch television.

'Mummy is TIRED,' she snapped at the rabbit. 'For God's sake, will you stop going ON AND ON?'

She sighed and looked at the heap of dirty dishes piled up in the sink. Sometimes, Mummy forgot things like there being no clean cups or dishes and Evie had to tell her again and again before she remembered.

When she'd eaten enough cereal that her tummy finally stopped rumbling, Evie crept to the living room door and listened. She couldn't hear any buzzing in there.

She opened the door the tiniest bit – too tiny a gap even for a wasp to slip out and sting her – but all was quiet in there. In a flash of bravado, Evie flung her blanket over her head and rushed over to the couch, snatching up the remote and turning on the TV.

Her eyes flicked wildly around the room and she ran back out, breathless, and slammed the door behind her again. She hadn't see one single insect but you couldn't be too careful. The wasps had been very well hidden in the pretty flowers that day. Too well hidden for even Mummy and Nanny to spot.

Plus, Mummy was still sleeping, and if the wasps came back, Evie didn't know where Mr Ethriz, the exterbinator man, lived. There would be no one to help her.

She shuffled back down the hallway, rubbing her eyes. She scowled at Flopsy Bunny, who watched her steadily from his chair.

'Don't you look at me like that.' She scowled. 'Like butter wouldn't melt.'

It was no fun being here in the kitchen where it was cold and quiet and there was nothing to do.

Evie heard a shout and someone laughing outside.

She pressed her nose up to the patterned glass but she couldn't see anything. Mummy had explained it was because of the oh-pake glass.

A funny yelp and another laugh. It sounded like someone was having fun in the yard. Maybe her nursery friends from Hemel had come to visit.

She bounded upstairs again.

'Mummy, wake up,' Evie called, shaking her arm. 'I want to go outside.'

But Mummy did not stir.

'Mummy, PLEASE!' Evie yelled into her ear. 'You've got to wake up NOW.'

Evie stood up and stamped on the bare floorboards. She ran back downstairs and into the kitchen. If her friends thought Evie wasn't here, they might go back home and she didn't want that.

The key was in the lock so Evie reached forward and wiggled it. She tried the handle but the door was firmly stuck. She twisted the key this way and that, took it out and then slid it back in. She turned it hard to the left and heard a click. This time when she tried the handle, the door opened. A rush of warm breeze caressed her face and Evie smiled, turning her face up to the sun.

But there was nobody in the yard.

Her smile faded and she sat on the step, tracing a pattern in the dust with her fingertips.

'Buster, fetch!' someone called out.

The funny yelp sounded again and a tennis ball arced over the hedge and landed on the grass.

Evie jumped up off the step and ran down towards it in bare feet and pyjamas.

A brown and white ball of fluff barrelled through the hedge and made the yelping noise again and again.

It was a puppy! A real, live puppy.

'Hello, cutie,' said a tall man with a spotty face on the other side of the hedge. 'What's your name, then?'

CHAPTER 17

Three Years Earlier

Toni

My eyelids flipped open. The bedroom was flooded with light. For a few seconds, I didn't recognise the room or know why I was there.

'Evie?' I called, coming to at last. No answer. 'Evie!'

I pulled on leggings and a T-shirt and rushed downstairs. The TV was on but the living room was empty.

I ran through to the kitchen to find the back door slightly ajar, the key hanging loosely from the lock on the inside.

In places, the sun had broken through the thick cloud covering and now weak shafts of light shone through the opaque glass in the door, illuminating the kitchen flooring in random patches. It felt like mid-morning but there was no clock in here so I couldn't be sure. How on earth had I slept so long?

'Evie!' I yelled as I shoved my feet into the flip-flops by the door and half fell into the tiny yard. I scanned the scrubby grass lawn and the edge of the ugly panelled fence.

I could see immediately that she wasn't there.

My breathing became erratic. I just couldn't seem to suck enough air into my lungs. I leaned heavily on a broken plastic garden chair near the door. One of the damaged legs gave way and I stumbled, twisting my ankle slightly.

I yelped in pain.

'Mummy!' Seconds later, a beaming Evie emerged, crawling on all fours, through a hole in the hedge that had been masked by overgrown foliage.

'What on earth are you doing?' I rushed towards her. 'Where have you been?'

'My fault, sorry.' The head and shoulders of a tall, skinny young man appeared over the hedge. He grinned, revealing blackened teeth. 'She wanted to see the new puppy.'

The oldest trick in the book, which every parent in the country warned their kids against.

'Who are you?' I snapped. 'I've been looking for her everywhere. I thought—'

'I'm Colin,' he said, the grin turning to a frown. 'Mam said she'd met you the day you moved in, yeah?'

This must be Sal's eldest son. The convicted criminal.

'You alright?' He stared at me with cold eyes. 'You look like you're about to pass out any second.'

'Of course I'm not fu—' I looked at Evie, who was wide-eyed, taking it all in. I bit back my language. 'I'm most definitely *not* alright. I come downstairs and find that a strange man, who I've never seen before, has taken my daughter out of the garden without my permission.'

'Now, just hold on a minute.' I noted the seamless switch to a more aggressive tone. 'The kid crawled through the hedge when she heard me playing over this side with our Buster. She's been out here on her own for bloody ages. More to the point, where have *you* been?'

'Evie,' I called in clipped tones. 'Inside, now.'

'Mummy, no! Colin said I can help him feed Buster.'

I bet he did.

'Inside. NOW!' I raised my voice.

Infuriatingly, Evie looked at Colin in the hope he might support her pleading.

'You'd best go inside, flower,' he told her. 'Looks like your mam's about to have a bloody hernia.'

I held out my hand in a gesture of affection to Evie but she stormed past me, back inside the house.

'It's NOT FAIR!' she yelled as she slammed the kitchen door behind her.

I turned and glared at Colin.

'Lovely little girl you've got there, missus,' he smirked, taking a deep drag on a roll-up. 'Sweet as sugar, she is.'

When I got inside, I felt grimy just from talking to him. Evie was back in the living room and had closed the door.

'Evie,' I said softly, walking in. 'Don't ever go out there again on your own without telling me. Do you understand?'

She sat under her 'wasp shield', as she now referred to her blanket, and ignored me, staring blankly at the TV. An empty cereal box lay on its side in the middle of the floor, a spoon flung further still. Evie still had on her pyjamas with grass stains on the knees that I could tell would never wash out. Her hair was tousled and loose and dry crumbs had collected at the corners of her mouth.

It was ten thirty. My daughter had probably been up on her own since 7 a.m.

I reached for the remote control and flicked the TV off. The silence reverberated, as if an invisible wall sat between us.

'Do you understand what Mummy is saying?' I tried again. 'You mustn't go outside on your own like that again, poppet. It's dangerous.'

'I tried to tell you, Mummy.' Evie turned to face me, her eyes wide and glistening. 'But you were still sleeping and you wouldn't wake up.'

I clamped my hand over my mouth and closed my eyes. A hot thread of revulsion wrapped itself around my throat like a burning wire.

Who on earth was I turning into?

CHAPTER 18

Three Years Earlier

Toni

Monday morning didn't turn out to be the calm, organised time I'd planned it to be. I felt groggy and out of sorts, even though I hadn't touched any tablets since the early hours of yesterday.

Evie was still clearly shaken by the wasp attack, aside from the physical discomfort of the still red, scratchy swellings on her arms and face.

'Can you button up my cardigan please, Mummy?' she asked in a small voice, her face forlorn.

'Come on, a big girl like you knows how to button up, don't you?' I chided her, tickling under her chin.

'I want you to do it.'

I'd plaited her blonde wavy hair into two braids. The red and grey uniform suited her, seeming to add a little colour into her pasty cheeks, which were still dotted here and there with the unsightly red blobs.

I buttoned her cardi up and pulled her gently to me and we had a little cuddle, silent in each other's affection for a few seconds.

Then Evie pulled away and looked at me.

'Mummy, are you taking me to school today?'

'Am I taking you to school?' I repeated with outraged amazement that brought the ghost of a smile to her lips. 'OF COURSE

I'm taking you to school, silly munchkin. I wouldn't miss that for all the tea in China.'

I tickled her belly and waited for the throaty giggle I loved so much. But Evie stepped away from my wriggling fingers, edgy and wary. Her face grew solemn again.

'Are you picking me up from school, too?'

I swear to God my daughter had an overdeveloped sixth sense. She could invariably pick up vibes from whatever was laying heavy on my heart at any given time of the day. Even when I thought I'd done a pretty good job of covering up the cracks.

'Are you?' she demanded.

'No, because Nanny is picking you up from school, isn't she? If you remember—'

'No!'

Mum had already called Evie on my phone this morning to wish her luck and to tell her she'd be seeing her at the end of school.

'Evie, don't start. Nanny wants to pick you up and hear all about your day. You don't want to upset her now, do you?' I felt rotten even as I said it. What kind of mother tries to silence a five-year-old with emotional blackmail? But I had to do something to stop the threatened tantrum I could feel hovering like an imminent storm.

'But I want *you* to pick me up on my first day, Mummy.' Her big blue eyes shone, pleading with me. Her bottom lip wobbled. 'Pleeease?'

I pinched the bridge of my nose and took a deep breath in.

Why did it feel like life always conspired to make parenting so damn difficult? Of all the days for me to get an interview for the job, it had to be this one.

It had all happened so quickly from me submitting my application, I could never have reasonably anticipated problems with Evie's first day at big school.

'Mummy, please?' Evie whined again, sensing weakness.

In the afternoon, after a sandwich and a quick shower, I dressed for the interview in my smart Ted Baker navy trouser suit and white blouse.

The outfit was now a few fashion seasons old but it still looked the part. Better than my custom leggings and T-shirt, at least.

I wondered if I'd ever be in a financial position that allowed me to shop for clothes at Ted Baker again.

It was clear I'd lost a bit of weight since I bought it a couple of years ago. Obviously, I'd noticed my clothes getting looser, but after I finished work, there was no need to dress for the office and I started to live in 'loungewear' – a nicer sounding word than 'scruffs' or 'comfies'. Clothes that felt the same, whatever your weight.

Losing weight through grief led to a scrawny, malnourished body. There had been no celebratory buying of new clothes when I'd dropped two dress sizes.

I stood in front of the wardrobe and scrutinized my image in the long mirror fixed to the inside door. I suppose I didn't look too bad, considering.

The jacket hung a little big on my shoulders and I could have done with a belt for the trousers. Luckily, as we were both a size six, Mum had been able to loan me a pair of M&S black court shoes, avoiding another unnecessary expense.

I pulled my shoulders back a bit and stood a little taller. I smiled widely at myself in the mirror to check I had nothing unsightly stuck in my teeth.

I'd already gotten out of the habit of wearing make-up. There really wasn't any need, stuck in the house most days. But today I'd used a bit of mascara and a pale pink lipstick I'd found at the bottom of my handbag. A dusting of bronzer and a slick of clear gloss on top of the lip colour and I looked fairly presentable.

I patted my chestnut brown hair, neat in its French roll that I'd pinned and sprayed to within an inch of its life. We'd not been able to afford a holiday again this year but my hair had a few natural highlights, pretty glimmers of gold harvested from hours spent with Evie in our old garden, where I would snatch reading time as she splashed in her small inflatable pool with one or more of her little friends from nursery school.

Confidence. That's what I needed to exude today.

I'd certainly lost all of the managerial demeanour I used to possess, but that wasn't necessarily a bad thing.

I intended to play down my previous work history as much as I could in the interview anyway. The last thing I wanted was to put them off because they thought they'd be employing a know-all done-it-all.

I checked I had everything in my handbag before I left, including two glowing references from the directors of the previous company I'd worked for, and headed out of the house.

It was cloudy but warm outside and I slipped my jacket off before getting into the car. I'd been unable to get Evie's pleading voice out of my head all morning, begging me to pick her up from school. 'Please, Mummy, please.' It echoed again at me now.

In the end, she'd gone into school quite happily, which had been a massive relief. There were lots of teachers on hand to take the new Primary-year-one children from reluctant parental hands on their first day.

Before we left home, I'd ended up agreeing that if it was humanly possible, I would pick her up from school. I said this knowing full well that with a three o'clock interview, there was no way on earth I was going to make it back to St Saviour's for three thirty.

I disliked myself for doing it, but the little fib had been worth it to put a smile back on Evie's face, and it had made our journey out of the house so much smoother.

I sat for a moment in the car and programmed the postcode of Gregory's Property Services into the satnav. It said the journey would take thirteen minutes and I was allowing thirty. Barring an alien invasion, there would really be no need to panic.

I pressed back into the headrest and took a few deep breaths in through my nose, out through my mouth, just like the relaxation app had suggested. I thought about the little brown bottle I'd salvaged from the bathroom cabinet and tucked away in the zipped compartment of my handbag. Just in case.

I'd done it just for insurance purposes, to make me feel a little more secure. A tablet might help with my heart rate and anxiety but I needed my wits about me more than ever today, and I had to drive, too.

I pulled away from the kerb and turned left out of the estate. Cinderhill Road was busy. It was a road that carried lots of traffic towards the big island at the top, funnelling vehicles on to the A610 and eventually the M1 motorway beyond that.

Today though, I was travelling in the opposite direction and the traffic flowed fairly lightly. The road swept steeply down, past cramped rows of terraced houses with weathered bricks and peeling cream sills, long overdue for a lick of paint. I continued over the tram lines at the bottom.

I glanced at the satnav screen and took a right turn at the mini roundabout and then headed out past Moor Bridge and towards Hucknall town centre. I passed young mothers pushing brightly coloured strollers and a group of hooded youths lounging on a bench with beer cans.

This morning, Evie and I had walked to school and it had taken us just under fifteen minutes. I'd silently rebuked myself yet again for missing our appointment to look around St Saviour's. Unfortunately, they had been unable to fit us in again before the start of the new term.

Evie had been quite the little chatterbox right up until the school's wrought-iron gates came into view and then she'd become suddenly quieter, the nerves kicking in.

'It's going to be fine, darling.' I squeezed her hand. 'You'll have such a lovely day.'

'But I won't know anyone,' Evie remarked. 'Daisy, Nico and Martha are my best friends and none of them are here.'

The four young friends had been inseparable in reception class at North View Primary, her old school. My stomach twisted at the thought of her sitting alone in class.

And then I remembered.

'There'll be lots of children here who don't know anyone,' I said as we neared the propped-open side gate. 'I bet you'll have tons of friends by the end of the day, and besides, you do know someone. Someone important.'

'Huh?' Evie looked up at me, her little forehead furrowing around two angry-looking stings.

'Miss Watson, of course,' I said brightly. 'You already know the *teacher*, so you'll be the best girl!'

Her face lit up. 'Yay, I'll be the best girl!'

She sang it on repeat as we approached the gate. I was so grateful to leave her happy and smiling. Of course, when I came away, I was the one who felt choked. I could see that most of the other parents of the new five-year-olds felt exactly the same.

But for us, it was even more significant. I was being a fairly crap mum at the moment, but when it came down to it, Evie being happy was number one in my priorities. If her first day at school went well, that would be a massive step towards carving out our new life.

My beeping phone broke me out of my thoughts, the satnav informing me I had now arrived at my destination. I parked up on a little side street and bought a parking ticket for a two-hour duration.

Slipping on my jacket, I grabbed my handbag and tried to ignore my heart battering against my ribcage.

I set off across the road towards the double-fronted, professional-looking estate agency that was Gregory's Property Services.

My heart felt light and hopeful; my stomach was riddled with knots.

CHAPTER 19

Three Years Earlier

The Teacher

After lunch, Harriet Watson led the small group of children into the infant library area.

The library was used only for literacy hour in the mornings, so she didn't anticipate being disturbed. Despite it being an open-plan design, she had a good view of the corridor outside in both directions.

Harriet had selected four children for today's group session. The idea was to remove children with particular difficulties or needs from the main class, making it easier for the teacher to manage and yet giving the small group more focused attention.

Years ago, the teacher was expected to run the whole group with no complaints, but of course, these days, they spoon-fed them. They fell out of university with their teaching degrees, and a whole roster of expectations and demands that were expected to be met by other hard-pressed staff like herself.

Fortunately for Harriet, this was the second year she'd acted as teaching assistant to Jasmeen Akhtar, a thin, meek young woman who seemed to rely on Harriet's advice and opinions far more than she ought. But Harriet wasn't complaining. It meant she got to choose the children she worked with. And she always chose the more pliant or interesting ones.

She glanced around the group. Some of them she recognised from last year's reception class. She'd take a group every now and then to get them accustomed to 'big class', as it was informally known within the school.

Today, there was Matilda White, an insipid-looking girl who barely said a word, Jack Farnborough, who was dyslexic, and Thomas Manton, who was just plain stupid, although, irritatingly, nobody was allowed to use that word to describe a child nowadays.

And, of course, there was the new girl who had caught her eye from the off: Evie Cotter.

Harriet relished being the one in charge in this neat little space. It was the best thing about her job, being able to get on with things with the children without Jasmeen quoting from her *Teaching and Learning Strategies* textbook. Harriet found it laughable; Jasmeen was barely out of nappies herself.

Harriet handed out the worksheets, the same ones she would use most weeks. Not as though this hopeless shower would notice.

The other children's faces already displayed bored expressions, but Harriet watched as Evie pulled her worksheet towards her and studied it carefully.

She also noticed that Evie kept glancing up at Harriet, as if seeking reassurance that she was doing OK, doing what the teacher expected of her.

This was always a good sign.

Harriet sat down at the head of the large, round table and looked around at them.

'Well, we *are* a lucky bunch today because we have someone here who is a newcomer to Nottingham,' she began. 'Welcome, Evie.'

Evie's eyes flickered over at the others before she looked down at the table again. She adjusted her worksheet and pencil so they sat a little straighter on the desk.

'Welcome, Evie,' Harriet said again.

'Thank you,' the girl mumbled, still looking down.

The others stared.

'I thought it would be nice if you told us a bit about yourself, Evie,' Harriet said, watching her blank face. 'Such as where you lived, before coming to Nottingham, and what sort of activities you like to do out of school.'

The rest of the group looked at Harriet and then expectantly back at Evie, as if a table tennis match was about to start.

The girl rubbed over her worksheet with an index finger, like she was trying to erase the print.

'Well?'

'We lived in Hemel Hempstead before,' Evie said slowly.

Harriet remained silent.

'And I like playing with Lego and watching television after school. And I like drawing.'

'Interesting.' Harriet nodded. 'Has anyone got another question for Evie?'

'Have you got any pets?' Jack Farnborough asked.

The girl began rubbing the corner of her worksheet again but she didn't speak.

'Evie?' Harriet prompted.

'We had a rabbit at our old house,' Evie said. 'A black and white one. His name was Carlos.'

'Carlos,' Thomas Manton repeated.

'What happened to the rabbit?' Jack asked. 'Did you have it put down when you moved house?'

An expression of pure horror crossed Evie's face.

'We gave him to Mr Baxter,' she said. 'For when his grandchildren, Daisy and Tom, come round to visit.'

'Any more questions?' Harriet looked around at the blank faces.

Nobody spoke.

Evie breathed out and looked down at her worksheet.

'What about your family, Evie? Tell us a bit about them.' Harriet smiled.

She watched as the child's breaths grew shorter, noticing her cheeks turning pink. She didn't speak.

'Your grandma?' Harriet prompted her.

'Nanny had a cat called Timmy but he got old and then he went to live with the angels and now she has a cat called Igor.'

'Igor,' Thomas repeated under his breath.

'And your mummy and daddy, what do they do?'

Evie lowered her chin and mumbled something incoherent.

'Look up and speak clearly please, Evie, so that everyone can hear,' Harriet said.

'Mummy used to sell houses to people.'

'And your daddy?'

Harriet watched, fascinated, as two dark pink patches appeared in the middle of the child's cheeks.

'He was a soldier.' Her voice was barely audible.

'He *was* a soldier?'

Evie fell silent.

'Can I go to the toilet, please, miss?' Thomas Manton asked.

Harriet glared at the boy and he shrank back down into his chair.

'Explain to us what you mean by saying your dad *was* a soldier,' Harriet said, turning to Evie again.

'He had an accident,' Evie said.

'What kind of an accident?' Jack said.

Evie looked down.

'Jack asked you a question,' Harriet said. 'Again, Jack?'

'What kind of an accident?' Jack repeated.

'He fell off a cliff, in Af – Af-gan-stan,' Evie said, her voice cracking. 'He died.'

She wiped her eyes with the back of her hand.

'He fell off a cliff, Jack,' Harriet repeated.

Jack's mouth dropped open.

'Well, there we go. That's Evie's story,' Harriet said brightly. 'Her mummy doesn't work anymore and her daddy used to be a soldier but he fell off a cliff and died.'

Matilda giggled.

Evie let out a sob.

'You mustn't blame yourself, Evie,' Harriet said. 'It's unpleasant, but it's something you must learn to face. And we are here, as your friends, to help you do that. Isn't that right, children?'

'Yes, Miss Watson,' the blank faces chanted glumly and in unison.

CHAPTER 20

Three Years Earlier

Toni

The estate agency was spacious and bright inside, and the layout was more or less exactly as I'd expected. There were four desks dotted around the large shop with an agent sitting at one of them, currently dealing with customers. I looked back at the windows and found that, just like my last office in Hemel, I could barely see out onto the street due to the property posters that were dotted over the entire glass frontage.

Not wanting to interrupt the busy agent, and having arrived ten minutes early, I pretended to be absorbed in looking through the available lettings folders. The shop was warm because of all the glass and I felt a trickle of perspiration snaking down my back.

I leafed blindly through the property details, wondering what Evie was doing in class. I hoped she was having fun making new friends and settling in well.

'Can I help you?'

A tall, athletic-looking man in his late thirties came striding towards me. He had on a smart brown suit, cream shirt without a tie and, crowning it all, a shock of bright red and somewhat unruly hair. The result of this rather eclectic mix was unexpectedly attractive.

'Toni Cotter.' I held out my hand. 'I'm here for the interview. I'm afraid I'm a bit early.'

'Ahh yes, of course. Toni.' He smiled and his green eyes creased up until I could barely see them. Close up, his face was a mass of freckles so dense, it looked like he had a patchy tan. 'I'm the owner, Dale Gregory. Really pleased to meet you.'

We shook hands and I pasted on a smile, trying to remember how I used to act when I had confidence in my abilities.

'If you'd like to come through, I'll introduce you to Bryony James, our residential sales and lettings manager.' He turned back and smiled at me as he walked. 'Just the two of us interviewing you today, Toni. All very informal, so nothing to worry about.'

Did I look so obviously terrified? I actually felt slightly better. I liked Dale and the friendly atmosphere of the place was reassuring. I even dared to think that I could probably imagine myself working here.

If I could only get this job, it would be such a massive step forward for both me and Evie.

Dale led me through the shop and into a short, cooler hallway at the back that was lined with four doors. Dale pushed open the one that was already ajar.

A woman wearing an immaculate black suit and crisp white linen blouse, who I assumed was Bryony James, sat scrolling through property details on a tablet on one side of a large conference table that took up most of the space in the room.

Her jet-black hair fell in front of her face like a straight and glossy curtain. Her nails were long and oval and painted in the fashionable new slate-grey shade that I'd seen in the expensive fashion magazines I often leafed through on the shelves at the supermarket.

I bent my own short and bitten nails in towards my palms and pressed them to my sides.

'Here we are. Please, take a seat, Toni.'

As Dale walked around the far side of the table to sit next to Bryony, she glanced up at him and smiled. I tried to catch her eye to smile too, but she looked back down again to flick off her screen.

I sat opposite them and waited while Dale turned off his phone and Bryony opened her notepad. At the side of her, I recognised a printed copy of the application form and CV I'd emailed over on Friday and I swallowed hard.

Bryony had small, pinched features that were set just a tad too close together on her face, leaving her forehead and cheeks appearing a little too wide to be beautiful.

Something about the way she repeatedly straightened her notepad, pen and tablet made me wonder if she always subconsciously made amends for this physical flaw by ensuring that everything else about her and around her looked nothing less than perfect.

The characterless room was small and airless and my previously loose jacket had started to feel tight and constrictive across my back and under my arms.

I jutted out my bottom lip and blew my fringe away from my sticky face.

Bryony choose this exact moment to make eye contact for the first time. She appraised me coolly and didn't return my harried smile.

Dale introduced himself again and turned to her.

'As I mentioned, this is Bryony James, our residential sales and lettings manager. If you're successful, Bryony will be your line manager.'

I smiled again and nodded to Bryony, who simply pressed her narrow lips into a tight line by way of a compromise against remaining completely sour-faced.

Dale laced his fingers together on the desk in front of him and leaned forward slightly.

'So, why don't you start by telling us a little bit about yourself, Toni, and why you've applied for the position?'

I started off well, giving a quick resume of my education and career to date. I was careful not to dwell on my senior position at the last agency and I made sure I retained eye contact with them both as I spoke.

'You don't have a degree?' Bryony remarked.

'No, I finished my formal education at A levels,' I said. 'From there, I worked my way up.'

'Nothing wrong with that,' Dale said cheerfully. 'Shows substance.'

'I notice there are a couple of gaps in your CV.' Bryony glanced down at her copy of my application. 'Five years ago there seems to be a year missing and then it looks like you haven't been working for the last couple of years at all. Fancy a bit of a break from selling property, did you?'

A flare of resentment spiked in my chest.

Actually, Little Miss Know-It-All, I've worked bloody hard these last two years, I wanted to say. *Harder than I've worked in my life. Just to stay sane and get through the crap.*

'Five years ago, I took twelve months maternity leave when I had my daughter, Evie,' I said, and wondered if I'd imagined the wisp of disapproval that appeared to flit over her face. 'And two years ago, I had to stop working for personal reasons.'

I'd already considered how I was going to handle Andrew's death if it came up in conversation. I'd decided I didn't want to discuss it in an interview situation; it just didn't seem right and I'd put myself at risk of getting emotional.

'Personal reasons?' Bryony raised an eyebrow.

'Yes,' I said. 'I had no choice but to stop working temporarily.'

'Go on.'

'Circumstances were out of my control at that point in time but happily my situation has now changed.'

How many different ways did she want me to say it?

We stared each other out in silence.

My heart thumped, my ears rang and my face burned. But job or no job, I'd made my mind up. I wasn't going to be bullied into baring my soul. Not here, in front of people I'd only just met.

Dale coughed and fiddled with his copy of my CV.

'You've certainly got a wealth of experience, Toni,' he said approvingly. 'On both sides of the business, too. Sales *and* lettings.'

I broke eye contact with Bryony and nodded at Dale, grateful for his intervention.

'I enjoy working in both areas,' I said. 'I know this opening is for the lettings side, but I'm happy to be flexible.'

'But you're aware this is the *assistant's* position?' Bryony frowned. 'Isn't this job rather a step down for someone with your experience?'

'It's true I've had a wide range of experience, but less responsibility suits me better at this point in my life.'

The heat in my face seemed to be building. I wished I had a glass of water and that they'd open the door behind me, to let a little air circulate through the stuffy space.

'You mentioned a daughter. Is she at school now?' Bryony asked. 'I assume you have flexible childcare arrangements in place, because there are occasions you might be asked to work late or come in a few hours early in busy periods.'

I opened my mouth to answer her and then closed it again.

Would she have asked a male candidate that question? A twisty heat begin to simmer in my chest.

'Let's remember this position is only part-time, Bryony,' said Dale. 'I'm sure Toni would be willing to be flexible if required.'

'Of course,' I replied, looking at Dale and avoiding Bryony's incisive stare.

They asked me a few more questions.

What kind of pay was I looking for? Did I have any pre-existing holidays booked? When could I start?

'No holidays and I could start tomorrow,' I said quickly. 'If you wanted someone that soon. And I'm flexible regarding pay.'

'We do have another candidate to consider,' Bryony said quickly. 'So we'll let you know our decision later today.'

Dale looked at her sharply and, for a second, something resembling irritation burned in his eyes. Then it was gone.

'Thank you so much for coming, Toni.' He stood up and began walking to the door. 'I'll show you out.'

'Nice to meet you,' I said to the top of Bryony's head as she scribbled something in her notepad.

'Yes.' She looked up and pulled her mouth into a shape that fell somewhere between a smile and a grimace. 'Thank you for coming.'

Back in the shop, there were more prospective customers browsing the properties and I saw that the agent, a woman, was still sitting at her desk dealing with clients.

Dale insisted on checking he had the right telephone number to reach me on.

'I'll definitely be in touch later.' He glanced around and dropped his voice lower. 'Just between you and me, we'd be fools not to snap you up, all those years of experience.'

Reading between the lines, it felt like his words were weighted and he was trying to tell me I had the job. But knowing me, I was probably imagining it, so I swept it aside.

We shook hands and, for the first time since the interview started, I felt a little lighter.

As I stepped outside and turned to pull the door closed behind me, I saw Bryony leaning against the wall in the hallway, watching me leave with narrowed eyes.

CHAPTER 21

Present Day

Queen's Medical Centre

Dr Shaw shines a light directly into my eyes.

I squint hard against the brightness, but regardless of what I do, my eyes remain motionless; wide open and staring.

The doctor bends down closer, humming softly as she peers at my pupils and then stretches each eyelid wide.

I can see the large, open pores in her nose and chin and it reminds me that I had a tub of face cream in my bathroom cabinet at home that was supposed to close the pores up, so you looked younger. She ought to use something like that.

I wonder how old Dr Shaw is – I'd say maybe early forties. Somehow, I can't imagine her with kids. Maybe she has a husband who is also a doctor. They might meet up after work and then cook a meal together to unwind when they get home.

It's far more likely they grab a sandwich and fall fast asleep after work, knackered from attending to hopeless cases like me all day long.

If only they had a machine that could translate the anxious thoughts that fill my brain. I could tell them how Evie was taken from me, beg them to help me find her before it's too late.

Every day I remember a little more. I'm putting together the pieces of how it happened, of how she disappeared.

Sometimes it's hard to know if my memories are real or just imagined.

Dr Shaw's face hovers close to mine and I catch the slightest trace of smoke on her breath that she has tried, unsuccessfully, to disguise with a mint.

I blink at her in a mad flurry but the connection inside me is broken and nothing happens.

'So, how's Matt?' I hear Dr Chance say from across the room. He is out of my limited range of partial vision. His voice is deep and sincere but I think I might detect a hint of amusement in his tone.

'Oh, you know, overworked and underpaid like the rest of us.' Dr Shaw squeezes a pipette and a drop of cool, soothing fluid slides onto my dry eyeball. Her face instantly blurs above me. 'Actually, he's still planning our escape to the country.'

'And will you go?' Dr Chance asks. 'Open that B&B you've always talked about?'

'No.' I watch a shadow settle over Dr Shaw's features. 'It's Matt's pipe dream and I'm guilty of indulging him. We've no equity in the house and without jobs it's nothing but a fantasy.'

Do it, I tell her in a bold, urgent tone. *Open your B&B, breathe in the clean, fresh air. Get away from the rat race and live the life you want, while you still can.*

'Oh!' She snatches back her hand from above my eye.

'What is it?' I hear Dr Chance's shoes clip briskly across the floor and now there are two faces peering down at me, hovering in front of my eyes.

His features are rugged with a faint shadow of stubble. His nose looks slightly off-centre, as though it might've been broken when he was younger. Flinty, grey eyes look down on me with vague but genuine concern.

I can see you! I cry out.

I stretch my mouth wide, blink my eyelids, wrinkle my nose.

They continue to stare down impassively.

Dr Shaw frowns. 'I don't know. For a second I thought there was something there.'

'Did she move?'

'No, it was just – I saw this sort of *gleam* in her eyes, that's the only way I can describe it. It was odd.'

Yes! Behind it all, I am still here. My eyes gleamed. They did!

'It's probably just the pupils contracting with the serum,' Dr Chance says, staring down at me without expression. 'Or a trick of the light.'

Look again! I shout. *Please, look again.*

'You're probably right.' She tilts her head, studying me. Still reluctant to look away. 'For a second it just felt there was some sort of presence there, behind her eyes, you know?'

'We all want to believe that,' Dr Chance says, stepping away. 'It's hard to accept the loss of life, when the patient looks so normal.'

'You're right,' she says, finally looking away from me. 'But in some ways, I suppose anything is better than this.' Her eyes flick back to me and she squeezes them shut briefly, before opening them again. 'It sounds harsh, but death has got to be better than barely existing.'

CHAPTER 22

Three Years Earlier

Toni

I stepped out of Gregory's Property Services and into the street. I felt a little better after inhaling a few deep breaths of fresh air. Being cooped up in that tiny office, under pressure, had been testing to say the least.

I slipped off my jacket, folded it over my arm and began walking briskly down the street towards my car. Soon, my heart rate would calm down and my face would stop burning.

I had plenty of time left on my parking ticket. But it was nearly three forty-five and Evie would already be home from school.

I was so excited to hear about how her first day had gone.

I fired off a quick text to say I was on my way and how was Evie, but Mum didn't reply. I felt a stab of annoyance. Of all days, you'd think she would let me know how Evie had coped on her first day at big school.

There was more traffic on the journey home than I'd expected but I didn't mind because it gave me a little thinking time. I wound the windows down slightly, enjoying the warm breeze but wishing the car had air con.

Maybe, just maybe, this job could get me a newer car and a weekend break away for Evie and I. Those things might not be as unreachable as they felt right now.

There had been a point during the interview when Bryony seemed to be so openly hostile that I questioned if I really wanted to work there.

But why should I let someone so obviously bitter put a dampener on my plans for a better life? I really liked Dale and although I hadn't had a chance to speak to the other female agent at the desk, Gregory's seemed a nice enough place to work.

I managed to find a parking space outside the house and as I got out of the car, I expected to see Evie banging excitedly on the living room window, desperate to tell me about her day.

We'd already developed a habit of using the back kitchen door, rather than the front door which led directly into the living room, so I walked around the side of the house.

I noticed that the yard was overgrown with more weeds than actual grass and it looked like the entire population of the estate's cats were used to treating the borders as the local litter tray.

Mum was adamant we should always keep the doors locked 'in an area like this' so I wasn't surprised when I tried the handle and the door didn't open.

Rather than start ferreting in my bag for the bunch of keys I'd just thrown in there, I tapped on the opaque, patterned glass and waited. Nobody came to the door.

I eventually found my keys and unlocked it.

'Hello?' I called as I stepped inside the house.

Something about the silence and the stillness of the air within told me nobody was home, which was surprising. I glanced at the kitchen clock. It was nearly four fifteen, a full hour after Evie had finished, and I knew from this morning that walking at a leisurely pace to school took only fifteen minutes.

I pulled my phone out of my handbag and checked for messages. Nothing.

I dialled Mum's number and it went straight through to answerphone.

My heart rate started to pick up pace again.

'It's fine,' I murmured out loud. 'Everything is fine.'

I dialled St Saviour's and waited for the administrator to answer, but a recorded message informed me that the school office was now closed.

I sat down at the tiny kitchen table, my chest rising and falling far too fast. Since Andrew's accident, my mind went straight from nought to a hundred miles per hour, seeing a crisis in everything. It sped to the worst case scenario every time.

Mum wouldn't have forgotten it was Evie's first day, I knew for sure she'd have been there to pick her up. So where could they be?

I couldn't just sit here, doing nothing. I dumped my jacket and handbag and dashed from the house, clutching only my phone and keys.

So many awful *what if* scenarios sped through my mind, I could barely keep track.

What if there had been a road accident involving Mum and Evie?

What if Mum had collapsed and Evie had run into the road in a panic?

What if Mum was ill and unconscious somewhere and Evie had somehow managed to wander home on her own?

I emerged on to the street, my eyes prickling and mouth dry, and that's when I saw them. Turning the corner into Muriel Crescent.

'Yoo-hoo!' Mum called, waving.

Evie had an ice cream in her hand and seemed subdued. Usually, I'd expect her to break away from Mum and run to me.

'Where were you?' I rushed up. 'I was worried sick.'

'Heavens, Toni,' Mum said in her *there you go again with your completely illogical reaction* tone of voice that always made me feel incredibly stupid despite the high level of panic Mum had managed to provoke. 'It's a warm day and you were at your interview. There's no sense in Evie being cooped up in the house.'

Mum's infuriatingly logical reasoning. Why couldn't I have told myself the same thing before I launched into imagining my whole world ending?

'But I thought . . . Anything could have happened. I texted you.'

'My phone's out of charge.' Mum shrugged. 'I left it on the side in the kitchen. Please don't make a scene about it, love.'

Me make a scene? I spent most of my time walking on eggshells so as not to annoy Mum. Still, I let it go.

I realised Evie hadn't said a word. I stepped in front of her and sank down on my haunches. My heart was still hammering but I knew it would calm down soon, now I knew she was safe. 'Do I get a cuddle from my big girl, then?'

She gave me a weak smile and a half-hearted hug and that's when I saw she'd been crying. I looked up at Mum.

'Besides, Evie got herself a little bit upset, didn't you, petal?' Mum shot me a meaningful look. 'I thought a little walk to the park and an ice cream might help.'

When we got back inside the house, Evie went straight to the living room door and waited there. I went in first and did my waspie walkabout. This was what we now called our new routine. Before Evie felt comfortable entering this room, I had to check every inch of it for wasps that might have escaped Mr Etheridge, the world's greatest pest controller.

When Evie was satisfied the room was safe, she turned on the TV and, despite the heat, snuggled under her fleecy comfort blanket with her thumb in her mouth. She wouldn't entertain the window being open anymore. I was hoping that in time the trauma would fade. Just like the stings seemed to be doing at last.

When I was sure Evie was settled, I went back in the kitchen, flicked on the kettle and looked at Mum.

'What happened?'

'I'm not sure,' Mum sighed. 'For starters, you told me the wrong time, which didn't help.'

'What?'

'School finishes at three fifteen, Toni, not three thirty. The other children had been collected and when I got there poor Evie was sat all alone.'

I frowned. I could have sworn that when Harriet Watson visited, she'd made a point of telling me that pick-up time was three thirty.

'Anyway, when I picked her up from class, Miss Akhtar, her teacher, said she'd had a good day.'

'I thought her teacher's name was Miss Watson?'

'No, it was definitely a Miss Akhtar, she introduced herself to me. A nice young woman she was, looked as though she was just out of university.'

That description didn't match the middle-aged, rather stern Harriet Watson, who had visited us earlier in the week. I seemed to be getting all the details mixed up in my head.

I made two coffees and we sat down at the table.

'I thought Evie seemed a bit quiet, and when we got out of the school gates, she burst into tears,' Mum said, tracing a deep scratch on the thin wooden veneer of the tabletop.

'Why was she so upset?'

'She wouldn't tell me, Toni.' Mum looked up at me and I could see she felt troubled and confused about Evie's reaction. 'All she kept saying was that she doesn't want to go to school tomorrow. Don't get annoyed with her.'

'Why do you keep saying that?' I took a big gulp of steaming hot coffee and swallowed it down, wincing as it burned my throat. 'When have I ever caused a scene or got annoyed?'

Mum looked at me.

I did feel a twist of blame towards her for not finding more out from the school. If she'd noticed Evie was overly quiet, then Mum should've asked the teacher a few more questions.

'It's a shame you couldn't have been there to pick her up on your first day,' Mum said, on the defensive again and weirdly accurate. 'Then you could have asked her teacher yourself.'

I wasn't going to get into a fight with Mum. I couldn't handle it today.

'By the way, my interview went well,' I said pointedly. 'They're ringing me later to let me know if I've got it.'

'Oh good,' Mum said, her tone conveying that, in her opinion, it was actually the exact opposite of good. She stood up and picked up something from the counter that was wrapped in a clean tea towel. 'Here, I made a quiche for your tea.'

CHAPTER 23

Three Years Earlier

The Teacher

After she'd photocopied more worksheets for the next day, Harriet began to collect up the numerous sheets of the children's dried artwork from the six square tables that were dotted around the classroom.

Without doubt, this was her favourite time of day. Most of the staff and all of the children had gone home and the classroom assumed a tranquil, reassuring ambience that never failed to calm her nerves.

Harriet was in no rush to go home. She was never quite sure, until she got through the door each day, what mood her mother would be in. It wasn't difficult to hazard a guess, of course. Nine times out of ten, it was a foul mood.

It had seemed such a long summer break this year. At times it had felt never-ending. Each time there was a school holiday, she was always among the rare few who were glad to get back to work.

At school, Harriet felt as if she was *somebody*. She was respected because of her experience and people generally seemed keen to listen to her views and opinions. It was a far cry from being stuck at home with her constantly criticising mother. But, regardless of what *she* thought, Harriet knew that the work she did was important. Children were vulnerable, they needed guidance to help them navigate through the pitfalls of life as they grew older. Many of them received little guidance and learned few suitable life skills from their parents, or rather *parent* in the singular, as Harriet observed had increasingly become the norm in many homes.

Take little Evie Cotter. Mollycoddled in one sense and yet woefully neglected in another. It was vital that the child learned to face up to the unexpected death of her father and began that process as early as possible, to harden herself against the cruel jibes that were bound to come when she got a little older and, in particular, when she went to the high school in a few years' time. There would be no stopping them then.

Other children could be vicious, cutting in the extreme with their remarks if they detected a soft centre, and Harriet was thoroughly convinced that this would leave lasting damage if the child concerned was unprepared.

Harriet froze for a few moments as thoughts whirled in her head, her hands full of colourful paintings depicting stick figures and various other indecipherable shapes.

The horror of being singled out and bullied at school left deep wounds that would weep inside you forever, where no one could see. The scar on her forehead began to itch again. It always did when she thought about the gang of girls who had tormented her for most of her senior-school years.

Harriet coughed, her eyes refocused and she took a hold of herself again. Now was no time to be lingering in the past or remembering that day they had cornered her with the broken bottle after school.

She had work to do. There were children here who she could save from a similar fate. Impressionable youngsters who depended on her, needed her guidance.

Evie Cotter was one of them.

CHAPTER 24

Three Years Earlier

Toni

After Mum left, I felt so tired that I half dozed off while Evie watched her cartoons. I didn't ask her any questions about what had upset her at school. We had the whole evening to get there and I knew from experience that Evie wouldn't be rushed into talking about it if she didn't want to.

I felt Evie sit up a bit straighter, tilting her head to one side as if she was listening. That's when I snapped fully awake.

'Mummy, your phone's ringing,' she said.

I jumped up and ran into the kitchen to find I'd missed a call from an unknown mobile number. Immediately, I thought it might be Dale, about the job.

But whoever it was hadn't left a message. Stupidly, I'd left the phone in here instead of having it next to me. I tossed it onto the countertop in frustration and just then it began to ring again. I snatched it back up.

'Hello?'

'Toni? Dale here, from Gregory's Property Services. I thought I'd give you another try, just in case.'

'Hello, Dale. I'm so sorry I missed you, I left the phone in the kitchen and—' I was babbling like an idiot. 'Sorry, I'm going on a bit.'

'Thanks so much for coming in today,' he began, and I filled in the blanks. *It was a really hard decision but in the end there was someone that suited the position better . . .* 'We were really impressed with your interview and I'd like to offer you the job. Starting tomorrow, if that's still convenient for you?'

'What? I mean, wow, thank you! That's brilliant.' I couldn't believe I'd done it. I'd got the job. 'And tomorrow is great for me, thanks. Thanks so much.'

'Perfect,' Dale laughed. 'Well, congratulations, and we'll see you at one o'clock tomorrow afternoon. Have a good evening.'

I stood for a moment when Dale rang off, the phone still in my hand. I felt a bit dazed.

A good thing had just happened to me. *A good thing!*

'I'm hungry, Mummy,' Evie announced, walking into the kitchen, trailing her blanket behind her. 'What's for tea?'

I pulled out a chair and picked Evie up, sitting down with her on my knee.

'Listen, munchkin, Mummy has some really exciting news for us.' My stomach fizzed as I heard myself say the words. 'I just got a job!'

'A job?'

'That's right. I'll just be working afternoons, so I can still take you to school each day.'

'But I don't want to go to St Saviour's anymore.'

My heart seemed to slip a notch in my chest.

'Come on, poppet. It's only your first day, it's natural for things to seem a bit strange. Tomorrow will be so much better, you'll see.'

'I don't want to go.'

Evie shuffled off my knee and stood in front of me, holding her blanket up to her pursed lips.

'Why don't you like school, Evie?'

'I just don't.'

'Who's your teacher? Nanny said it's not Miss Watson.'

'Miss Watson isn't my teacher.' Evie frowned. 'She just helps Miss Akhtar.'

It was puzzling. I felt sure Harriet Watson had told me she was Evie's teacher. I must have misheard her.

'I had to go with Miss Watson into the library with some other children,' Evie said.

'That's good. Miss Watson already knows you,' I beamed. 'I bet you're her favourite.'

'I'm not.'

'OK, so what did you do in the library?'

'She made me talk,' Evie scowled. 'I didn't want to talk to the other children.'

It sounded to me like Miss Watson was trying to get Evie to come out of her shell a bit, to mix with the other kids. As far as I was concerned, that could only be a good thing.

Evie needed to make some friends. Although she was chatty and confident at home, I'd noticed in the last few months that she could be stubbornly silent and a bit moody around new people.

'It's just a first-day thing, Evie,' I reassured her. 'Everyone has to do that when they're new, I'll have to do it tomorrow when I start my new job. It'll be different tomorrow, you'll see.'

'I'm not going tomorrow,' Evie said, her jaw firmly set. 'Nanny said I don't have to.'

CHAPTER 25

Three Years Earlier

Toni

When I opened my eyes the next morning, my heavy heart told me there was something to worry about before my mind caught up with exactly what that was.

I was going to have a big problem in getting Evie to school.

Fortunately, I'd woken early – it was just six thirty. Plenty of time to get myself psyched up and organised, ready for the battle that undoubtedly lay before me. Evie might be small and endlessly cute, but she was a fearsome opponent when she dug her heels in. Any nerves about my first day in the new job melted into oblivion when I thought about the problems it would cause if every weekday became a battle with Evie. The stakes were high and I needed to try to sort things out before they escalated.

I'd already laid out my work clothes last night so I showered, washed my hair and got myself ready for the day ahead. That was the easy part.

Downstairs, I prepared a bowl of Evie's favourite cereal, poured her a small glass of orange juice – without bits – and prepared to wake her at seven thirty, which was in five minutes time.

Last night when Evie was watching TV, I came into the kitchen and rang Mum to tell her that I thought I'd solved the mystery of what had upset her.

'Miss Watson tried to get her to tell the others a bit about herself,' I had explained. 'Because she's new to the area.'

'Well, I'd be surprised if that's all it was, Toni, she was so upset,' Mum replied. 'Anyway, Evie's a sociable enough girl, she doesn't need to be put on the spot like that.'

'Evie isn't as sociable as she used to be, Mum,' I tried to reason. 'Also, she said Nanny told her she doesn't have to go to school tomorrow if she doesn't want to. If that's true, can you stop saying it? Because it really isn't helpful.'

'You didn't see her sobbing outside the gates,' Mum shot straight back. 'I said what I could to calm her down after that Watton woman, or whatever her name is, upset the poor mite. The woman is overbearing.'

'Her name's Miss *Watson*, Mum, and as far as I'm concerned, being encouraged to talk to her classmates can only be a good thing. I'm sure it was just first-day nerves on Evie's part, nothing more than that.'

'Hmm, well we'll soon see, won't we?' Mum was on her high horse now. 'Because I'll tell you now, if she's in tears when I pick her up this afternoon, I'll be going straight back inside and asking them why she's so unhappy.'

'Don't get on the wrong side of the school, Mum,' I said, trying to keep my voice level. 'Evie doesn't always know what's best for her, she's just five years old.'

I had almost felt Mum's irritation trickling down the handset and dripping into my ear. She made some inane excuse and rang off.

I shook off the memory of last night's conversation and checked the time. It was just gone seven-thirty now, so I was going to have to wake her, which wasn't ideal.

I padded softly up the stairs and stood outside Evie's door, listening to her soft, regular breaths. There had been a couple of nights where she'd come into my room and woken me, upset from a bad dream she'd had about me. It was only natural, after her Daddy had gone from her life so tragically and quickly, that she'd worry that I might leave her too.

I pushed the door open and crept into the room. Fortunately, the previous owners had left the curtains, but they were thin and barely kept out any light at all. Their choices would have to do for now, but I was going to make sure Evie had the princess bedroom she deserved once I had a regular wage coming in.

I stood for a moment and drank in the sight of my beautiful girl, her golden hair spilling across the pillow. She had Andrew's lashes, long and dark.

My heart squeezed in on itself when I thought about what she'd been through. She was dealing with a never-ending hurt she didn't fully understand. Her daddy had been there one minute and gone the next, and now upheaval had struck again in the shape of a new home and a new school.

Was it any wonder she'd withdrawn into herself a bit and didn't want the spotlight on her in class? I blamed myself. I should have made it clearer to Harriet Watson the day she'd called at the house, but I wasn't sure what else I could have said. Don't try to help her integrate or make friends? Leave her completely alone? Ignore her? Of course not. In the long run, Miss Watson's efforts would pay off, I felt sure of it.

'Morning, Mummy.' Evie stretched and yawned and smiled at me sleepily.

'There she is, my best girl.' I smiled back. 'My clever, clever girl who goes to big school now.'

A shadow passed over her face and her fingers clawed at her comfort blanket.

'Your favourite breakfast is awaiting you downstairs, Your Highness.' I swept my arm grandly.

'Frosted Shreddies?' Her face lit up.

'Frosted Shreddies indeed.' I grinned. 'And fresh orange juice WITHOUT the bits.'

'Yum!'

Evie pushed her blanket away and shuffled over to me for a cuddle.

'Now, are you going to be a brave girl for Mummy and go to school again today?' I ventured. 'It's my first day at my new job and I'm a little nervous, too. Can we do it together, do you think?'

'Yes, Mummy.' She nodded in full agreement and I silently thanked the great God of Tantrums for giving me this temporary and most welcome respite.

An hour later, Evie was washed, fed, dressed and standing in the corner of the short hallway with her arms folded, refusing to leave the house.

'Evie, please,' I tried again. 'You have to go to school.'

'Nanny said I don't have to go.'

'You do. Nanny just said that because you were upset.' I ran my hand through my still-damp hair. 'Every little girl and boy has to go to school or their mummy could go to jail. It's the law.'

She looked mildly concerned for all of two seconds. 'I DON'T want to go.'

This was getting ridiculous. If we didn't leave the house in the next five minutes, Evie was in danger of being late.

'You have to go to school, simple as that,' I repeated sternly.

'I want to go to school,' she said, her eyes shining. 'But not *that* school. I don't want to go to horrid St Saviour's.'

'It's the only school around here,' I said, reaching for her arm. 'You have to go there, Evie.'

'I don't want to.' Her voice ramped up an octave as I gently tugged at her arm.

'Let's just walk together and see how you feel. Look, it's a lovely day out there, we can look on my phone and see if there are any Pokémon around to capture on the way.'

Her eyes widened. 'OK, Mummy, but if I don't want to go in when we get there, can I come back home with you?'

'Ooh, look,' I said, tapping at my phone as if I hadn't heard. 'We might find one of these!' I flashed the screenshot of a suitably monstrous-looking creature.

We walked quite briskly and I led her past hedgerows and seat benches that all might be concealing Pokémon. It worked brilliantly. Until the school gates came into view.

'I've decided I don't want to go in after all, Mummy.' She stopped dead in her tracks and folded her arms.

'Evie, I told you. You *have* to.' I took her arm and gently pulled her along.

'I don't want to. I DON'T WANT TO!' Then the tears started, streaming down her cheeks, which she rubbed all over her face, dampening her fringe.

'Evie, *please*.'

Parents and children were staring now as Evie started to pull the opposite way, strange faces displaying varying degrees of sympathy, disapproval and fascination. It was becoming impossible to keep hold of her arm and pull her through the side gate without hurting her.

'Good heavens!' A voice thundered in front of us. 'What's happening here?'

I let go of Evie's arm in alarm and she stopped struggling immediately. We both looked up to see Harriet Watson standing at the gates, hands on her hips.

Evie froze.

'Surely this can't be Evie Cotter, who was such a good girl yesterday?' She shook her head at me, aghast. 'Do you know,

Mummy, Miss Akhtar said there might even be a sticker for Evie if she behaves as well today.'

Evie inhaled a little sob and wiped her eyes, staring all the time at Miss Watson.

'A sticker, you say?' I repeated.

'Yes, and we don't give stickers out to many of the children, you know,' Harriet said. 'Only the *very best* behaved girls and boys.' She took a few steps forward and held out her hand. 'Now, Evie, if you come along with me, and we walk into class together, Miss Akhtar doesn't need to know about this little upset this morning, does she?'

Evie shook her head and grasped Miss Watson's hand, looking up at her with undisguised hope of being given one of the hallowed stickers.

I let out a breath when I saw she'd actually stopped crying.

'It can be our little secret.' Harriet tipped her head at me meaningfully and I turned quietly to walk away. 'Now then, we're doing some very exciting work in class today. Do you like art?'

'Nanny says I'm a very good drawer,' I heard Evie say as the two of them disappeared through the gate. 'And I can do lots of different sorts of art, even painting faces.'

I watched them go, Evie nodding and answering Miss Watson's questions. She never even looked back to see if I was still there. An invisible weight lifted from my shoulders and I stretched my neck left and right to try to ease the trapped tension.

Mum might not be impressed, but as far as I was concerned, Harriet Watson was my hero.

CHAPTER 26

Present Day

Queen's Medical Centre

I am trying, so desperately, not to sleep.

If I sleep, they could come in and turn me off. It could easily happen, just like that. The flick of a switch, the press of a button and *bang* – I'm gone.

No one to stop them, no one to miss me.

Dr Shaw will sign the papers that will go to the coroner. They'll quickly reduce me to a pile of ashes, and once the death certificate is filed, no one will be any the wiser that I was ever here. Alive in my invisible prison.

And then what will happen to Evie?

I know that somewhere, my beautiful girl is behind her own glass wall, unable to find her way back home. Without me, they'll write her off, forget her. She will just become a statistic, another unsolved case.

That's why, no matter how hopeless it seems, I have to fight. I have to find a way to make them see I am still here. That I am worth taking a chance on.

I have such vital things I need to tell them. Things that might just find Evie. I'm starting to remember everything, even the seemingly uneventful, everyday things. The truth is in there somewhere.

Beep, hiss, hiss, hiss, beep.

My chest rises and falls as the respirator pumps life into my lungs.

Tick tock, tick tock.

The clock on the wall taunts me. Every second that passes, I move nearer to certain death at the hands of the doctors.

Unless I can crack the glass, that is. Shatter this unseen prison inside myself.

I search for the archived lessons of my school human biology class.

The diaphragm is the muscle that promotes effective breathing. It moves up and down and it is located just under the ribs.

I try to feel its presence; my *diaphragm.* I conjure up in my mind a horizontal band of thick, powerful muscle. Muscles can move, they can twitch of their own accord. Muscles have a memory.

For a few seconds I concentrate, willing my diaphragm to move.

Up, down, up, down. Relax.

And again. Up, down, up, down.

Nothing happens.

But it's a start.

CHAPTER 27

Three Years Earlier

Toni

When I got back home after taking Evie to school, I made a coffee and sat drinking it in the kitchen, waiting for my mood to stabilise. I had that horrible feeling again. It was hard to explain it, but suffice to say it was a powerful feeling that something awful was about to happen, although I knew that was hardly rational. Enough awful things had happened already to last me a whole lifetime.

I ought to be feeling hopeful. Surely things were looking up. With any luck, Evie would settle into school, and I'd landed a job way before I could've reasonably expected to. Yet even though I knew I'd be able to cope easily with the duties at Gregory's, bearing in mind my previous experience, my hands began to tremble when I imagined myself walking in there this afternoon. The new girl all over again at thirty-five years of age.

Evie was just five years old. Why was I even remotely surprised she was having teething problems at St Saviour's? My daughter had a good excuse; I had none. I was all grown up and had to take whatever life threw at me.

Tara had included a telephone number and email address in her recent letter. I could call her. I used to enjoy our chats; she was always so pragmatic and sensible, I remember she had this knack of calming me down.

And then I remembered the recent bad news about her health. There's no way I could ring, burdening her with my silly little problems in comparison. I would call her soon, but I wouldn't be bleating about how hard *my* life was.

Slowly these thoughts began to drift and one image filled my mind. That of a little brown bottle.

I placed my mug down on the table and stood up. As I climbed the stairs I thought about one little tablet and the tremendous power held within it. It would relax me but there was a risk it would make me overly sleepy, too. Half a tablet would be just perfect. Half a tablet still had the power to calm me down, making me appear confident and relaxed on the first day in my new job, when I most needed it.

Bryony James, my new line manager, hadn't seemed overly impressed with me at the interview. I wanted to put that right, but the way I was feeling at the moment, I doubted she was going to get the impression I would turn out to be any kind of asset to the team.

I opened the bathroom cabinet and scrabbled my fingers towards the back of the shelf, pushing through the half-filled packs and boxes of various toiletries. I plucked out the bottle and cradled it in my hand, like it was something precious I was afraid of crushing.

The bottle was about half full of tablets. I hadn't taken one for two days.

If I was honest with myself, one of the reasons I'd delayed moving house for so long was because I was afraid it would affect my ability to continue collecting Andrew's repeat prescriptions. I had managed to collect an extra month's supply of the sedatives by pretending we were all going on holiday. Me, Andrew and

Evie. 'An extended family break,' I'd told the regular pharmacist, who'd been only too pleased to authorise additional supplies.

I'd packed the new bottle away at the bottom of a box of old photographs and greetings cards. I had no intention of taking those tablets, of course, but it gave me a warm glow to know I had them there. Should I need them.

I'd read in a magazine that some prescription drug addicts couldn't manage even for an hour or two after the effects began to wear off. I'd gone two days already, so I felt satisfied that I wasn't remotely near addiction.

The instructions stated that patients shouldn't drive or operate machinery whilst taking the sedatives but I was just going to take *half*. That reduced dosage was hardly going to render me useless and incompetent.

I unscrewed the bottle and shook one tablet out into my palm. It sat there like a lucky charm. I looked around the bathroom for something to cut it in half with, but, of course, there was nothing that was suitable.

In the few moments it gave me to think, I was seized by a sudden rush of optimism. We had a new house, a new school for Evie and I had a new job which miraculously fit in with school hours, meaning I could still take Evie to class each morning.

I could do this.

My husband had died in a terrible tragedy but I was still forging on and I was nearer to coming out the other side than I'd ever been. Some people, like Tara, for instance, hadn't been so fortunate.

I had years of experience at management level in the property business. I could do the new job with my eyes closed. I knew it.

I didn't need the tablet. I could cope on my own.

I tipped it back into the bottle and tucked it away in the cabinet again.

* * *

Dale Gregory had said that if there was a free spot, I could park around the back of the offices. As I turned in to the small grid of marked places, I was pleased to see a free space right outside the back entrance.

It had just started to rain. I nabbed the spot right away, noting how the wipers on the Punto seemed a bit stiff and were leaving the windscreen still wet and smeared. They would probably be the next thing that needed attention on my list of jobs that I couldn't afford.

I bit down on my lip. This might be a good time to stop expecting the worst. Today had been a good start so far. Everything was going to be fine. I reached for my handbag and slipped my feet back into Mum's black court shoes.

I tried the back door of the shop but it was locked so I walked around to the front. I cursed as the fine drizzle settled on my hair; the last thing I wanted was to walk in looking a damp, frizzy mess when my line manager, Bryony, obviously put such great stock on looking well groomed and slickly professional.

Out on the main road, I took a deep breath and pushed open the door, striding into the shop with confidence, as if I'd worked there for years.

My optimistic mood dropped immediately as I stepped inside. The shop was empty. No customers and, even worse, no staff. I had a flashback to briefing my own team at the agency in Hemel.

'Please make sure there is a member of staff out front at all times,' I told them when I was first appointed branch manager. 'Even if you have to stagger nipping to the loo or making a drink. Nothing looks worse to customers than walking into an empty shop.'

When I got the chance, it might be a good idea to suggest the same to Dale or Bryony to make a good, early impression. It didn't hurt to bring something to the table as the newbie, illustrate right away that you were adding value.

I'd been standing there for a minute or so when a small, plump woman appeared from the back of the shop. She clutched an oversized soup mug and beamed at me.

'Hello there, sorry to keep you waiting.' She raised the mug and grinned. 'Lunchtime. How can I help you?'

'I'm Toni Cotter.' I smiled. 'It's my first day here and I—'

'Of course! Toni! I saw you when you came in yesterday but I was tied up with customers so couldn't say hello.' She plonked her mug down carelessly and the croutons floating on top made an easy escape onto the desk. 'I'm Jo Deacon, assistant sales agent.'

We shook hands and I found I liked Jo immediately. Her light brown, natural curls settled loosely on her shoulders, her warm brown eyes sparkled and dimples danced in full, lightly rouged cheeks. Everything about her came together to make me feel welcome, and finally I felt the tendons in my neck relax a little.

'Dale's out on a commercial valuation but Bryony will be back very soon.' She dabbed at the soup spill with a tissue. 'Can I get you a cup of tea or anything?'

'No, thanks. I'm fine,' I said, looking around. 'Do you know which one will be my desk?'

Jo blew at her soup and took a sip, grimacing as it scalded her mouth.

'That was Phoebe's desk, your predecessor.' She nodded to the far desk located by the main door and I immediately thought of the constant draught the person sitting there would have to endure. 'That will probably be your desk now, but who knows. Bryony likes to mix things up sometimes, you know?' Jo rolled her eyes.

I felt a kind of comradeship with her already. I'd worked out for myself that Bryony was the kind of boss who could be a bit pedantic.

I perched on the edge of the desk behind me.

'So, I heard Dale say you've just moved to the area?'

I nodded.

'With your family?'

'With my daughter,' I said. 'My mum lives close by, too.'

That was all I was willing to say at the moment. I liked Jo but I wasn't yet ready to open up and tell her all about the reality of how crap my life was.

'How long have you worked here?' I asked her, just for something to say.

'Far too long.' Jo grinned, sitting down and making a half-hearted attempt to tidy the strewn papers on her desk. 'It'll be six years this Christmas.'

'What did you do before?'

'Oh, you know, this and that.' I got the distinct feeling she perhaps didn't *want* to remember. That was fine by me; I knew exactly how it felt to want to keep your distance from the past. 'It's OK here, the hours and the pay aren't too bad, I suppose. Above the minimum wage, anyway. It's just that—'

The front door flew open then and Jo immediately clamped her mouth shut as Bryony appeared. She was dressed in an immaculate black suit she'd paired with a silver-grey silky blouse and towering red heels. Her expression was thunderous.

'Hi, Bryony,' Jo called brightly.

'Who the hell does that old Punto belong to in the car park?' Bryony demanded. 'Some idiot has only gone and dumped their heap of crap in *my* space.'

CHAPTER 28

Three Years Earlier

Toni

'I'm really sorry, Bryony,' I said breathlessly when I finally got back into the shop. 'It won't happen again.'

I'd had to park up on a side street and scuttle back to the office as fast as I could.

'Let's hope not,' she said sourly, her words laden with unspoken threats of what might happen if it did.

I glanced over at Jo, who appeared to be suddenly absorbed in sorting out a pile of glossy leaflets. I'd been in the new job for all of fifteen minutes and had already managed to rub my line manager up the wrong way. The worst thing was that I had to admit it was all my own fault. Only when I'd reversed the Punto back out of the parking spot, carefully avoiding Bryony's glistening white Audi TT, did I spot the 'Reserved' sign clearly displayed on the wall. I'd been in such a hurry to get into the office on time that I hadn't noticed I'd poached my boss's space.

The shop door opened and Bryony's face lit up, the sour fury melting away and being rapidly replaced by a winning smile. 'Mr and Mrs Parnham, how lovely to see you. Please, come through to my office.'

A heavily perfumed and coiffured Mrs Parnham swept by me and grasped Bryony's outstretched hand, her diamond-studded Rolex glittering under the stark fluorescent lights.

Only when they were safely ensconced in Bryony's office did Jo look up from her leaflet shuffling. She let out a long breath and pulled a guilty face. 'Sorry about the misunderstanding. I never thought to check where you'd parked. It's one of Her Majesty's pet hates, people nicking her spot. One of her *many* pet hates, I should add.'

'My fault.' I shrugged. 'I don't know how I managed to miss the reserved sign.'

'You can relax now, anyway, she'll be in there ages.' Jo grinned. 'Bryony adores the Parnhams. Well, she adores their wealth, I should say. They move house every couple of years or so, always on the lookout for the next ostentatious property to show off to their jet-setting friends. But this time, they're looking to spend their most yet. I wouldn't be surprised if Bryony's commission is more than our salaries put together.'

'Ahh, I get it.' I smiled, everything falling into place. No wonder Bryony's face had lit up when they walked in – the promise of a hefty commission can have that effect on people. The Parnhams had got me off a hook, anyway, so good luck to them.

I turned back to Jo. 'Can I help you with anything? I feel like a bit of a spare part.'

'You could file these property details away, if you don't mind. Thanks.' Jo picked up an unwieldy pile of stapled brochures and pushed them across her desk. 'They need to go in the folder in postcode order, hope that makes sense.'

I smiled and nodded. It made perfect sense. Filing brochures was one of the duties I'd done as an apprentice, too many years ago to think about. In the space of a few days, the last twenty years of my career had melted away and it felt like I was back to square one.

I collected the pile of papers and carried them over to Phoebe's old desk.

The phone rang once or twice, and Jo answered, but there were no more customers. Jo and I worked in companionable silence for a while.

'Is it usually this quiet?' I asked eventually.

'Varies.' Jo shrugged. 'It's been busier since Phoebe left.'

I liked to be busy. I'd worked with people before who seemed to get a thrill out of doing as little as possible all day, or by making simple jobs last twice as long. I found time dragged that way; I'd rather have too much on than too little. Less time to brood and overthink things, which was always a bonus in my book.

I slotted the property details in their rightful places in the laminated ring binder and glanced at the wall clock. Evie would have had her lunch and be back in class now. Maybe she'd do some artwork to bring home later. They would probably go through their spelling or handwriting drills, both of which Evie would be confident doing because we'd always spent time doing lots of reading and writing at home, even before she'd started nursery. I couldn't wait to see her later and hear all about it.

'Hello, is anybody there?' Bryony's hand swept in front of my face. 'Goodness, Toni. That's the third time I've spoken to you.'

'I – I'm so sorry,' I mumbled, feeling heat instantly channel into my cheeks as Mr and Mrs Parnham stared at me. 'I was miles away.'

'Weren't you just!' Bryony turned and grinned at the Parnhams, but I sensed a concealed threat hanging behind her words. 'Can you photocopy these details for Mr and Mrs Parnham? They have another appointment in town, so quick as you can, please.'

'Of course.' I stood up and took the thin wedge of property brochures from Bryony, who was already distracted again, gushing about Mrs Parnham's rather vulgar-looking clutch purse that had what looked like a jewelled knuckleduster for a handle. The new Alexander McQueen range, apparently.

I hadn't been shown where the photocopier was yet but I sensed this was not the time to interrupt Bryony's charm offensive on her most valued of customers. I walked around them and headed for Jo's desk to ask her. But the phone rang and Jo began an animated conversation with a builder who, from what I could gather, hadn't turned up for a customer's viewing of a brand new apartment near the train station that morning.

I walked into the back hallway and looked around. I'd operated enough photocopiers in my time to know that extracting a few back-to-back copies wasn't rocket science. I just had to find the damn thing.

I surveyed the available doors. The one to the right was the small boardroom I'd had my interview in. The door at the end bore a sign that read 'Staff Toilet'. That left two others.

I opened the first one and stepped inside. It was quite a large room and held a sleek blonde wood desk and a beige leather chair. A couple of aesthetically beautiful filing cabinets stood against one wall with tastefully framed secluded-beach prints hanging symmetrically on either side.

I stood for a second and surveyed the longest wall, lined floor to ceiling with shelves that housed what seemed like hundreds of perfectly colour coordinated and immaculately labelled files. Not your regular dull black or grey office binders but those expensive, elaborately coloured designer folders from a specialist supplier. The desk was dotted with other products of the same brand; a complicated post-it holder, a stapler and hole punch, all obviously part of a matching range.

I turned to another door, tucked away in the corner of the room. Often, unsightly copiers were hidden away in walk-in cupboards so I put the stack of brochures down on the desk and tried the handle, but the door was locked.

'What the hell are you doing, snooping around my office?' Bryony's voice cracked like a whip behind me. I jumped and spun around. 'The Parnhams are still waiting for their details.'

'I – I was just looking for the copier,' I stammered. 'I haven't been shown where anything is yet.'

'Well, it's fairly obvious there's no copier in here,' she snapped, her tone acerbic. 'Try the next office.'

I hurriedly gathered up the papers from Bryony's desk, at the last second spotting one that had fallen on the floor by her chair.

'Sorry,' I mumbled, silently berating myself for failing yet another task on what was promising to be the worst first day ever. I pushed open the door of the tiny room next to Bryony's office and there it was: an all-singing, all-dancing photocopier that took up most of the floor space.

I braced myself for further problems as I peered at the complicated computerised control panel but breathed a sigh of relief when I saw there was no passcode and straight forward back-to-back copying seemed to be a case of pressing a single button.

A few minutes later, I was back in the shop and I handed the details to Bryony.

She took them without thanks and turned back to Mr and Mrs Parnham, and I found myself as good as dismissed.

CHAPTER 29

Present Day

Queen's Medical Centre

As the daylight dims I begin my routine.

First, I count the ticks of the clock. Thousands and thousands of seconds, stacking up into wedges of lost time.

I can't see the actual hands, just the round shape of the clock face, but I can hear the tick tock, marking the seconds that turn into minutes. My life ebbing away.

Two hundred and thirteen, two hundred and fourteen, two hundred and fifteen . . .

Precious seconds slipping by, and still Evie is gone.

I am floating inside myself, amongst my frozen cells. I imagine reaching out to touch Evie, wherever she is. Perhaps she is sitting quietly somewhere not too far from here, or maybe she is on the opposite side of the world.

I like to think there is a delicate, unbroken thread that joins us and that she can feel a glimmer of something, she's just not sure what. A feeling, a memory of me that brings her a sliver of hope, of comfort.

I'm losing track of the clock count now; time to switch to the respirator.

In, out, space. In, out, space.

Pieces of Evie flash through my mind.

Her pale feet and perfect, shiny toenails like new shells on the beach. Small, neat teeth flashing as she laughs. The fine, downy hair on the side of her face.

That freakily warm day when she sat in the garden of the new house, soft toys arranged around her in a tea-party circle. She chattered to them as if they were real, her silvery giggle floating out, over the fence and down the lane. All these tiny pieces are bound together and by some kind of mysterious synergy they all amount to Evie.

The seconds turn into minutes, hours, days, then weeks, and finally the months turn into years that roll steadily on and the image of Evie grows a little dimmer in everyone's mind.

It's a long time since her picture appeared in the newspapers. Beautiful, vibrant Evie has somehow become old news. And I find myself wondering, for the millionth time, where is Evie now, this very second?

Will she even remember my face? Part of me hopes not.

I'm not a bad person, I just made some bad mistakes. I got distracted.

I let her down badly. Perhaps I was never meant to have her. She deserves so much better than I could ever give her. I do understand that now.

I begin my diaphragm exercises.

Up, down, up, down. Relax.

And again. *Up, down, up, down.*

Nothing happens.

The door opens and I hear it close again, softly.

Someone is in the room.

CHAPTER 30

Three Years Earlier

Toni

The rest of the week plodded on. At least Evie wasn't sobbing and threatening that she didn't want to go to school each morning, but she seemed subdued and her beautiful, blue eyes took on a sort of dull cast. Even the new Lego set Mum bought her couldn't seem to raise Evie's old sparkle.

I didn't see a lot of Dale at work because he had lots of county-wide valuations on, but Bryony was in the office for the majority of the time. She gave me Phoebe's old desk and I decided to keep my mouth shut about the potential draught problem. She looked on sourly when I took out a small, framed photo of Evie and placed it on my desk.

'My daughter, Evie,' I said, by way of explanation. 'It's OK to keep this on here, isn't it?'

'Of course,' Bryony replied frostily. 'The odd photograph is fine, just don't let the place get cluttered up with personal items.'

As I recalled, there had been no photographs displayed on the immaculate desk or walls in Bryony's office. I also noted that Jo had no photographs out on her desk.

I'd become quite practised in answering the phone and helping Jo with her workload, but I was also itching to carve out my own duties and make the job my own.

'I could come with you, if you like,' I offered, when Bryony announced she was leaving shortly to show a client to show around a property in Linby, a leafy village no more than a couple of miles away from the shop. 'Just to get some practise in.'

'That won't be necessary, Toni. You aren't a branch manager now, remember? Your duties don't include client viewings. Your job is to remain here, in the office.'

'Fair enough.' She could please herself, I was only trying to show willing.

'Jo is going to show you how we send a targeted mailshot out. That should keep you busy.'

Jo performed an exaggerated yawn for my benefit behind Bryony's back.

The phone rang and I dealt quickly with a query about our opening times. When I came off the call, Bryony hadn't moved. She stood at the side of my desk, still staring down. I was about to ask her if she felt OK when I realised what she was gazing at so intently.

It was the photograph of Evie.

When Bryony left, Jo made us both a cup of tea. I decided that now might be a good time to get Jo's opinion on my boss's bad attitude.

'She's very prickly, isn't she? Bryony, I mean.' I nodded my thanks as Jo handed me a steaming mug of tea and a two-finger Kit Kat. 'I feel like I can't do right for doing wrong. If I sit twiddling my thumbs she asks me if I've nothing to do but shoots me down if I try to show some initiative.'

'She'll calm down soon enough,' Jo offered. 'You're right, she is very prickly, but it comes from a place of insecurity.'

I nearly choked on my tea. Insecurity? Bryony? Two words that didn't go together.

Jo caught the look on my face. 'I know she seems uber-confident and sorted, but she isn't, not really.' She put down her mug and sighed. 'Look, if I tell you something about Bryony, do you promise not to breathe a word?'

'Course.' I gulped, wondering what Jo was about to say. Truthfully, I felt a bit uncomfortable, gossiping about my boss my first week in the job, but anything that would help me understand Bryony would be a massive help in breaking down the apparent barrier between us.

'We had a staff night out about eighteen months ago. There were supposed to be four of us at the meal, but Phoebe had a stomach upset and Dale's mum had a bad fall. So in the end, it was just me and Bryony rattling around on a table for four at Hart's restaurant.'

I couldn't imagine a worse scenario than being stuck on my own with Bryony, trying to make conversation, even if it was at one of the best eateries in the city.

'You can guess how the evening went. We ate too much and drank far too much good wine. Towards the end of the night, Bryony suddenly opened up to me. She said it was a relief to talk to someone.'

No matter how hard I tried, I couldn't reconcile the picture of the person Jo was painting with the Bryony James I'd just met. We were talking about a woman who seemed so sorted and so in control of her life. I honestly couldn't imagine her confiding in anyone at all.

'Turns out she'd just started her third programme of IVF.' Jo's voice dropped low, as if she was somehow afraid Bryony might overhear us from Linby. 'It was destroying her. She said she couldn't sleep properly anymore because the need to have a child was literally taking over her life.'

'Oh God,' I murmured, feeling immediate sympathy.

'And as I said, that was eighteen months ago,' Jo continued. 'She's had another course of treatment since then. I think the whole baby thing has chipped away at her and she's just dealt with it by developing an icy, protective shell.'

I thought about the way Bryony had stared just a little too long at Evie's photograph. What I'd taken as being a slightly creepy expression was probably nothing more than pure longing. Unknowingly, I'd witnessed a deeply buried sadness surfacing in Bryony's cool demeanour.

'Is she embarking on another course of IVF?' I asked.

'Dunno, she's been a bit distant the last few months,' Jo replied. 'She's avoided personal chat with me, probably because she can't face talking about it. Not that I can blame her.'

'It must be so hard,' I agreed.

'Her husband seems a bit of a cold fish. I've only met him once. He's a consultant at the hospital,' Jo said, breaking off a finger of Kit Kat and biting it in half. 'They live in a fabulous house at Ravenshead. I haven't actually been there but she brought me pictures of their new kitchen and the extension. It's immaculate.'

'Like her office,' I remarked. 'There's not a thing out of place in there.'

'You know, I think that's her way of coping,' Jo said through a mouthful of chocolate wafer. 'She keeps everything in her life so ordered and perfect, even herself. I reckon it's the only way she can make sense of it all.'

I nodded, feeling another twinge of guilt at our casual armchair psychology, dissecting a colleague's most private personal life.

'Thanks for telling me, Jo,' I said, meaning it. It had already helped me to see Bryony in a new light, even though I had the distinct feeling she wasn't going to be the easiest person to work with.

'You're welcome,' Jo said. 'Just don't drop me in it. She'd never forgive me if she knew I'd been blabbing to you.'

CHAPTER 31

Three Years Earlier

Toni

I'd just come off a call when the shop door opened. I expected to see Bryony walking in but it was Mr and Mrs Parnham again.

Jo looked up but she'd just begun a customer call she'd been waiting for all morning. I was fine with that, I felt confident I could cope.

'Mr and Mrs Parnham, how nice to see you again.' I stood up and stepped forward to shake both their hands. 'I'm Toni.'

'Hello there,' Mr Parnham said, craning his neck towards the back of the shop. 'We were hoping we might catch Bryony.'

'I'm sorry, she's out on a valuation,' I explained. 'She should be back very soon though.'

The Parnhams looked at each other.

'Is there anything I can help you with?' I offered.

'Actually, perhaps there is. Those details you copied for us the other day?' Mrs Parnham fished a property brochure out of her handbag and handed it to me. 'There's a house here that we're extremely interested in and we'd like a few more details, if possible?'

'No problem at all.' I smiled, indicating for them to sit down at my desk.

Although it only seemed to irritate Bryony, my previous experience meant I knew exactly how to locate the property database and extract additional details.

I glanced over at Jo and she widened her eyes at me and shook her head. Mr Parnham noticed me looking across the room and twisted round, catching Jo's expression.

'There's not a problem here, is there?' Mr Parnham frowned, shifting in his seat.

'Not at all,' I said brightly. 'I'm just bringing the property up now. Here we go.'

I rotated the monitor, so the Parnhams could see the additional online interior photographs.

'I can't understand why Bryony didn't mention this house, it's exactly what we're looking for.' Mrs Parnham tapped her long, red nails on the edge of my desk. 'She said she had nothing with more than five bedrooms and nothing located in the Berry Hill area. Yet this property has both.'

I frowned and scanned the details on the screen. For some reason, it looked like the property had been flagged as under offer when it was clearly still for sale. I felt relieved it wasn't my error.

'I'll get you the full details,' I said, pressing the print button. 'It's a stunning property and it's been with us for a few weeks now. Between you and me, the owner might well be open to a reasonable offer.'

'Oh, I'm excited.' Mrs Parnham turned to her husband, her leathery skin flushed against her startling, over-backcombed orange hair. 'When can we view?'

'I'm sure Bryony can sort you out a time when she returns,' Jo called helpfully from the other side of the office, her call having just ended.

'Bob, I don't want to wait a moment longer,' Mrs Parnham appealed to her husband. 'I'm worried someone else will make an offer.'

'Could you contact the owner while we're here, please, Toni?' Mr Parnham said firmly.

'Of course.' I beamed. 'His number is right here.'

Five minutes later, I'd made an appointment for the Parnhams to view the property on Saturday morning.

'Someone from Gregory's will meet you there,' I reassured them, unsure quite who it would be.

'Thank you so much, Toni.' Ms Parnham took my hand in both of hers as the office phone started ringing again. 'We're so grateful.'

I showed them out of the shop and closed the door. I turned to Jo, beaming. My smile faded at the look on her face.

'Shit, Toni. What were you thinking—'

Just then, the door walloped open behind me and caught me hard on the shoulder.

'Oww!' I turned, expecting an apologetic customer. Instead, I got an irate-looking Bryony.

'I've just bumped into the Parnhams,' she fumed, slamming the door shut. 'What the HELL have you just done?'

Jo buried her face in her hands.

'How dare you?' Bryony rounded on me. 'I knew you were going to be trouble from the moment I set eyes on you. And you!' She hissed over at Jo. 'Why the hell did you let her—'

'I was on an important customer call,' Jo said calmly. 'Had you instructed Toni not to deal with the Parnhams?'

'I didn't think I needed to,' Bryony spat, her face thunderous. 'Anyone with an ounce of common sense would know that—'

'Is everything OK in here?' Dale stood in the hallway. He'd obviously let himself in the back door, directly from the car park. 'Sounds like World War Three is kicking off from where I'm standing.'

It seemed I'd misjudged Dale. There was no trace of the mild-mannered personality he'd displayed during my interview.

'Bryony?' he said sharply. 'What's happened?'

'I pop out for one hour, that's what. One bloody hour! And your new appointment, Miss Cotter here, loses me a shitload of commission by poking her nose in where it's not wanted.'

I took in a sharp gasp.

'Bryony, please.' Dale frowned. 'Try to keep it professional.'

'You won't say that when you find out she's probably just lost us one of our biggest customers. The Parnhams.'

Dale's mouth opened and closed again. He looked at me.

'They came into the shop looking for Bryony,' I said, my mouth instantly turning dry. 'I told them she'd be back any time but they asked if I could get them details on a property they were interested in. I thought I was helping by—'

'That's the trouble,' Bryony snapped, beside herself with fury. 'You didn't *think* at all.'

My years of experience were telling me that something wasn't adding up here. All I'd done was furnish the Parnhams with some additional property details and arrange a weekend viewing. A completely normal task in any property agency – it's what we were there for.

'You shouldn't be introducing them to properties. They're *my* clients. That's *my* job.'

I'd held back long enough. Bryony was trying to cover something up and by the look on Dale's face, if I didn't watch it, she was going to successfully pin the blame firmly on me.

'They already had the property details, Dale.' I picked up the original brochure the Parnhams had brought into the shop. Bryony lunged for it but Dale was quicker and took it from me.

'Th – they shouldn't have had that one,' Bryony stammered, reddening. 'I thought I'd kept it back. I never gave them that one.'

'Dan Porterhouse's property,' Dale mused, looking at the brochure. 'Why would you not give them details of this one, Bryony?'

'They said it was perfect, just what they were looking for,' I added, earning myself a killer glance from Bryony. 'It had somehow been incorrectly tagged as under offer on the system.'

'Mr and Mrs Parnham wouldn't leave until Toni tried to make a viewing appointment with the owner,' Jo explained. 'She didn't really have a choice.'

I looked over gratefully at Jo.

'If you didn't give them these details, then who did?' Bryony said, as if she'd caught me out.

I suddenly remembered that I'd picked up a stray property brochure from the floor of Bryony's office when I'd been looking for the photocopier. I'd assumed I'd dropped it, but . . .

'Why does it matter so much that they were interested in the house, Bryony? You should be congratulating Toni that she's managed to make a viewing appointment on a 1.5 million pound property,' Dale said sternly. 'A property you've somehow managed to mark as already sold. Can you come through to my office, please?'

Bryony followed him a little sheepishly, but not before she'd thrown me yet another hateful look.

'Oh God,' I sighed, sitting down heavily at my desk. 'I've made a complete balls-up and I don't even really know what I've done yet.'

'That's what I was trying to tell you when I was on the phone,' Jo said in a low voice. 'Never, ever attempt to deal with Bryony's clients. You never know what shady deals she's pulling off.'

I looked at her, puzzled.

'She plays clients off against each other,' Jo explained, glancing nervously though the back to check we were still alone. 'She'll be keeping the Parnhams away from that property so they buy another mega-expensive one. Meanwhile, she'll have another client lined up to buy Dan Porterhouse's property. That way, Bryony gets double commission. She's pulled it off loads of times.'

I shook my head, incredulous. That wasn't ethical or honest behaviour in anyone's book. Worst of all, it was betraying the trust of loyal clients like the Parnhams, who'd been coming to her for years.

Jo and I both worked in silence for a while. My hands felt a bit shaky and my heart was pounding.

Ten minutes later, Bryony whisked through the shop, clutching her coat and bag.

Jo had customers again by this time and Bryony came close to the edge of my desk.

'I'll get you back for this,' she muttered, too low for anyone else to hear. 'I'll fucking teach you not to mess with me.'

And then she was gone, leaving the glass door shuddering behind her.

CHAPTER 32

Three Years Earlier

The Teacher

Harriet dodged the delicate china cup, full of tea, that flew past her and shattered on the wall behind.

'Tea is supposed to be hot,' her mother screamed. 'HOT. Not tepid. You know I hate tepid anything, you stupid bitch.'

Harriet turned and watched for a second or two as the dark brown liquid streamed down the cream wall like dirty tears.

'When will she be here? When will you get off your useless backside and *do* something?'

'Mother, I've told you—'

'I don't want to hear it.' The old woman cupped her hands over her ears. 'I don't want to hear you or see you. I never wanted you.'

Harriet turned and walked out of the bedroom without uttering a word, closing the door quietly behind her.

Her mother continued to scream insults as Harriet walked calmly back downstairs humming 'Annie's Song' and thinking about John Denver's lovely, kind face. She could still hear the obscenities back in the lounge with the door closed and her earplugs in.

It was all so *unnecessary*.

Harriet sat down in front of the antique writing desk and took some deep breaths. As she felt the wave of pain rising, she closed her eyes against it, trying to form a barricade against the disappointing person that she was.

She smoothed her hands over the desk's fine oak planes, still glowing with quality after all these years. This wonderful piece of furniture had belonged to her father. The desk was the only tangible thing left of him, her mother had made sure of that.

Harriet had vivid memories of hiding behind the couch, clutching moth-eaten Ted and watching her mother stuff bag after black bin bag full of her father's suits, shirts and shoes. Then she'd been made to help drag them out into the back yard, where they'd sat for months on end, disintegrating in the inclement weather.

But when Harriet sat there at her father's desk, she almost felt part of him again. Lately, she'd felt a thread of steel growing within her, dissolving the pain of her mother's disappointment. Silently guiding her, giving her hope.

Tonight though, Harriet felt an unwelcome prickling in her chest.

Harriet liked to call herself a teacher but she hadn't gone on to higher education in the end. She'd left college to become a trainee teaching assistant – 'a teacher's lackey', her mother called it.

She was so much more capable than most of the trained teachers at St Saviour's, but because she hadn't got a piece of paper from a university to validate her, her skills counted for virtually nothing.

Life would have been different if her father had been alive. She should have gone to university to study and her father would have supported that.

He'd tripped on an uneven paving stone and stumbled under the wheels of a red London bus on Oxford Street when Harriet was just five years old. The age all her children in her class were now.

Her mother had never liked London, and after the death of Harriet's father, she couldn't get away from the city quickly enough.

They'd made the move to Nottingham within months, her mother snapping up a creaky old Victorian villa on a dreary back street in Lenton, an area she selected solely because it appeared in the *Domesday Book* in the late eleventh century.

A village back then, Lenton had been quite well-to-do at one time, but over the years the nearby houses had slowly been converted into bedsits and now they found themselves surrounded by students at every turn. But Mother steadfastly refused to move out of the area and into something smaller and more manageable.

'I'll leave this house when they carry me out in a box and not a moment before,' she liked to taunt Harriet.

Harriet sat up straighter and twisted the ornate brass handle in front of her, gently pulling the front flap of the desk down. A dozen tiny compartments and drawers faced out, intricate and pleasing to the eye. The desk reminded her of the human psyche. Deceptively simple on the outside but once you peeled the outer layer away, all manner of complexities were revealed inside.

Harriet remembered only too well how it felt to be a young child experiencing the rawness of tragedy whilst trying to cope with the tumultuous change that often followed it. The only way to get through it was to develop an invisible sheath of armour that would stop you hurting ever again. The trick was to develop it at a young enough age for it to be effective.

She slid open a long, narrow drawer and extracted a key. When her mother took her bath, Harriet would climb to the third floor of the creaking old house and continue her preparations on the room. She would make sure everything was just perfect for when their guest arrived. She'd come to realise it was the only way to placate her mother.

In the meantime, Harriet had an important telephone call to make.

CHAPTER 33

Three Years Earlier

DIARY ENTRY

6th September

TIMELINE
Arrival at watch point: 14.30 p.m.

14.35 p.m.	House observed for ten minutes. Zero movement.
14.45 p.m.	Enter back yard.
14.48 p.m.	Enter property.
14.52 a.m.	Commence full sweep of property. Locate required items.
15.12 p.m.	Exit property.

Departure from watch point: 15.16 p.m.

GENERAL OBSERVATIONS
- Property is in disarray.
- No landline/internet connection.
- No security alarm or additional locks fitted. No window locks.
- Awaiting further instruction.

CHAPTER 34

Three Years Earlier

Toni

After Bryony stormed out of the office so dramatically, I had to try and steel myself, pushing the unsettling incident aside so I could get through the rest of the afternoon.

At three o'clock, Dale called me through to his office.

'I'm sorry you've been put in an awkward position today, Toni,' he said. 'It won't happen again.'

'Has Bryony left? I mean, have you—' I felt horrified that I might have caused someone to be fired.

'No, no.' He smiled. 'Let's just say I've had words with her and fully explained the ethics that must be adhered to by all staff who are employed by this agency. As you've probably noticed by now, Bryony doesn't take well to being dictated to. She's damn good at what she does but needs reining in now and then, I'm afraid.'

I nodded but kept quiet.

'I'm impressed with how you're throwing yourself into the job.' Dale smiled. 'Don't let this put you off, I want to see you putting all that experience you have under your belt to good use here.'

I smiled my agreement but secretly wondered what Bryony would have to say about that.

'In your interview, you alluded to the fact you'd had some sort of upheaval in your life. I think you said "circumstances beyond your control".' Dale raised his hand. 'Don't worry, I'm not fishing. But if ever you need to talk, I'm here. That's what bosses are for, right?'

I shifted in my seat. 'Thanks, I appreciate that.'

'I know you've got a young daughter and you've just moved into the area, and now, a new job. Sometimes it takes time to settle in but I'm sure your family are supportive.'

It was kind of him to show an interest but I wished he'd just leave it there.

A couple of beats of silence gave me time to breathe.

'Yes,' I said. 'New starts can certainly be challenging.'

He looked at me.

I really didn't want to have this conversation, but he was being so nice and supportive that I didn't want him to think I was ungrateful. Perhaps it was time to get it over with.

'My husband died two years ago,' I said evenly. 'So it's just me and my daughter, Evie. And my mum, too, I'm close to her.'

'God, I had no idea, Toni.' His face crinkled with pity. 'I'm so sorry.'

'What can you do but get on with it?' I said lightly. 'We'll survive.'

Our eyes met for a second or two.

'Well.' Dale stood up quickly and walked around his desk, laying his hand on my shoulder. I felt the warmth of his fingers radiating through my flimsy blouse and reaching my skin. 'Don't forget my offer to talk. Any time.'

'Thanks, Dale.' I smiled, inhaling the subtle, musky scent of his aftershave. For a crazy second I had this mad urge to close my eyes and lay my head on his chest. I'd forgotten what it felt like to have someone to lean on, someone to make everything OK. I ached for it.

'You OK, Toni?' He took a step back and squinted at me, concerned.

'Yes, of course.' I blinked, moving towards the door. 'Thanks again.'

'Everything OK in there?' Jo looked up when I walked past her desk.

'Fine.' I smiled. 'Dale's a lovely bloke, isn't he?'

'Hmm,' she agreed, quickly engrossed again in her computer monitor.

Back at my desk, I kept glancing around her. I couldn't help wondering how bad things would be for me when Bryony returned.

'Don't worry about it,' Jo said, looking up and catching my expression. 'You've done nothing wrong.'

Somehow, it just didn't feel that way.

Half an hour before the shop closed for the day, Jo made tea and brought it through for us to sit and drink at our desks as we wound up for the day.

'This is nice. Thanks.' I cradled the mug, savouring the warmth in my hands. The rest of me felt icy cold, though the heating had been on all afternoon.

'You look tired out,' Jo said. 'You should run a nice hot bath with candles when you get home. Treat yourself.'

'Chance would be a fine thing,' I muttered, already imagining the long-gone luxury of an hour or two to myself to get lost in a book, to take a bath without worrying about anything and everything. I looked up to find Jo studying me. I gave her a small smile and brought my mug up to cover my face.

'Toni, I don't want to pry but are you a single mum? It's just that you mentioned something about just moving up here with just your daughter, ' Jo said tentatively. 'Don't get me wrong, I'm not judging. I've nothing but respect for single mums.'

'I am.' I managed a smile. 'Not by choice though. My husband, Andrew, he died.'

The last thing I wanted to do was bring it all up again after speaking to Dale.

'Oh God, I'm so sorry.' She put down her mug and covered her mouth with her hand. 'I didn't mean to intrude, I—'

'Really, it's fine,' I assured her. 'I wish to God it hadn't happened, but it did, and the best I can do is try to deal with it every day. I'm not sure I manage it most days though.'

I gave a little laugh but Jo's face remained serious.

'I can't imagine what you've gone through.' She shook her head. 'What you're *going* through, every day. And little Evie – did you say she's only five?'

'She just turned five two months ago.' I nodded, remembering all the tinies – around fifteen of Evie's nursery friends – wreaking havoc in the ball pool at her birthday party.

Afterwards, Evie said, 'It was the best birthday ever in the WHOLE universe of the world, Mummy.'

I'd looked at her flushed face and bright eyes and promised myself that, when we moved house, I'd give her even better birthdays with her new friends each year.

I didn't feel nearly as confident about that now.

Jo looked at me, too polite to ask more questions but obviously wondering. So, for the second time that day, I explained what had happened to Andrew. The accident.

Her face seemed to crumple, although thankfully she didn't start full-blown crying. I don't think I could have handled that. I'd have probably joined in.

I hated that, no matter how many times I explained how Andrew's accident had happened, he sounded incompetent. I felt guilty even thinking that word in relation to Andrew, but it seemed that whatever I told people, and however I said it, it sounded like it was his fault. There was no getting away from the fact that, on paper, he was the one leading the mission that night.

It was something that constantly bothered me but that I'd kept completely to myself. Thankfully, nobody else had been tactless enough to mention it.

Sometimes, in the early hours, I burned inside, wondering how he'd managed to make such a terrible navigational mistake.

But talking about it now to Jo, I just felt empty.

'I'm sorry, Toni.' Jo wiped at her eyes with her sleeve. 'I wasn't expecting that. You see, I know how you feel. My sister, well, her husband died on active duty, too, a few years ago. She's been through hell. Actually, she's still in it.'

'I'm sorry to hear that, Jo, her suffering sounds familiar.' I twisted up my mouth in sympathy. I hoped she didn't want to tell me all about it, I didn't feel up to it.

'I do what I can, but it's hard, you know?' Jo said, staring towards the window. 'She lives down south. I manage to get down there a few times a year but most of the time it's a matter of supporting her as much as I can by phone or Skype. I'm not sure it's enough, really.'

'Your sister's lucky to have you.'

Jo shrugged.

'I don't know how much good I do. It almost destroyed her. But she hasn't got any kids,' Jo said. 'You do so well holding down a job, being a mum to Evie. I can't imagine what that takes.'

She glanced at the clock.

'Oh well, nearly closing time. I'll check the back door's locked and turn everything off, if you can put the shutters down.' She hesitated. 'Just one thing. I hope we can be friends and, maybe when we know each other better, I can get to meet Evie and even help you out a bit. I – well, I have nobody. But I have lots of time.'

I felt my face burning. It was so kind of Jo but I didn't feel ready to let someone I had just met fully into my life yet. Still, her concern had helped a little. Just knowing she had personal experience of something similar made me feel a little more normal.

'Thanks Jo.' I smiled. 'That means a lot.'

The Friday-night traffic driving home was particularly heavy and the car crawled along in gridlocked queues for several miles. A fat raindrop exploded on the windscreen, followed by another and another. Within minutes, the shower turned into a torrential downpour. The windscreen wipers were unable to cope and suddenly I could barely see the car in front of me.

As the traffic was continuously crawling and then stopping, I had to wind the window down and keep wiping the windscreen with a grimy old cloth I found in the door pocket. The whole of my right-hand side was getting thoroughly soaked.

Thankfully the downpour eased quite quickly, but still, after the day I'd had, it was all too much.

Heat and pressure welled up inside my head and tears began rolling down my cheeks. That rotten feeling I'd hoped was finally behind me, the feeling that everything was going wrong again, well, it was back with a vengeance.

I found myself wondering if things could actually get any worse.

CHAPTER 35

Three Years Earlier

Toni

Evie was in a foul mood when I eventually arrived home, a full forty minutes later than usual.

Throughout the journey, I confess I'd kind of hoped that Mum had taken Evie back to her house for a couple of hours after school. A bit of down time alone, to try to get my head straight, would've been more than welcome today.

'I can't do anything with her,' Mum whispered behind her hand as we watched Evie jamming Lego bricks together so hard it was only a matter of time until she nipped her fingers.

'Calm down, poppet, it's Friday,' I said lightly, even though I probably felt as frustrated as she did. 'That means no more school until Monday.'

'I don't want to go anymore,' Evie scowled, staring down at her bricks. 'I don't like it there.'

'What don't you like, Evie?'

No response.

'I can't help you if you won't talk to me about it,' I pressed, feeling my heartbeat speed up a notch. 'Is someone being unkind to you in class?'

'I just don't like it,' Evie repeated. 'I hate it. I hate everyone there.'

Mum turned to me. 'It's not helped, Toni, you getting this new job.'

'Mum, please.'

'Well, it's true, love. Evie needs some stability at this point. She needs you to be there, not chasing a career all over again.'

'I wouldn't call a few part-time hours a week "chasing a career",' I snapped. 'There are bills to pay and I take Evie to school every day, which is more than some mums are able to do.'

'Yes but their kids haven't been through what Evie has been through, Toni. You need to—'

'Mum.' I cut her dead. 'Just leave it. Please.'

Mum was so bloody brilliant at telling me what I needed to do, how to run my life, how to raise my daughter. The list went on.

'Tell you what, why don't I just take myself off home?' she said tersely, standing up and snatching her handbag. 'I know where I'm not wanted. Bye, Evie, darling, Nanny will call you tomorrow.'

She blew a kiss across the room but Evie didn't respond.

'Mum, please, I didn't mean to—'

She stalked by me and slammed the door on her way out.

My neck ached and I felt queasy and hot.

I looked longingly at my handbag a few times, imagining the relief that awaited me, tucked away in the zipped inside pocket.

It was the weekend. I'd had one hell of a week, in all the wrong ways, but I didn't have to drive tonight and I didn't have to keep my wits about me at work. Now, I could finally relax.

I was so pent up, I could do with a little help. What was the harm?

Something about it being still the afternoon felt prohibitive, like having a drink mid-morning. Only alcoholics did that. Maureen, the ex-manager at the estate agency where I used to work, would disappear into the back office like clockwork every morning.

The mints didn't cover the smell of alcohol on her breath when she came back out, but she was so much more chilled out after her first few swigs of the day. It was a secret standing joke amongst the rest of us and I hadn't really understood back then why Maureen did it.

But I understood well enough now.

When Maureen retired, I had been successful in applying for her job. I wondered where Maureen was now and if she still had her mid-morning tipple.

Sometimes it felt like I might be turning into her.

At the same time, I also knew I was a million miles away from having a serious problem, like Maureen obviously did. The odd pill was neither here nor there. It wasn't as if I was addicted or anything. In the end, they'd had Andrew dosed up with so much medication he didn't even know what day it was most of the time. A blessing, as it turned out, for the short, painful time he had left.

The pharmacists had always shelled out his tablets like sweeties, no questions asked. There was no reason to believe it would be any different here in Nottingham, if I wanted to continue to submit his prescriptions.

I often wondered if the government wanted people like Andrew to just disappear from public view and quietly fade away in their own private, medicated bubble. At the time, I'd almost envied Andrew his invisible chemical shield. That buffer from the pain and trauma of the real world.

I could really do with a pill now.

I looked down at my fingers and saw that I'd bitten my nails so low that a couple of them were actually bleeding. This level of anxiety was no good. If I didn't do something, it would get a hold of me and I'd find it difficult to function.

I unzipped the small compartment in my handbag and took a tablet to calm my frayed nerves. Just the one.

It was no shame to admit I needed help coping at the moment. Even the most sorted person needed a helping hand now and again. But I didn't want it documented at the GP surgery, have gossipy clerical staff knowing all my business. I didn't want anti-depressants. I'd heard all the horror stories about how easy it was to get hooked and become a zombie.

On the face of it, society seemed to be getting more open and tolerant towards mental illness, but privately, words like 'nutter' and 'freak' were still whispered behind the backs of those who suffered.

I knew for sure the stigma was still alive and well in the workplace. Anxiety or depression on a medical certificate was still widely regarded by some employers as skiving, and it was this hidden loathing that would always stop me seeking legitimate help.

I watched Evie, now half-heartedly slotting her bricks together. The savagery had gone from her play since Mum had left, but there was no denying she was far quieter than usual.

The pain of Evie's suffering felt sharp, like fine needles sticking in my skin. I couldn't bear to acknowledge she was so desperately unhappy. That hadn't been the plan in moving here.

On a whim, I picked up my phone and fished out Tara's letter from my handbag. I tapped in the number and waited. She picked up on the third ring.

'I'm so happy you called me, I could cry,' she gasped, and we laughed at her being so corny. Within five minutes, the years had melted away and we were just us again.

I told her about my bad day.

'You know, Toni, we've been through enough that things like disagreements at work really don't mean anything. Just ignore your bitch boss.'

It was good advice . . . when I was feeling this brave.

I tried to discuss her illness, the multiple sclerosis.

'Don't want to talk about it,' she said firmly. 'This call is about you and Evie, I want to know all about your fresh start.'

So I told her all about our crappy house and how Mum was driving me up the wall and how I was just making such a mess of everything and we laughed some more. Twenty minutes later, I finished the call and felt like I'd been on a spa break after all the stuff I'd offloaded to Tara. My heart rate had steadied somewhat, I felt lighter inside and I was beginning to think a little more logically.

Evie was happy in her own little world for the time being, so I climbed the stairs and headed for my bedroom. If I could begin to make inroads into getting the house organised, it would give me a sense of achievement instead of the sense of foreboding I got every time I put the key in the door.

I opened the bedroom door and stared at the piles of bin bags in there. Immediately, I felt like turning round and going back downstairs, but I didn't. That would get me precisely nowhere. I took a few steps forward, trying to cultivate a non-existent feeling of determination from somewhere. I stopped dead and looked all around me, my eyes scanning every inch of the floor space.

Something felt different about my bedroom.

It had looked just the same at first glance but . . . I don't know, the air just felt *different* in here, somehow.

When I'd packed up our stuff, I'd tied the tops of the bin bags in loose knots. A few of them were untied now. The hairs on my arms prickled.

I walked over and peered inside. As far as I could tell, everything seemed to be there. It was difficult to determine amongst such chaos. All manner of stuff had spilled out when the bags were transported upstairs from the living room.

I shook my head, smiling ruefully at my imagination. Maybe this was how the descent into madness began. When you became utterly convinced of a certain reality and the people around you nodded and smiled indulgently but threw concerned glances at each other the second you turned away.

I closed the door and walked back downstairs, holding on to the handrail as the bottom step looked a bit fuzzy from up here.

I felt nothing but relief that Evie's first week at school was finished. Hopefully, over the weekend, we'd be able to spend some time together, and once Evie felt more relaxed, I would gently broach the subject of school again. I felt sure I could coax her to reveal what was troubling her. The first few weeks in any new situation were bound to be difficult, everyone knew that. Evie was no exception and I was probably worrying too much.

That was my trouble: I worried too much about *everything*.

Just as I picked up my barely touched crime novel to read while Evie played, the phone began to ring.

I snatched up the cordless handset. 'Hello?'

'Mrs Cotter? Harriet Watson here, from St Saviour's. I'm just calling to discuss how Evie's first week went at school.'

'Oh, hello there.' I stood up and walked into the kitchen, pushing the door closed behind me. Although a part of me wondered why Evie's teacher was calling, the tablet was already working its magic. I felt relaxed and able to deal with the conversation. 'I hope everything is OK, Miss Watson?'

A few moments silence, as if Harriet was waiting for me to say something else.

'Evie has had a quiet first week,' Miss Watson said. 'She seems cautious when it comes to getting fully involved in lessons and mixing with her classmates. But I'm sure she'll get into the swing of things before long.'

'I don't think she's made any friends yet.' Without warning, my eyes prickled. 'She got upset again today, said she didn't want to come to school on Monday. But she won't talk to me about it.'

'Evie doesn't seem to be adjusting quite as readily as we'd hoped,' Harriet agreed. 'One of the reasons I've called is to tell you that I've included her in my small group work, to give her a little more personal attention. I hope that's acceptable.'

'That's really good of you, Miss Watson,' I said gratefully. 'Thank you.'

'I do hope you don't feel I'm interfering, but in my experience it's very important we do as much as we can in school to help children to integrate effectively right from the start, particularly when there have been . . . rather difficult personal circumstances,' Harriet said. 'I'm going to be running some after-school workshops two or three days a week. They'll be one-to-one sessions, designed to build confidence and social skills and to prepare children for the challenges that may lie ahead. I can only take one or two pupils, but I have selected Evie because I believe she'll benefit tremendously from attending. If you'll agree to it, that is?'

There were a few seconds of silence as I processed what she'd said.

'Absolutely,' I said at last. 'Thank you, that sounds ideal.'

I felt the weight on my shoulders lift. At last, someone was trying to help me instead of placing yet another obstacle in my path.

I listened as she gave me details of the forthcoming sessions.

'It's best if you don't keep asking Evie about school,' Harriet continued. 'We can tell her she's been specially chosen for the after-school club, which indeed she has, and hopefully we'll see better results next week.'

This woman seemed to really understand my daughter. In just a week, she had noticed Evie's reluctance in class and had already acted upon it. I felt quite overcome with gratitude.

'Thanks so much for your help. Things are a little difficult at home at the moment and I really appreciate . . .' My voice faltered.

'Say no more. I do understand, Mrs Cotter,' Harriet soothed. 'I'll be in touch with the days you'll need to pick Evie up a little later from school.'

'I'll tell my mother,' I said.

'Sorry?'

I fell silent. For a second, I couldn't remember what it was we were talking about.

'Mrs Cotter?'

It came back to me.

'Yes, I bring Evie to school each morning but her nanny picks her up at the end of the day,' I explained. 'I work until five o'clock, you see.'

'I see,' Harriet replied, a little tightly. 'Perhaps you could change your hours? It's very important we work together to help Evie settle in.'

'Yes, of course,' I said quickly, shamed by a flash of guilt. 'I'll ask at work but I've only just started, so it might have to be my mum for a little while yet.'

When Harriet ended the call I felt flushed and fidgety. She'd made me feel like Mum did, like I was making purely selfish decisions about working that would impact negatively on my daughter. I should have told her to mind her own business.

I shook my head to disperse the feeling of being got at. I had to remember that at least Harriet Watson was trying to help me. Although we were nothing alike, part of me felt she somehow understood me. Knew where I was coming from.

CHAPTER 36

Three Years Earlier

The Teacher

Harriet replaced the phone in its charging cradle and turned to see her mother standing in the doorway.

'When?' the old woman croaked, hobbling over to the table where Harriet sat. 'When are you going to get everything sorted out?'

'Soon,' Harriet said. 'I keep telling you, Mother, everything will be sorted very soon.'

'It had better be. I've waited too long, listening to you and your pathetic promises. She needs us.'

Harriet watched her mother as she stalked from the room. It wasn't lost on her that it would be Halloween in a matter of weeks, and from the back, the old woman resembled a sort of living ghoul, her hair scraped over her scalp in a transparent bun, her voile nightdress floating above the floor as she moved.

Soon Harriet would creep upstairs herself and make some final preparations to the room on the top floor. She knew it wasn't the right thing to do, but Mother had set her mind on what must happen and, as Harriet knew only too well, there would be no changing it now.

Harriet listened, waiting until the noise of the stair lift had abated and her mother's feet hobbled across the landing above her. The bedroom door opened and then closed.

Silence.

Then the slap of a wheelie bin lid in next door's yard, a group of young female students striding by the window, laughing and bursting with a confidence Harriet had never managed to conjure within herself.

Sometimes, in her quieter moments, she wondered what the future would bring. When her mother was gone and she was still here, in this big, old, crumbling house, alone. What then?

She yearned for a new start, a family of her own. Specifically a child, to give the love and affection she'd never experienced herself but that she'd seen other people give their offspring.

It just didn't seem fair that there were people out there who had everything but failed to value it. They fully deserved to have their precious things taken away, given to someone who would care and cherish them.

Someone like Harriet.

CHAPTER 37

Three Years Earlier

Evie

Evie lay awake in her bed, staring up into the darkness. The new starry nightlight that Nanny had bought for her birthday was supposed to make night-time friendlier. At least that's what it had said on the box. But it didn't seem to be making any difference at all here.

Even though Mummy was an adult, she had gone to bed at the exact same time as Evie because she had said she was very, very tired. Evie had seen that her eyes were doing the staring thing again.

Mummy was already asleep. Evie could tell just by listening to her breathing, which she could clearly hear because both their bedroom doors had been left a bit open. Sometimes Mummy woke her up, shouting in the night, but when Evie went into her bedroom, she was still asleep. When Evie sat on the edge of the bed, she'd wake up and say, 'Have you had a bad dream, poppet?' and Evie would reply, 'No, it was you,' and Mummy would say, 'Ahh, you've had a bad dream about Mummy?'

Evie just didn't know exactly how to explain it and she always felt so dreadfully tired in the middle of the night, so mostly she just went back to her own bed.

Deep and slow breaths like now meant Mummy was properly sleeping.

She wouldn't know if Evie slipped out of bed and tiptoed downstairs for a biscuit or another glass of juice like she sometimes did, even though she wasn't allowed more than one drink before bed because Mummy said she'd be up weeing all night.

Now the darkness was thick and heavy, like when she covered her eyes up with her comfort blanket. There were no streetlights shining in from outside, like there had been in her old bedroom.

She tried to focus on the tiny nightlight stars scattered on her ceiling but they seemed dull here, not bright and glittering like they used to be in her old bedroom. Evie sometimes wondered if Daddy was looking down on her while she slept, amongst the real stars in the real night sky. Nanny said he definitely would be.

'But how do you know?' Evie had asked her more than once.

'There is no doubt in my mind that your Daddy is *always* looking out for you, sweetheart, day and night,' was all Nanny ever said.

Sometimes it worried Evie that Daddy might be watching her. Like when she'd stolen a biscuit before dinner or the time she gave Nanny's cat, Igor, two treats instead of one, even though Nanny said it might give Igor the runs. The last thing Evie wanted to do was to let her Daddy down.

She didn't like this stuffy new house, the way it was so silent at night, like everything in it was dead.

Their old house had creaky pipes and comforting traffic noises from the main road nearby. She had never felt alone there. Sometimes, when she was playing with her Lego, Evie used to imagine Daddy was still there behind her, sitting in his armchair and watching Sky Sports or reading his cycling magazine.

She wouldn't cry. She wouldn't.

Crying was for babies, that's what the other children at school said all the time.

Evie had vague memories of Mummy and Daddy taking her to a pizza restaurant as a treat. Sometimes, Daddy used to take her swimming while Mummy had a bit of peace to read her book.

All that had stopped, of course, after the accident. And now Daddy wasn't coming home ever again.

At first, Nanny had promised her that Daddy would get better in the Afghanistan hospital and would be 'good as new', but that hadn't happened.

Then Nanny stopped saying it, and later . . . well, that's when Mummy told her that Daddy had gone to be with the angels. It had all happened very fast.

Nanny and Mummy had always told her that she could go and talk again to the nice lady at the hospital about Daddy's accident. If she wanted to, they said, Evie could talk to *them* about how she felt and about how everything had changed. But she didn't want to.

Evie didn't like talking to people about things that made her feel sad. She hadn't made friends yet with anyone in class and she didn't like Miss Watson questioning her about stuff in that horrid small group.

Miss Watson told Evie she wanted everyone to get to know her because she was new to the area. She also said Evie had to be a good girl at home for Mummy. But her questions made her feel all funny inside, like Evie's nice round pink heart had been ironed flat. So it felt like a grey pancake hanging inside her chest.

It was really hard to make the adults understand it all, so Evie decided it was better to just stay quiet. Today, when they'd got home from school and Evie had been upset, Mummy had looked at her as if she was disappointed, somehow.

Evie hadn't known what would happen. She hadn't known Daddy would fall off that cliff and get all broken into little pieces.

At her old school, Arthur Chapman's Action Man got stamped on at break and had to be thrown away by Miss Bert because it simply couldn't be mended.

When the last bell sounded today, she'd been so happy it was Friday and there was no more stinking school for two days, but then Mummy had taken that phone call in the kitchen and been all pretend-bright afterwards, with her beaming smile that she used when she really wanted Evie to like something that wasn't very nice.

She told Evie that next week she would be doing a special after-school club, *on her own*, with Miss Watson.

'Everything is going to be fine.' Mummy had held her hand a bit too tight and her eyes looked all misty again, like she was struggling to see Evie properly. 'Miss Watson has got a lot of faith in you, Evie. She wants to help you settle in.'

Evie was never going to settle in. Not here in this house or at St Saviour's Primary School.

She just knew it.

CHAPTER 38

Present Day

Queen's Medical Centre

The room appears quiet and perfectly still, but something in the air has changed. Whoever the person was who very quietly opened and closed the door, they're still in here. I can sense their presence.

There's a long beat of silence, during which the walls seem to press closer to my face. It feels harder to breathe. If I had to breathe of my own accord, that is.

When it comes, her voice sounds coarser than I remembered.

'I heard about what happened to you but I had to see it for myself before I could really believe it.'

I hear her pad forward from the door a few steps. It's almost inaudible, but I am instantly alert to the faintest muted rustle of soft soles on a hard floor. My ears have sharpened. It's as if my body is trying to make up for the fact that almost all other bodily functions have been rendered useless by the stroke, or whatever condition since then has paralysed me.

I catch a whisper of breath and that tells me she has moved a little closer to my bed. But I still can't see her.

'What happened to Evie, it's your fault.' Her voice sounds fairly level but there is a wobble behind it, a sort of worrying unevenness.

It's true. It's my fault Evie was taken. I don't need *her* to tell me that. Of all people, she is far from blameless. I should never have listened to her poisoned words.

My heartbeat wallops against my chest wall and, worse than that, I can feel nausea rising in my chest. If I bring back my liquid food, I could choke to death before the nurses even get here.

I hear the soft rustle again. She's on the move but sticking close to the walls, staying purposely out of my view.

With her last step, she comes into focus.

A vague shape of unidentifiable colours, over on my right hand side. She stands adjacent to my head but well back.

If only I could swivel my eyes, just slightly to the right . . .

'They say you can't move, not even a millimetre,' she says. 'They say it's not known whether you can see or hear, but I've got some things I want to say to you all the same.' She shuffles slightly. 'I've got something I want to show you, too.'

I don't like the way she says that.

I start to shake my head violently from side to side, and stretch the fingers of my left hand until it hurts, stretching towards the emergency button that hangs on a thick cord, just centimetres away.

I shout and yell for the nurse to come and help me, to make her go away.

But of course, in the real world, I remain completely still and unresponsive.

Now she has stopped speaking, there is only the ticking of the clock, the rasp of the respirator and the thick, cloying air that settles on the surface of my skin like a toxic sheen.

I wonder how she got past the nurses. Do they even keep a check on who is coming in here? The medical staff check on me around three or four times a day, taking their readings, maintaining my life support. In addition, Dr Shaw and Dr Chance pay their brief visits also.

The cleaner came in early this morning, whisking quickly under my bed with a mop and leaving the air thick with the acrid disinfectant that chafes at my throat. Another cleaner will drop by later.

None of them will take a moment to really look at me. Nobody will speak to me. Unless the nice nurse comes back, that is.

But for now, I am alone with someone I thought I would never see again. Someone I hoped I would never breathe the same air as again.

Evie, I whisper.

'Do you still think about Evie? Think about what you did?'

Every day. Every day, I think about her.

'You just had one job that mattered and that was to take care of her.' The coloured shape draws nearer to me. 'It's laughable you could even think of yourself as worthy. She wasn't taken, you let her go.'

I didn't let her go, I screamed. *She was taken. Somebody took Evie away.*

And then, swiftly, she is right next to my bed and her face is above mine. Directly above my eyes, staring down at me, her lips set in a terrible grimace of something that falls between hatred and anger.

She pulls back her arm and then whips her hand in front of my face. For a moment, I think she is going to punch me in the face but then I see she is clutching something between her fingers, something white and stiff.

She flicks the piece of card, holds it squarely above my eyes. A photograph, of Evie. Her beautiful face is older; eyes like azure pools of sadness. The strawberry-shaped birthmark is partly visible on her neck.

It has been three years since I saw her, when she was five years old. In this photograph she looks about eight.

A force rises up from my solar plexus, I feel the thrust of it travelling up through my body, chest, throat and suddenly it's there, filling my head like liquid explosive.

And I blink.

I actually blink.

Above me, her face freezes and then sort of collapses. She steps back in shock.

'They said you couldn't move, they said—'

Her voice falls away and she steps forward again. Her face looms in front of my eyes. She thinks she might have imagined it and she is checking me again.

I really did blink. I try to do it again and nothing happens.

I squeeze my eyelids together, or I try. But they are glued apart, and once again I am moving only in my head.

I blink repeatedly. Fast, hard, squinty blinks, one after the other.

Nothing happens.

I don't know what I did that time, how or why it was different. I don't know how to blink again.

The door opens and she gasps and looks round.

'Ms McGovern?' I hear Dr Chance's voice. 'The nurses said you were here.'

My heart seems to leap up into my throat.

Tell him! I cry out the words. *Tell him I just blinked.*

'Yes,' she says, turning away from me. 'Pleased to meet you. I'm her sister.'

'I take it someone has spoken to you about your sister's current condition?'

I haven't got a sister.

'Y-yes.' Her voice breaks with emotion. It's an impressive performance.

'We're very concerned there has been no sign of any movement whatsoever. Your sister can neither breathe nor swallow independently. There will need to be' – he pauses – 'some important decisions made, quite soon.'

Tell him I blinked. Please tell him.

'Of course, I understand. It's so sad,' she says and I hear sniffling and the swish of a tissue being whisked from a handbag. 'I've been here talking to her and watching her and there's nothing at all, no reaction. I don't feel she's with us anymore. It's like she's already gone.'

'Indeed,' Dr Chance says softly. 'And perhaps it is kinder to think of it that way.'

I am here, I shout. *I am still here.*

'If you'd like to come with me, Ms McGovern, we can go to my office for a chat. Dr Shaw, my colleague, may be able to join us.'

The door opens. And closes.

And I am alone again.

The room is silent in between the tick tocks and the rasps, which I hardly notice anymore.

The light is fading. The sun has moved round to the side of the building, leaving my room cold and clinical.

The blur of leaves sweeps to and fro across the glass as the wind picks up, lifting the branch to the window. On my face they would prickle and scratch, but from my bed they sound muted and soft. Like Evie's breathing at night.

I stare at the white, glossed ceiling with blurred eyes and try to blink. Nothing happens. The sensation of an explosive fullness in my head has gone now. I feel completely hollow, devoid of life.

I project the photograph of an older Evie onto the ceiling above me. She dangled it in front of my eyes for mere seconds but it was long enough. I have it now, here in my mind. I conjure up Evie's smooth, plump cheeks and the soft gleam of her hair cascading onto the shoulders of the red tartan dress with the white lace collar. I block out her never-ending tears, captured by the flash.

I try to un-see the fear and sadness in her eyes, but it is all I can ever think about.

I repeat *her* cutting words: 'You just had one job that mattered, and that was to look after her.'

I know I am totally to blame for what happened to Evie.

It was all my fault.

CHAPTER 39

Three Years Earlier

The Teacher

Harriet Watson had entertained certain suspicions about Evie Cotter's mother, but now she was utterly convinced that her suspicions were correct.

It had begun when Harriet noticed Mrs Cotter's odd drowsiness, evident on the day she visited the family home. During their tea and conversation in the kitchen, there had been a second or two, just here and there, of distracted silence on the other woman's part.

Perhaps the unpaid bills and maxed-out credit card statements had something to do with that. Toni had soon whisked them away when she realised she'd left them on the table.

Still, Harriet hadn't been *completely* certain of Toni Cotter's dependency.

But today on the telephone, the woman had clearly been slurring her words. It had been pronounced enough that Harriet herself had hesitated on the call, waiting for Toni to explain why she was having trouble speaking.

There had been no explanation. Toni had simply fallen silent herself until Harriet began speaking again. She was obviously completely unaware of how she sounded. Which is what had given her away. As the call continued, Toni became emotional, eventually teetering on the edge of tears, so Harriet had hastily finished the call.

She replaced the phone in its cradle and sat down on a breakfast stool. Staring out of the kitchen window, her eyes settled on the damp rot of next door's fence.

From this vantage point, she could see the two odd socks that had been hanging on their neighbour's line for months and months, through all weathers. The cotton had started to unravel; soon there would be nothing left.

At least fifteen years ago, the house next door had been converted into four separate student flats with communal kitchen and lounge areas. But Harriet could still remember when Mr and Mrs Merchant lived there and everything had been shipshape. Fences regularly treated with creosote and not a sign of the tangled, weed-strewn flowerbeds that now encroached onto the narrow front path.

Keeping the house and garden in order seemed to be a dated pastime for many these days, Harriet thought. Even that shoebox of a house that the Cotters had moved into looked in dire need of sprucing up.

If her suspicions proved correct, then Harriet doubted Toni Cotter was actually capable of organising a good, thorough clean up and providing a stable home for her daughter.

Harriet continued to stare through the rain-spotted glass, but she had stopped seeing anything now. Her mind had begun to ponder other concerns. What was little Evie getting up to while her mother was mooching around in a drugged haze? Who was the GP who'd been dishing out sedatives like Smarties to an obviously healthy young woman?

Harriet took her responsibilities seriously, and, as she had already made the decision to take Evie Cotter under her wing, so to speak, she would be unable to turn a blind eye to her mother's behaviour. It was obvious she had stumbled on a rather unusual situation. You might say the mother was as much in need of Harriet's guidance and support as her child was.

Harriet would make it her job to find out exactly what was happening when the door of 22 Muriel Crescent swung closed to the outside world.

In Harriet's opinion, it amounted to the worst sort of neglect.

CHAPTER 40

Three Years Earlier

Toni

I didn't hear anything at all from Mum on Saturday. She called my mobile while I was upstairs and Evie answered and spoke to her briefly. I wasn't worried; sometimes she was just best left to get over her strop in her own good time.

I refused to lie around feeling sorry for myself all morning, so I decided I'd take Evie into Hucknall.

'Do I get to see where you work, Mummy?' Evie asked, delighted. It was a pleasant change to see her smiling and upbeat.

'That's right, poppet,' I replied. 'And you'll get to meet Mummy's work friends, too.'

Impressively, aside from being the final resting place for the great poet Lord Byron, Hucknall was a convenient place for shopping. Once a thriving market town, it was much smaller than Nottingham city and I preferred the shops and layout to what I'd seen so far of Bulwell. A morning trip would be ideal to combine keeping Evie entertained and getting some errands done.

I parked up on the usual side street near work and walked into town, hand in hand with Evie. I felt so proud of my daughter, full of questions and energy, bright and eloquent in her conversation. This was Evie as she used to be, back at home. Happier, vibrant.

And it was no coincidence that this happier, more vibrant Evie had appeared at the weekend, when there would be no school.

We dawdled a little as we made our way down the bustling High Street, a chilly breeze occasionally brushing our cheeks but leaving no lasting discomfort. If anything, it reminded me of the fact that Christmas was looming on the horizon, and in turn, as it always did, the fact that Andrew and Christmas family time no longer existed for us.

For the first time in a very long time, I wondered if I could make Christmas a more jolly occasion for me and Evie. A little spare money and this fresh start might just swing it in our favour, making the best of and showing gratitude for what we still had, rather than what we'd lost.

We walked past shops, several with Halloween displays in the windows, even though it was still a few weeks away. Evie spotted a witch's outfit she loved in the window of a quality greeting card shop.

I made a mental note to buy it, once I got my first wage from Gregory's. It would be far more expensive than my original plan of hitting Poundworld for all the witchy components, but hell, this was why I'd taken the job in the first place.

It wasn't until the shop front of Gregory's came into view that it occurred to me that if Bryony was in the office, she might well take umbrage at me popping in with Evie. The last time I'd seen her she'd swept by me, issuing what sounded very much like threats but what I hoped was just temper.

Still, my stomach twisted when I thought about it and I felt glad I hadn't had any breakfast before we left the house. I opened the door to the shop and walked into the stuff of nightmares. Everyone – Dale, Bryony and Jo – was there. Their heads swivelled to the door as we stepped inside.

'We just popped in to say hello,' I said lightly, leaving the door ajar behind me so Bryony would see I wasn't staying to chat. 'I don't want to disturb you.'

Bryony looked startled and her eyes immediately focused on Evie. She rushed over.

'Hello, Evie, I'm Bryony.' She held out her hand and I was proud that Evie shook it confidently. 'I've seen your picture on your mummy's desk but you're even prettier in real life.'

Evie glanced at the framed photograph on my desk and her face broke into a wide grin. She was a sucker for compliments.

My mouth fell open. Bryony was the closest thing I'd ever seen to a person with a split personality. The fire-breathing dragon was gone and in her place was this sweet, good-natured woman who had instantly put Evie at ease.

'Hello, Evie.' Dale smiled. 'Have you come in to help us sell some houses today?'

Evie shook her head solemnly. 'Just to say hello to Mummy's work friends.'

'Ahh, I see,' Dale said, winking at me. I noticed he looked far more casual than I'd seen him before, wearing black jeans and a striped polo shirt. He mustn't be taking any clients on viewings today, although I felt sure we had some booked in.

'Shall I make a drink?' Jo stood up from her desk and walked across to us. I felt bad, like we'd been ignoring her. 'Evie, I'm Jo. Would you like some orange squash and maybe a biscuit?'

Evie looked at me and I nodded.

'Yes, please,' she said.

Jo held out her hand. 'Come and have a look then and you can choose which sort you'd like.'

To my surprise, Evie took Jo's hand and disappeared through the back without displaying an ounce of clinginess.

'Toni, she's adorable,' Bryony gushed. 'I don't know how you manage to come to work, I'd want to be with her constantly.'

'Well, she's at school now,' I said, wondering if she was having a dig. 'So it fits in really well with the job.'

'I wouldn't let her out of my sight,' Bryony said dramatically. 'Little angel, she is. I could eat her!'

Five minutes later, Evie walked back into the room, gingerly carrying a plate full of assorted biscuits.

'You're doing a marvellous job there, Evie,' Bryony praised her.

'Mummy, Jo took some photos of me in the kitchen.'

'Oh, you spoilsport.' Jo grinned, carrying in a tray of drinks. 'It was supposed to be a surprise, remember?'

I frowned, not sure what she meant.

'We were going to surprise you with a screensaver of Evie on your computer for Monday.' Jo rolled her eyes. 'But now Evie's gone and spilled the beans.'

'Ooh, can I have an Evie screensaver?' Bryony beamed.

I smiled and nudged Evie but she didn't smile back.

I hoped one of her tantrums wasn't looming. She didn't appear to need a good reason lately.

CHAPTER 41

Three Years Earlier

Toni

Sunday morning at ten, Mum called round to take Evie to the park as planned.

'Do you want to come in for a cuppa?' I asked her as she told Evie to get her coat from the front door step.

It wasn't much of an invite, I admit.

'No, I'll get straight off, I think,' she said, in the wounded tone she liked to use when I'd done something wrong but she didn't want to discuss it.

'What's the matter?' I said, unwilling to let it go. 'I can't say a thing lately without you getting the hump.'

She gave me a rueful smile and shook her head.

'You know, Toni, I'd like to live in your world. Where nothing you ever do is wrong and you very conveniently forget about the needs of others.'

I didn't have a clue what she was getting at.

'Anyway, it's not me I'm worried about.' She scowled and discreetly tipped her head towards Evie.

'She's fine,' I sighed. 'Or she will be, if you'd stop trying to give her a complex.'

'She's retreating into a shell.' Mum's face darkened. 'She's nervy and uncharacteristically quiet, Toni. Surely you can see that?'

It felt like something had loosened inside of me, something that wanted to shut Mum up.

'Don't be ridiculous,' I snapped. 'There's nothing wrong with her. Lots of kids have a problem adjusting to a new school.'

'I'm not just talking about school,' Mum said quietly. 'She's not sleeping properly, she's losing weight. Look at her.'

Evie shrugged on her light jacket and beamed up at me. 'Bye, Mummy,' she sang. 'See you later.'

There didn't look much wrong with her to me.

'Fine,' I said. 'We can talk about this later.'

But I had no intention of doing so.

I bent to kiss the top of Evie's head. 'See you soon, poppet. Have fun.'

Mum took her hand and I moved to close the door behind them.

'You might want to clear that mess up while we're out,' she said, nodding towards the corner. I followed her line of sight but the chair was in the way of whatever she was looking at. 'I'll bring her back after she's had her tea.'

And with that, they were gone.

I clicked the front door closed, leaned against the wall and closed my eyes. Peace at last. A few hours where I had no responsibilities, expectations or a paranoid mother to contend with. There were a thousand and one jobs that needed doing in the house but I pushed all thoughts of hard work out of my head.

First job was coffee. The next a long, hot bath with the book I'd been picking up and putting down for the last two weeks.

I walked into the kitchen and filled the kettle. A tap on the window made me look and my heart sank when I saw it was Sal from next door. I cursed my bad luck at being in full view in the kitchen. I would have happily hidden behind the door until she went away again.

'Looks like I'm just in time,' she said when I opened the door. She gave me a gappy grin and nodded to the kettle as she stepped inside without being asked. 'Seeing as you never came round for that cuppa, I thought I'd do the honours instead.'

'Oh right,' I said tightly. 'Thing is, Sal, Mum's just taken Evie for a couple of hours and I've got loads of unpacking still left to do.'

'I'll help you,' she said cheerfully. 'I don't mind, I'm at a loose end all day.'

She and both her sons were at a loose end *every* day, from what I could see.

'Thanks but there's no need,' I said firmly, imagining the horror of being stuck with her for hours on end, with no escape. 'But I can take ten minutes out for a chat.'

'So,' she said as I put two steaming mugs of coffee down on the table. 'I hear you met our Col the other day?'

'Yes,' I said, imagining the names he'd probably called me. This was my chance to tell Sal the truth. 'Did he tell you what happened?'

She took a noisy slurp of her coffee and nodded, grinning at me. 'Gave you a fright, I hear.'

'Actually, Sal, he really did.' Something clawed at the inside of my throat. 'I really thought Evie had gone. I didn't know what the hell had happened to her.'

'Yeah, but he said you'd left her on her own all morning, love.'

'Rubbish!' How dare she come round here, virtually accusing me of neglect. 'I was upstairs, that's all. I've still got loads to do up there and—'

'Your little 'un told our Col you were still in bed, said she couldn't wake you.'

The thought of her slimy son questioning my daughter made me feel sick to my stomach.

'Well, she was mistaken.' Her eyes flicked to my hands and I realised I was gripping the edge of the table like a vice. I wiggled my fingers to relax them. 'I'd got a bit of a headache, that's all. I was just having a lie down, I wasn't asleep.'

'Ahh, I see. Kids, what're they like, eh? They tell you anything.'

The last thing I wanted was a confrontation but it was important to make my position crystal clear. This was my chance.

'More to the point, Sal, Colin should never have encouraged Evie to come over to your side without checking with me first,' I remarked. 'That was really irresponsible of him. People could get the wrong idea.'

Her face darkened and the good-natured grin slipped.

'What are you trying to say?'

I swallowed. 'I'm just saying, a grown man taking a five-year-old girl without her mother's permission might not look good to—'

She slammed her hand down flat on the table and I jumped up from my seat. She was reducing me to a bag of nerves in my own home.

'Enough of that. You can just shut your mouth,' she hissed. 'Our Col has enough fucking trouble from the coppers without you starting to spread your vile lies.'

'Sal, I'm not saying Colin was up to no good.' I sat down again, pressing the air with my hands as I tried to placate her. 'I'm just saying it doesn't look very good. All he had to do was tell me—'

'You were out of it, drugged up in bed.'

'I told you, I was just having a lie down—'

'You were out of it.' Her eyes flashed in slight hesitation and then spite got the better of her. 'I know that because our Col couldn't wake you up.'

A cold chill crept up my back. A second or two of silence stretched between us as the meaning of her words dawned on me.

When I spoke, my voice was shaking. 'Are you telling me he came into my bedroom?' I stood up, placing my fingertips on the table to steady myself.

She pressed her lips together, smug and accomplished.

'You'd better go,' I said, with as much dignity as I could muster. 'And you can tell your son, if he ever sets foot inside my house again, I'll ring the police.'

She stood up and purposely let her mug drop to the floor, coffee and smashed shards spattering to the furthest corners of the room.

'What the hell are you doing?' I yelped, stepping back to protect my bare feet. The woman was a maniac.

'Don't even think of trying to cause trouble with the coppers, love.' She waved her phone at me with a menacing look. 'Or someone might just have to show 'em why your kid was on her own for hours on end. It's all on here. You should be thanking our Col. She could've run out onto that main road, or fell down the stairs.'

I opened my mouth in retort but found there were no words waiting to be spat out in reply.

There was absolutely nothing I could say to defend myself.

CHAPTER 42

Three Years Earlier

Toni

I stood, silent and rooted to the spot, as Sal stormed out. The door crashed shut behind her so violently that I didn't know how the glass remained intact. Fury at the thought of her creepy convict son intruding into my house had already morphed into acute embarrassment and shame. How long had he stayed in my bedroom? How many pictures or videos did he take of me in that state? What if he'd . . . I could hardly bear to think the words . . . *touched* me?

My head fell forward and I squeezed my eyes shut. I felt my fingernails push deep into my palms.

How could I have allowed this to happen?

He could have done anything to me or my daughter. How fucking dare he?

Why on earth hadn't Evie mentioned anything about him coming into the house?

I opened my eyes and walked over to the window. Pulling down the blinds, I locked the back door and went into the sitting room. In there, I closed the curtains, leaving just enough of a gap to let a little bit of light in. Without thinking, I picked up my phone and called Tara. I needed to speak to someone; needed to offload before I exploded.

My heart sank when the call went straight to Tara's voicemail. I should have just ended the call but before I could think better of it, a torrent of anguished words poured out of my mouth and down the line.

I ranted about Bryony at work, Evie at school and about Colin the creep from next door. I was just about to embark on Mum's attitude when a disembodied voice announced the voicemail was now full. I hadn't even had a chance to ask how Tara was feeling.

I tossed my phone aside, annoyed at my own neediness.

A strong urge to hide away in the dark and never come out washed over me.

I grabbed my handbag and before I could think better of it, swallowed two tablets with cold tea I found in a mug on the floor, praying they'd work quicker than usual.

I felt desperate for a few hours of blissful oblivion. I couldn't face the thoughts and possibilities that were ricocheting around my head.

A man in the house with my daughter, while I was sleeping. While I was completely *out of it*.

Before sinking down onto the couch, I remembered Mum's sharp comment about cleaning up the mess. I snapped on the light and peered into the corner by the chair. My hand flew to my mouth and I stood for a few moments, blinking hard and trying in vain to process the evidence in front of me.

Two months before he died, Andrew had bought me an exquisite crystal glass vase for our tenth wedding anniversary. He'd had it engraved with our names and the date of our big day and I treasured it as the last thing he gave to me.

Now it lay in pieces in the corner of the room, broken beyond any hope of repair.

Only yesterday, I had carefully peeled off copious amounts of bubble wrap, washed it gently by hand and set it down by the fireplace.

That, I could remember. But how it got broken was a complete mystery.

Yet when I looked down at the splintered shards of crystal, I found myself flinching.

I took a step back. Something wasn't right.

I was beginning to realise that little pieces were missing, ripped here and there from my memory, like sticking plasters, leaving smooth gaps of time that remained a mystery.

My hands began to shake.

I rushed upstairs to the bathroom, hung over the loo and stuck my fingers down my throat.

Twenty seconds later, the contents of my stomach were at the bottom of the pan, hopefully along with the two sedatives I'd just taken. I prayed I'd caught them in time.

Following a quick shower, I put on my fluffy dressing gown and came back downstairs. I ran a glass of cold water from the kitchen tap and took it through to the living room, sitting down in the gloom and trying to get my thoughts straight.

I knew, without any doubt, that the smartest, most effective thing I could do for myself right this second was to flush the remaining tablets down the toilet.

I wanted to do it, I really did.

I could just take the damn things out of my handbag, walk upstairs and flush them down the loo. And then I could go to my bedroom, open the shoebox under my bed, take out the birth, marriage and death certificates and reach for the other two small brown bottles hidden under there, full of tablets. I could flush those away too.

But even as I walked through the steps in my mind, I knew I couldn't do it. Not yet.

Those tablets were all I had. They were the only buffer between me and a very messy meltdown. Since Andrew's death, they had served as a dam against a tsunami of pain and grief that had been waiting to crush me.

I picked up the glass of water and gulped it down in one.

I couldn't face getting rid of my sole defence, not yet. It wasn't that I wasn't going to do it, I just had to give myself time to get used to the idea. Grow stronger.

After all, it would be totally counterproductive to get rid of the pills and then find myself unable to function.

It was true that, most of the time, I felt ashamed to call myself a mother. Yet, pitiful as I was, I still managed to fulfil some parental duties most days. And that was preferable to finding myself trapped in some institution, leaving my daughter to face life without me.

I had to keep the tablets for the time being, purely as a safety net. I realised I couldn't manage without them, but continually sabotaged myself by using them.

I was trapped, caught in my own personally created hell.

CHAPTER 43

Three Years Earlier

Toni

On Monday morning, Evie was quiet and a little withdrawn.

I helped her on with her coat in the hallway. 'What's wrong, poppet?' I said, knowing full well it was her dislike of school that was behind it all.

She stared at the wall, saying nothing.

I hadn't gone into great detail with her about Harriet Watson's after-school club. I didn't want to add to her stress by asking her to cope with yet more new things. Hopefully, she'd enjoy having some one-to-one time with an adult other than me or Mum; it would make her feel special.

Harriet had advised me not to press her to talk about school, so I quickly changed the subject.

'How about we swing by McDonalds later?' I said. 'A fast-food tea. Whaddaya say, kiddo?'

She gave me a tiny smile but it was far from the jumping up and down and squealing that the offer of a McDonald's meal on a school day would usually bring. I almost wished I hadn't suggested it. It was an expense I could ill afford and which would get me little or no payoff, judging by her subdued response.

I ignored my headache and overcompensated for Evie's silence by chatting too much on the way to school. When we arrived, I was relieved there was no refusal to go through the gates and no pulling away to go back home.

There seemed to be a new, quiet acceptance from my daughter that almost concerned me more than if she'd thrown one of her tantrums.

The effects of yesterday's set-to with Sal were paired with a feeling of lethargy and sluggishness that made me think traces of the two tablets I'd tried to vomit up might have been absorbed, after all.

I made a coffee and lay down on the couch with my book, setting the alarm on my phone for two hours' time, just in case I dropped off.

I opened the book and tried to pick it up where I last left it weeks ago. None of it made any sense, so I went back to the beginning.

My concentration span was short. I began reading about the main female character, who was a bit of a sap, to say the least. She suspected her fiancé was having an affair with her best friend, so she quickly embarked on an unsophisticated plot to kill them both.

If only life were that easy.

I closed the book and let it fall to the floor before closing my eyes.

'Bryony's in the back,' Jo said in a low voice when I got to the office. 'I was going to text you over the weekend but didn't want to intrude. I couldn't believe the change in her when you popped in with Evie.'

'I hope her change of heart wasn't just for show in front of Dale,' I said wearily.

'Just act normally,' Jo advised. 'Offer to make her a cup of tea or something.'

Jo was doing her best to help, but I didn't see why I should brown-nose Bryony when, actually, I'd done nothing wrong. *She* was the one who had been swizzing her most loyal of customers. Of course, my brave indignation deserted me the moment she showed her face.

'Could you call the Wiltons, please, Jo,' Bryony said, handing Jo a piece of paper and showing no signs she'd even noticed me in the office. 'I've written down some possible viewing times for the converted barn.'

She had on a black skirt, bright red jacket and impossibly high black stilettos. Her hair sat perfectly in a neat chignon.

I stood up and spoke to her back. 'Hi, Bryony, I'm just going to make a hot drink, would you like one?'

She turned and her nose wrinkled slightly, as if she'd detected an unpleasant smell.

'No, thanks,' she said curtly. 'Toni, I'd like you to go through some of the archived boxes of old property details this afternoon. They're in the back office, in a bit of a mess. Everything needs filing in alphabetical order.'

Behind her, I saw Jo's eyes widen. If I had to dream up the most mind-numbingly awful job I could give someone in an estate agency, then this was probably it.

'Fine,' I said brightly, ignoring the burn of muscles tightening across my shoulders and neck.

'And when you've done that,' Bryony continued, 'you can go through the property database and make sure no fool has tagged anything as sold when it's still available.'

She turned on her heel and stalked out before I could reply.

'Ouch.' Jo grimaced. 'That's a bit brutal, even for her.'

CHAPTER 44

Three Years Earlier

Toni

It seemed luck was on my side, because it turned out to be one of the busiest afternoons since I'd worked there. There was a steady stream of customers and Jo was pretty much continually occupied.

'You'll have to leave the archiving until later,' Bryony sniffed. 'It'll wait, I suppose.'

I processed a bond deposit and booked in a viewing for a student bedsit conversion that had just gone on the market that morning.

Something had been niggling me about my desk since I'd got into work, and as I reached for a notepad, I suddenly realised what it was: Evie's photo was missing. I opened my pedestal drawers and peered in, but the photograph was nowhere to be found. Just as I was about to mention it to Jo, a young couple came in.

'We're interested in the two-bedroomed house that's just come up for rent on Muriel Crescent in Bulwell,' the girl said, pushing back a long mousey-brown fringe. 'Our friend told us about it. Number sixty-one.'

I smiled and opened my mouth to tell her that I lived on Muriel Crescent, but then thought better of it. I didn't want them knocking on my door at Christmas when the boiler had bust or something similar.

'Take a seat, please. I'll just get the details up,' I said, tapping at my keyboard.

'I'm afraid that property has already gone,' Bryony said from behind them, seemingly appearing from nowhere. The clients turned around in their chairs to look at her. 'It went this morning. But I'm sure Toni can find you something similar in the vicinity.'

'Of course,' I said, frowning. I'd not seen a lettings board on my street and I tended to make browsing new lettings one of my first jobs in the afternoon, so that I had an up-to-date overview for clients. I didn't know how I'd missed it.

Within twenty minutes, I'd found two similar properties for the couple and set up viewings for both of them. After they'd left the shop, just out of interest, I submitted a search for properties to let on Muriel Crescent. Nothing had been registered on the database.

Bryony came through and placed a stack of index cards on the corner of my desk. I got a powerful waft of her sickly-sweet, flowery perfume.

'Can you rewrite these customer contact cards, please, Toni,' she said without looking at me. 'They're getting a bit dog-eared. And I'd like you to at least make a start on the archiving before you go home, please.'

I glanced at the wall clock. She was overloading me on purpose for the last hour.

'I thought all our customers' details were computerised?' I said, lightly.

I couldn't help myself. Who, in this day and age, handwrote contact details anymore? I wanted her to know that I knew she was just being an arse for the sake of it.

'Did I ask for your opinion?' she snapped, her perfectly plucked eyebrows shooting up. 'When I ask you to do something, I don't expect to be questioned, Toni.'

'Fine,' I sighed, reaching for the cards. Then I remembered. 'Oh, there's no property on Muriel Crescent on the database,' I said. 'Do we have a hard copy of the details?'

'Toni.' Bryony's expression was pained, as if I was causing her actual physical discomfort. 'The property came in and was snapped up by a tenant before it even got to that stage. I dealt with it personally. Now, please get on with your job, you've wasted enough time wittering on as it is.'

'Probably another one of her dodgy deals,' Jo whispered behind her hand after Bryony had disappeared back into her office.

'Have you seen Evie's photograph?' I asked her, pointing to the space where it had been. 'It's disappeared.'

Jo pulled a face. 'I haven't. That's strange.'

'It was still here on Saturday when I popped in.'

'Ask Bryony.' Jo shrugged. 'It wouldn't be the first time she's taken it upon herself to move people's personal items.'

A few minutes later, Bryony came through into the office and I asked her if she'd seen the photograph.

'What do you mean, have I seen it?'

'Well, it's gone from my desk,' I explained. 'I just wondered—'

'What you mean is, have I taken it?'

'No, I didn't mean that, Bryony, I just . . .' I couldn't seem to get my words out. She towered above my desk, glaring down at me. I could feel myself becoming flustered, so I backed off. 'Sorry, I didn't mean to sound like I was accusing you. Maybe I've mislaid it, I don't know.'

She turned without saying another word, pinned something to the customer notice board and walked back into her office.

* * *

I worked steadily and got half of the contact cards rewritten.

Evie would be in her first after-school session with Harriet Watson now. I hoped and prayed Harriet could help counteract the morose mood Evie had slid into. Despite Mum's reservations, Harriet seemed to be working hard to build up a rapport with my daughter and I felt grateful to her for that.

Finally, the shop had quietened down, so I took the opportunity to go into the back office to start the archiving task.

'If I'm not out in half an hour, come and get me,' I told Jo. 'I might just fall asleep in there, given it's such an enthralling task.'

Jo snorted in reply.

The archived boxes were piled up next to the photocopier, which was noisily churning out property brochures by the dozen.

There were at least twenty boxes from the previous year, labelled A–C, D–F and so on. I sighed and picked one at random. I bent down to pick it up and screamed as something touched my back, my hand flying up to my throat.

'Sorry!' Dale backed off, his hands in the air. 'I'm so sorry, Toni, I didn't mean to startle you. I did say hello but you didn't hear me over the noise of the machine.'

He'd tapped me lightly on the back to let me know he was there. My heartbeat was in overdrive.

'Oh God, I'm turning into a nervous wreck.' I gave a little laugh. 'I didn't hear you, sorry.'

I looked up at him and felt my face flush as I inhaled. He was wearing that nice aftershave again.

'I wanted to ask if you've been OK today,' he said. He glanced at the door and leaned forward to speak quietly into my ear. 'I hope it's not been too . . . difficult?'

We both knew exactly what – and who – he was referring to.

'It's been OK,' I began and then, in a moment of madness, decided to be a little more candid. 'Bryony has got me doing senseless tasks though, it's ridiculous. There are far more important things I could be doing.'

Dale nodded. 'I hear you. Let me keep an eye on things for the next couple of days. I'd hate to think we're wasting all your experience.'

Wasting it? They hadn't even tapped into it yet.

'I've got to refile the archived property details.' I nodded to the box that had toppled from the pile when I'd jumped back.

'Here, let me get that for you.' Dale moved past me and stumbled slightly, grasping hold of my shoulder, his face embarrassingly close to mine. We locked eyes for a moment.

'Oh! Excuse me.' Bryony stood in the doorway. 'Am I interrupting something here?'

Dale coughed and stepped away from me.

'I was just helping Toni,' he said quickly. 'With the archive boxes.'

'I see.' Her mouth set into a tight little line and she glared at me. 'Toni, you can carry on writing the contact cards in the office,' she said. 'Leave the archiving for today.'

I nodded and walked out of the office without looking at either of them again.

When I got out into the corridor, the door clicked shut behind me, and as I walked away, I heard raised voices.

Back in the office I relayed what had happened to Jo. 'She looked furious,' I said. 'Anyone would think she was the owner and Dale was her assistant.'

'You've worked out why, haven't you?' Jo smirked. 'Surely you can't be that naïve.'

'Worked what out?' Then it came to me. 'They're having an affair?'

Jo had just taken a sip of her tea and nearly choked. She shook her head. 'Bryony's got a crush on Dale but the attraction isn't mutual. Dale was engaged to his childhood sweetheart. They'd just started to plan their wedding when Mia was killed in a car accident. It happened about eighteen months ago.'

'Oh no,' I whispered. No wonder Dale had been so understanding when I told him about Andrew. He knew exactly how I felt.

'Since then it's been embarrassing.' Jo rolled her eyes. 'Bryony started coming to work dressed to the nines. She's not even subtle about her intentions anymore.'

'But she's married,' I said. 'You said they were desperate for a child.'

Jo rolled her eyes again. 'Like I said, Toni, no offence, but you're a bit naïve. Don't you realise that some people just want it all?'

CHAPTER 45

Three Years Earlier

The Teacher

Harriet Watson placed the small dish of seedless grapes and sliced strawberries on the desk in front of Evie and beamed. 'A nice snack I prepared for you earlier.'

Evie looked at the fruit but didn't touch it.

'So, what do you say?' Harriet prompted her.

'Thank you,' Evie muttered.

'Well, aren't you going to eat it?'

The child picked up a seedless grape, inspected it and popped it into her mouth. 'We're going to McDonald's for tea.'

Harriet's stomach burned. 'Fast food will rot your innards,' she said tightly. 'Your mother shouldn't be taking you to those places.'

'It's a treat.' Evie frowned. 'It's my favourite.'

'Fast food contains very high levels of sugar and salt,' Harriet told her. 'If you eat too much of it, your taste buds will only want that sort of food and you can even become addicted.'

Evie looked at her. 'It's just a treat.'

'Anyway, enough about that. I'd like to get to know you a little better, Evie. You can start by telling me all about your friends at your old school.'

Evie popped another grape in her mouth and took her time chewing it.

'I'd like to know their names and the sorts of things you used to do together.'

'My best friends are Daisy, Nico and Martha,' said Evie, perking up a bit. 'We used to play together at break and eat our lunch together. And we sat next to each other at story time, too.'

'How lovely,' Harriet remarked. 'You said they *are* your best friends but they're not, anymore, are they?'

'They are,' Evie replied swiftly. 'They *are* my best friends.'

'But you never see them. They live back in Hemel Hempstead.' Harriet's voice dropped lower. 'I heard they have a new little girl as their friend now. I'm afraid she took your place when you moved house.'

'They're still my friends.' Evie pushed away the bowl of fruit. 'Mummy says we might go and see them soon.'

'Oh, I think Mummy might just be saying that to make you feel better.' Harriet smiled. 'She's always promising things that never quite happen, isn't she?'

Evie thought for a moment but she didn't respond.

'You see, it's no use getting upset about losing your friends, because *you* left *them*, didn't you? You left all your friends behind to come and live here, in Nottingham.'

'I didn't want to,' Evie said, knotting her fingers together on top of the desk. 'I didn't want to live at Muriel Crescent.'

'But Mummy wouldn't listen, would she?'

Evie looked at Harriet, a mournful expression on her face.

'And neither would your Nanny,' Harriet went on. 'It was all your Nanny's idea, you know, taking you away from your friends and moving you up here. Did you know that?'

Evie gave a slight shake of her head and stared down at her fidgeting hands.

'Mummy and Nanny don't tell you things because they think you're just a silly little girl,' Harriet told her. 'But I will tell you the truth, Evie. I am your friend and you can always trust me because I know what's best for you.'

Evie didn't speak.

'Do you understand? I am your friend and you can tell me anything you like in our little sessions together.' Harriet crossed her chest. 'I won't tell anyone what you say, I promise. Cross my heart and hope to die. Do you promise, too?'

Evie sat very still and then nodded.

'Pardon?'

'Yes.'

'Because if you're a very good girl, I might be able to get your friends to come up to Nottingham and see you,' Harriet said brightly. 'Would you like that?'

Evie nodded.

'Sorry?' Harriet cupped her ear.

'Yes, Miss Watson.'

'Excellent. Now, tell me about Mummy's friends.'

Evie began to hum.

'Kindly stop playing with your fingers and look at me.'

Evie spread out her palms and pressed them into the table. She looked up at Harriet. 'She just has Nanny.'

'There are no friends who Mummy meets for coffee or who come to the house to chat with her?'

Evie considered this and shook her head. 'Just Nanny.'

'And did Mummy have friends when you lived at your old house?'

Evie nodded. 'Paula and Tara.'

'Paula and Tara,' Harriet repeated. 'But Mummy doesn't see them anymore?'

'No. She hasn't got any friends anymore, just Nanny.'

'Perfect.' Harriet smiled. 'Well, isn't this nice, chatting together, just you and me?'

'Yes,' Evie replied blankly.

'Perhaps I could be Mummy and Nanny's friend too.'

'Nanny doesn't like you,' Evie said quickly. 'Because you're over a bear ring.'

'Is that what she says?' Harriet's smile fell away. 'Overbearing? Now, that is interesting. And did Nanny say anything else about me?'

'She said you weren't a proper teacher like Miss Akhtar.'

'I'm afraid that's a common error lots of people make,' Harriet said, tapping her fingertips on the table. 'But I *am* a proper teacher. You know that, don't you, Evie?'

Evie studied Miss Watson's steely eyes and the taut curve of her mouth that was supposed to look like a smile but didn't.

'Yes,' she said.

CHAPTER 46

Three Years Earlier

Toni

I turned the car into Muriel Crescent, but instead of pulling up outside the house, I drove around the full crescent, which wasn't very big, and slowed outside number sixty-one. All the blinds were pulled down and even though there was no to-let sign up, it did have a vacant look about it: nothing on the windowsills, a free newspaper sticking out of the letterbox and the tiny patch of front lawn was slightly overgrown.

Whoever had snapped up the property before it even came onto the market obviously hadn't moved in yet.

I executed a sloppy three-point turn in the road, briefly holding up a black Audi with heavily tinted windows that had just turned into the crescent. Even though I couldn't see the driver through the darkened glass, I raised my hand in apology, but the car motored by at speed as if to make a point, as if they were furious to be delayed for even twenty seconds.

As soon as I got through the door, I said hello to Evie, kissing the top of her head. She grunted, already engrossed in building a Lego structure.

Mum put down the TV guide she'd been reading, stood up and scooped up her car keys and coat.

'There's no need for you to rush off,' I said, although I wasn't in the right frame of mind for making amends, especially when Mum was obviously still in a mood. 'Unless you've got somewhere you need to be?'

She stopped for a moment and stared straight ahead, as though she was having an internal battle. Then she put down her coat. 'I'll have a quick drink with you.' She followed me into the kitchen, placing her car keys on the worktop. 'I'll be truthful, Toni, I'm finding it difficult to be around you. I'm worried about the signs I'm seeing but you don't want to listen.'

Not this again; we'd already discussed it to death. I filled the kettle and turned it on at the wall.

'I do listen, Mum,' I sighed. 'I agree that Evie's been a bit withdrawn but she'll soon come out the other side again. She's had some big changes to deal with, it's a natural reaction.'

'I'm not talking about Evie,' Mum said. 'I'm talking about *you*.'

I stopped reaching up into the cupboard for mugs and looked at her.

'You keep forgetting things and you fly off the handle at the slightest thing.'

'Have you got an example?' I challenged her. Talk about exaggerating, Mum was an expert at it.

'Well, you've told me the wrong times for picking Evie up, for starters.'

'No, I think the school – Harriet Watson – gave me the wrong times to begin with.'

'And then you lose your temper and forget you've done it,' Mum continued, ignoring my line of defence. 'Like when you threw that vase at the wall because the television was on too loud and woke you up. You need to go to see the doctor, Toni, it's not natural you being so tired and irritable all the time. Sometimes you can barely focus and that's not fair on Evie.'

Something gripped at me hard inside my chest. For a few seconds I couldn't say anything. I knew I'd come to a crossroads. This was my chance to admit to Mum I'd been relying on the sedatives to cope.

This was my chance to ask for her help and support.

I almost opened my mouth and told her, I *almost* did. But then my mind presented me with flash-forward images of Mum fretting about me and Evie, losing sleep and badgering me to throw the tablets away and see the doctor. I couldn't handle all the drama that would ensue. I just didn't have the energy for it.

'Look, it's been hard for all of us,' I said, trying to change the subject.

'I know how much that vase meant to you,' Mum pressed. 'That reaction, it wasn't you, love. What's going on?'

'You weren't here when I threw the vase.' I was hedging my bets, as I had no memory of whether she was here or not.

'No, but poor Evie was. It scared her, Toni, she told me all about it the next day. I actually thought she was exaggerating until I saw the mess.'

'I have felt tense and stressed out,' I conceded. 'I know you disapprove, but this new job is important to me, Mum. I'm trying to make a good impression there; the money will come in so handy. And I've also been really concerned about Evie not liking school.'

'I don't like that Watton woman,' Mum said.

'Miss Watson,' I corrected her again.

'Whatever. You'd think *she* was Evie's nanny, the way she talks about what's best for her. I had to bite my tongue again today.'

'Why, what did she say?'

'Oh, she just hinted that it would be better if *you* could pick her up after her new later sessions. I get the impression she doesn't like me picking her up full stop. My own granddaughter.'

'I'm sure that's not the case, Mum,' I said, remembering that's exactly what Harriet had suggested in her phone call about Evie's private sessions.

I spooned coffee into our mugs and poured in boiling water.

'I don't know why Evie has to go to these silly sessions anyway, she'd rather be at home, I'm sure.'

'Well, I'm grateful to Miss Watson.' I went to the fridge for milk. 'She's going the extra mile to help Evie settle in. She seems very giving of her own time.'

We took our drinks into the lounge. Mum handed Evie a carton of orange juice.

'What did you do in your session with Miss Watson today, sweetie?' I asked Evie.

She looked up briefly.

'Just talking,' she muttered.

'Talking about what?' Mum chipped in.

'About friends,' Evie said, poking the straw into her drink. 'Mummy's friends.'

I raised an eyebrow at Mum. '*My* friends?'

'There's something I don't trust about that woman.' Mum pursed her lips. 'Why would she be poking her nose in your personal business?'

'I told her you hadn't got any,' Evie said, slurping juice through the straw.

'Oh, cheers, Evie.' I laughed, but it was sobering to realise it was actually the dismal truth.

'She said she could be your friend,' Evie added.

'Creepy,' Mum shuddered. 'I don't like the woman.'

'Miss Watson said she's going to get Daisy, Nico and Martha to come and visit me soon,' Evie went on, selecting her next brick.

I shrugged at Mum's disapproving glare. I felt sure Miss Watson hadn't promised Evie such a thing. It was fairly obvious she'd been encouraging her to speak about friends, and that was a positive thing, seeing as she hadn't managed to make any yet.

Her old friends visiting would be nothing but wishful thinking on Evie's part.

After all, our old life was firmly behind us. There was nothing left for us there anymore.

CHAPTER 47

Three Years Earlier

Toni

When Mum had gone home, I unpacked Evie's book bag. There was a slip of paper tucked inside her reading journal.

> *Mrs Cotter, would you be able to stay for a 5 min chat when you bring Evie to school in the morning?*
> *Regards,*
> *H. Watson*

My heart sank, wondering what it was she wanted to talk to me about. I hoped she wasn't still concerned about Evie settling into her new class.

I felt exhausted, far too tired to contemplate unpacking anything upstairs, so I decided I'd just make us a light tea and crash out on the sofa while Evie watched TV. Not the most nurturing plan a parent ever came up with, but I told myself that, sometimes, needs must.

'Mummy, when are we going to McDonalds?' Evie said.

I stared at her, this morning's forgotten promise echoing in my head. I felt like crying.

'You promised,' she said, watching me with narrowed eyes.

'We can go now if you like,' I said wearily. 'Get your coat and shoes.'

'Miss Watson said fast food is full of salt and sugar that add hicks you,' Evie remarked, buckling her shoes. 'But I still want to go.'

When we left McDonalds and drove home, the first thing I noticed, when we turned into Muriel Crescent, was that the lights were on in the kitchen of number sixty-one. The blinds were still pulled down and although I could see shadows moving around, the fabric was too substantial to make out any detail. As we drove by, I saw that the car parked outside number sixty-one was a black Audi, remarkably similar to the car that had sped by me earlier.

Later, before I climbed into bed, I turned off the light and peeked out of the curtains onto the road. Number sixty-one was almost directly opposite our house, and a dim lamp had just snapped on in the lounge, illuminating the room in a rosy glow.

A woman walked over to the windows to draw the curtains. I squinted at the shape behind her and realised that there was someone else there in the room too. Before she pulled the curtains completely closed, the woman hesitated and stared out for a few seconds, clutching the drapes close to her face.

If I was the paranoid type, I'd have sworn she was looking directly up at me.

The next morning, Evie and I walked to school under our matching ladybird-themed umbrellas, which served as both a novelty and a distraction for her.

I kept looking for signs that she seemed a little happier going to school, but I couldn't find any evidence of that. She didn't complain loudly or refuse to go in, like she had done previously, but her demeanour was virtually identical. She remained surly and quiet for most of the journey.

It was a tall order to expect Harriet Watson to work her magic in the space of a single one-to-one session. We were in it for the long haul, but I felt sure we'd get there in the end.

When we reached the school gates, Harriet Watson was waiting for us. Evie looked up at me, slightly alarmed, but I squeezed her hand to reassure her everything was fine and she wasn't in any trouble.

We all walked towards the building together.

'Now, run along to the classroom, Evie, and I'll be through in a few minutes,' Miss Watson said briskly when we got inside.

I bent down and got a peck on the cheek before Evie sauntered down the corridor towards Rowan Class.

Miss Watson led me into the pleasant open-plan library space. We moved from echoing wooden flooring onto a carpet that muted all the sounds. Shelves piled with colourful, tempting books of every genre lined the walls. Even the lighting seemed a little softer in here.

Although pupils were constantly walking by us to their classrooms, it was a surprisingly calm and private space, buffered as we were by the bookcases and carpet. We sat down at a round table next to the back wall.

'Thanks so much for coming in,' Harriet began, placing her hands, one on top of the other, on the tabletop. 'I wanted to tell you how the session went yesterday. Evie was very responsive and chatted openly about her friends and life at her old school.'

'She told me.' I nodded, smiling. 'In fact, Evie said you were going to arrange for her three friends to visit her here.'

We shared a chuckle.

'Oh dear, little Evie perhaps got the wrong end of the stick there.' Harriet smiled. 'I'm sure I never said anything of the sort.'

'Don't worry, I realised she must have got confused,' I said. 'I thought it was positive you'd got her talking about friendships though. I really hope Evie will make some new friends here very soon.'

'Quite,' Harriet Watson agreed. 'But try not to worry. I have every confidence Evie will soon forge strong friendships here at St Saviour's. Her involvement in my small group work during the day will encourage this, as she'll be working with the same group of classmates most days. We sit right here, in fact.' She patted the tabletop.

'It's a lovely space,' I said, looking around with approval.

'You're probably wondering why I wanted to speak with you,' she ventured. 'I just wanted to reiterate what I said about you making an effort to pick Evie up after the later sessions.'

I felt a prickle of annoyance.

'I will ask at work, but as I said, I've only just started the job, so it might be a bit difficult to change my hours at this early stage.'

'I understand work is important, Mrs Cotter, but—'

'I will ask,' I said again. 'But Evie is completely used to being with my mum, it's not as if a stranger is picking her up. She loves her Nanny and—'

'And I'm afraid therein lies the problem, Mrs Cotter.'

'Call me Toni, please,' I said. 'And sorry, what do you mean?'

'This is difficult.' Harriet sighed, pressing her hands into the desk and leaning forward.

'I'd rather you be honest,' I said, feeling a wave of tension steadily filling the space between my shoulder blades.

'I get the impression that your mother – sorry, remind me of her name?'

'Anita.'

'Of course. I get the impression that Anita rather thinks she knows best when it comes to Evie. Do you understand what I'm saying?'

I nodded slowly. I couldn't argue with her assumption.

'It strikes me that, although Anita obviously loves Evie with all her heart, she thinks she knows better than you, her mother, or indeed myself, an educational professional with decades of experience.'

But not a teacher. The thought flitted through my mind, but I had to admit, qualified teacher or not, she was talking sense.

She looked at me. 'Mrs Cotter – Toni – the last thing I wish to do is offend you but—'

'Not at all,' I interrupted. 'I'm not offended, honestly. You seemed to have worked Mum out. I'm impressed.'

'Really? Oh, well, that's somewhat of a relief.'

'I'm afraid me and Mum often clash over what we think is best for Evie.' I held back saying any more because it felt a bit disloyal to Mum. She'd be so upset if she heard us talking like this.

'I'll be frank, I'm afraid I got the distinct impression that Anita wasn't a fan of Evie staying for our one-to-one sessions.'

I bit my lip and stayed quiet, but inside I cringed. I hoped Mum hadn't said anything inappropriate to Harriet.

'And of course, we all know that children are like little sponges, soaking up the opinions and unspoken disapproval of the adults around them.' Harriet pressed her lips together. 'Toni, I'm so sorry to have to tell you this, but I think your mother is unknowingly sabotaging the work we are trying to do with Evie.'

'Oh.' A thickness collected in the middle of my throat, cracking my voice a little. 'I'm sure Mum would never—'

'Don't get me wrong,' Harriet said hurriedly. 'There's no doubt in my mind that your mother wants the very best for Evie – but that's the crux of the matter, isn't it? She doesn't really *know* what's best.'

I thought about how Mum said Evie was better at home than in Harriet's sessions, how she said the school staff were to blame for Evie not settling in as well as we'd expected.

'Toni,' Harriet said gently, 'what I'm saying is this: I think, to give Evie the best chance, you need to limit the time she spends alone with your mum.'

CHAPTER 48

Three Years Earlier

Toni

Harriet Watson made it sound a lot easier than it was. Limiting the time Evie spent alone with Mum wasn't something I could just do overnight.

'I'm relying on Mum with my new job,' I explained. 'I could have a talk with her, try to make her see that we all have to work together.'

Harriet gave a sardonic little smile.

'She listens to you, does she, your mum? Takes on board what you say?'

I sighed. She had a point there.

'I know things have been very difficult for you over the last few years, Toni,' Harriet said quietly. 'You've had to manage alone under an enormous amount of stress and strain.'

To my horror, a prickling sensation started up in my eyes and nose.

'I know your mother has been a great help to you in the past, but now Evie is at school, the welfare of your daughter must become your priority.'

I nodded, although Evie had always been my priority.

'Our next session is on Wednesday, so I urge you to speak to your manager today, if you can. We must work together to give

Evie the best start at St Saviour's.' Harriet placed a hand on mine. 'Other children can be so unkind and are quick to shun. We don't want her becoming an outsider, now, do we?'

I'd got myself looking fairly presentable for my appointment with Harriet Watson, styling my hair and putting on a little make-up, so when I got home, I changed into smart trousers and a blouse and left early for work.

I had one or two bits I needed to do in town and it wouldn't do any harm to get into the office a bit earlier. It might even get me into Bryony's good books, paving the way for me to broach the subject of tweaking my hours on certain days.

I parked the car and walked onto the High Street. On the spur of the moment, as I was passing, I decided to drop by the office and say hi to Jo.

I peered through the shop window and watched her for a couple of seconds, smiling and talking to her computer monitor. I realised she was probably Skyping her sister, which meant Dale and Bryony were out of the office.

I opened the shop door and Jo looked up, smiling, expecting to see a customer. The smile melted away when she saw me.

'Sorry,' I mouthed. 'You busy?'

She shook her head and held up her index finger. 'Sorry, sis, got to go now. Toni's here, the new lady I told you about.'

I grinned and walked over to her desk, intending to give her sister a little wave.

'OK, speak later, bye,' Jo said to the monitor, turning it off.

'Oh.' I stopped walking. 'I was just going to say hi to your sister.'

'Sorry, I'm just nervy,' Jo said, looking at the door. 'It would be just my luck for Bryony to come back and catch us Skyping. I shouldn't do it at work, really, but it's been a quiet morning and the internet speed is so much better than I get at home. Anyway, how come you're here so bright and early? Couldn't you keep away?'

I grinned. 'I just needed to do a few bits, pop to the bank, the chemist. Do you need anything while I'm out?'

'I'm good, thanks,' Jo replied. 'But seeing as you're in town early, I'll take my half hour for lunch for a change. Dale should be back soon. Fancy popping to the café next door for a coffee and sandwich, about twelve fifteen?'

'Perfect.' I smiled. Forty-five minutes was ample time to get my errands done. 'Meet you there.'

I got to the café a few minutes early but Jo was already in there, tucked away at a table at the back. I plonked down my shopping bag and handbag on a spare chair before dashing to the loo.

'Back in five.' I grinned, crossing my legs for comic effect.

When I got back to the table, Jo was studying the menu.

'It's really nice in here,' I said, looking at the homemade cakes lining the counter and inhaling the smell of freshly brewed coffee. 'We should do this more often.'

Jo rolled her eyes. 'I'd love to, but they'd have a fit if I wasn't in the office to answer the phones and work the front desk most lunchtimes.'

'You're entitled to a lunch break, you know,' I said, picking up the other menu and leafing through. 'You could insist on taking it.'

'Yeah, I could,' Jo said. 'If I wanted a miserable life. Bryony has this way of quietly torturing you if she's displeased. I really hope you don't get to see that side of her.'

'I think I'm getting pretty close to it,' I murmured. 'By the way, our little chat the other day really helped, thanks.'

'Aww, I just want you to know I'm here if you need to offload, that's all. I don't want to push you. I know sometimes it can be difficult to open up, especially as we've only just met.'

Jo couldn't possibly know that I found it hard to trust people I didn't know, but somehow, she seemed to sense it anyway.

'I find it easy to talk to you,' I said, rummaging in my handbag for my purse. 'You're a good listener.'

'Years of practice.' She smiled. 'With my sister, mainly.'

'Let's order, these are on me,' I said, frowning as I delved deeper into my bag.

'I don't think so,' Jo said firmly, standing up. 'These are definitely on me. What're you having?'

Jo went to the counter to order our sandwiches and lattes and I pulled my bag onto my knee, taking out items and laying them on the chair, determined to locate my purse. I found two of Evie's favourite glass hair bobbles we thought she'd lost months ago, an overdue electricity bill and a folded five-pound note that was covered in biscuit crumbs.

'Sandwiches are coming,' Jo said, putting down our coffees and peering at the stuff piled on the chair. 'Looks like you keep all your worldly goods in that bag.'

'I'm looking for my purse,' I said, tasting sick in my mouth. 'It's not here.'

Jo was immediately calm. 'Look again. Sometimes stuff gets tucked away behind other things.'

'But I've taken everything out.' I opened my bag wide so she could see. 'It's not there, Jo. Oh shit. Shit. Shit.'

'Was there anything in it?' she asked. 'I mean other than debit cards?'

'I'd just drawn my food money out for the week,' I said, the sting of tears blurring my eyes as I looked hopelessly around the floor. 'I seem to manage better when I use cash.'

'OK, first things first,' Jo said. 'Let's go back to the bank and see if you left it there.'

'I didn't. I went to the chemist after the bank and then the post office. I definitely had my purse in the post office.'

'So we'll try there. Someone might have handed it in.' Jo kept up her calm, reasonable tone but I knew it was just for my benefit. I mean, who was going to hand in a purse full of cash?

'Oh God.' My heart ached as I remembered. 'There was a letter in there from Andrew. He'd sent it before the accident and I received it two days after he died. I don't know why I was keeping it in there, I just wanted it with me all the time, I suppose.'

'Oh, Toni, no.' Jo grasped my arm. 'Come on, let's go back to the shops, it might not be too late.'

We left the lattes untouched on the table and Jo hurriedly asked the waitress to bag up our sandwiches to collect on our return.

CHAPTER 49

Three Years Earlier

Toni

'I'm sorry,' I said to Jo as we walked briskly back up the High Street together. 'I've ruined our lunch, being so careless with my purse.'

'Don't be daft,' Jo said, linking her arm through mine. 'We've all done it.'

In the post office, Jo took charge and walked straight to the front of the queue. Unsurprisingly, nobody had handed in a long, black purse stuffed full of cash. We scouted round the shelves full of envelopes, Sellotape and packs of pens but it was hopeless.

'Are you certain this was the last place you had it?' Jo asked me.

My mind was just a mess. I couldn't remember even getting my purse out in here, but I must have done, in order to buy the stamps.

Then I suddenly remembered. 'I put the stamps in my purse.'

'And then you put the purse back in your bag?'

'Yes, definitely. That's what I did.'

'So maybe it dropped out somehow when you walked to the café,' Jo suggested.

We walked back to the café in subdued silence, scanning the pavements in vain. The street was busy with shoppers and workers on their lunch break, everyone scurrying around trying to maximise their time.

That's why the tall, stationary figure, staring from across the road, drew my eye. I squinted through the moving bodies to see if it was someone I recognised but whoever it was stepped aside and melted back into one of the alleyways between the shops.

I silently berated myself. I was becoming paranoid, as well as ridiculously forgetful. I waited outside while Jo popped back into the café for our sandwiches. Not that I had any appetite left whatsoever.

'I just don't know how I could've lost my bloody purse between here and the post office,' I said as we got to the office door.

'You two are back early,' Dale said, his mouth full of food.

'There's been a bit of a disaster,' Jo told him. 'Toni has lost her purse.'

We had to go through the whole story again for Dale's benefit. Halfway through, Bryony came back from lunch and waded right in.

'Let me get this straight,' she said. 'You can't even remember when you last had your purse?'

'I do remember. I definitely had it in the post office,' I said. 'I bought stamps, put them in my purse and then put it back into my handbag.'

'Maybe you thought you did but left it on the counter instead.'

'I didn't. I put it back in my bag.'

'But it isn't in there. So you either missed your bag and it fell on the floor, or—'

'I think I would've noticed that,' I said. I felt hot and I couldn't seem to get my breath properly. 'I would have noticed.'

'Well, then, someone must have taken it out of your bag.' Bryony looked at Dale. 'Maybe we should call the police?'

'And say what?' Jo remarked. 'Toni has no description of a thief, she doesn't even know if there *is* a thief.'

I shook my head glumly.

'Sadly, under the circumstances, I think you might have to put this down to experience,' Dale said. 'It's painful, I know, but under the circumstances—'

'You seem to be mislaying rather a lot of things lately,' Bryony said. 'You managed to lose a framed photograph from your desk and now your purse. I wonder what will be next.'

They all exchanged a glance.

'Excuse me,' I said abruptly, and walked quickly into the back, locking myself in the loo. I splashed some water on my face at the little sink and took a few deep breaths. I really needed that money I drew out of the bank today. What was I going to do, go cap in hand to Mum again? I wasn't exactly her flavour of the month at the moment. It would just give her more ammunition to beat me into submission.

And losing Andrew's letter, the last thing he ever wrote to me. How could I have been so utterly stupid?

Then there were the debit cards; I'd have to ring the bank as a matter of urgency. It was all so overwhelming.

A faint tapping sounded on the door. 'You OK, Toni?'

I unlocked the door and walked out. 'I'm fine, Jo. Just angry with myself.' I smiled weakly at her. 'Thanks so much for all your help though.'

She dismissed my comment with a wave of her hand.

'Look, maybe you've just got a lot on,' Jo said kindly as we walked back into the office. I was relieved to see that Dale and Bryony were no longer in there. 'Let's go out for a drink after work one night, let our hair down. What do you say?'

'I can't afford it now,' I said. 'And I can't really ask Mum to babysit at the moment with everything else she does.'

'OK, then I'll come round to yours,' she said brightly. 'I can sit and read Evie a story while you have a nice bath. No arguing, OK?'

'OK.' I smiled.

But it wasn't OK, not really. The house was such a mess and I felt anxious about letting someone into my life when I was struggling to cope with even simple everyday things. Not to mention the little pockets of forgetfulness I seemed to be having.

Jo meant well but I wished she'd just leave me alone to sort myself out.

CHAPTER 50

Three Years Earlier

Toni

For the rest of the afternoon, I couldn't really concentrate for worrying about what I'd lost in the purse, but I was able to bury myself in the mindless writing of customer contact cards.

When I checked my phone I had a missed call from Tara. She was probably ringing to see if I'd finally flipped over the edge, after my rant to her voicemail the other day. I couldn't face talking to her at the moment; I didn't want to tell her about today's crisis. I felt so completely incompetent.

I never thought I'd feel grateful to Bryony for giving me such a boring job, but it turned out to be the ideal task for getting me through the hours until I could finally leave for home. When the cards were finished, I picked up the stack and took them through to her office. She wasn't in there, but the door was wide open so I went straight in and placed them neatly on the edge of her immaculate desk.

I'd just turned to leave when I noticed the door to the small store room in the corner was ajar. Something glistened as I moved, drawing my eye. I took a step towards it and then froze as I recognised what had caught my attention.

There, perched on the end of a shelf and just visible through the open door, was Evie's silver-framed photograph. The one that had disappeared from my desk.

I stared, trying to make sense of what I was seeing.

'What are you doing in here?'

Bryony's sharp, cool tones behind me made me visibly jump.

'Oh! I was – I just brought you the contact cards through.' I nodded to the neat stack I'd placed on her desk.

She folded her arms and leaned against the door frame.

'It's the second time I've found you in here, snooping around.' Her eyes narrowed. 'Kindly keep out of my office when I'm not here. And why are you looking at me like that?'

'I just – well, something caught my eye in there,' I stammered, looking back at the store room door. 'It's – it looks like Evie's photograph, the one I had on my desk.'

'What?'

She stalked by me on her killer heels and pushed the store room door open wider. 'Where? Oh, here.' She picked it up, looked at it and smiled, her face softening. 'She's a little sweetheart, isn't she? What's it doing in here?'

'I don't know,' I said, taking the photo from her outstretched hands. 'I didn't put it in here.'

'Well, I certainly didn't.' She shook her head. 'Don't look at me like that, the cleaner probably found it lying around in the main office and put it in here for safekeeping.'

'Yes, of course,' I said. 'That must've been it.'

I'm assuming the cleaner would have known it belonged on my desk. After all, it had been there almost a full week before it disappeared.

'You'd better take extra care where you put things in future.' Bryony frowned as I moved towards the office door. 'It seems that losing stuff is getting to be quite a habit of yours.'

I didn't respond to Bryony's veiled criticism, but carried on walking and went back to my desk. I sat for a moment, staring at Evie's photograph, which I'd laid flat in front of me.

The door closing behind an exiting customer broke me out of my doleful reverie.

'You OK there, Toni?' Jo asked, her face creased with concern.

'Sorry.' I shook my head and smiled. 'I'm fine. Just thinking about something Bryony said.'

'You look upset,' she said cautiously, as if she was worried about me bursting into tears. 'Hope she hasn't said anything to make your day even worse.'

'No, she hasn't. She said something that's made me think, though. Look.' I held up the 'lost' framed photograph. 'It was in Bryony's store cupboard.'

Jo pulled a puzzled face. 'What was it doing in there?'

'Bryony said the cleaner might've put it in there. She reckons I've got a problem with losing stuff.'

'That's not fair.' Jo frowned. 'Anyone can lose a purse.'

'It's not just the purse though, is it?' I shrugged. 'This photo went missing from my desk, and then, at home, I keep forgetting important times and stuff. I mean, what if I'm losing my marbles and I don't realise?'

Jo laughed and shook her head.

'Toni, you might be a bit scatty because you've got a lot on, but I'm willing to bet you're still sane. Mostly, anyway.'

I smiled at her quip but then my face fell again. 'Sometimes I worry I'm not coping very well,' I said, surprising myself that I was actually voicing this worry. 'I'm a crap mum to Evie at the moment, too.'

Jo shook her head. 'You're too hard on yourself, love. We've all done stuff we're not proud of. Jeez, I know that more than anyone.'

She must have been referencing her past. I stayed quiet, wondering if she'd elaborate, but she didn't say anything else.

'I just – I don't know. I hate this feeling of not being in control of myself, of what happens.'

'Yeah, I know what you mean,' she replied, but I doubted she did.

She didn't know about the tablets and the gaps in my memory. And I certainly wouldn't be mentioning that. I didn't say anything else, letting the whole subject go.

But underneath, something was still niggling at me. Something didn't feel right.

CHAPTER 51

Three Years Earlier

Toni

'Mrs Cotter? I'm Di Wilson, a nurse at the accident and emergency department at the QMC. Your mother has had a fall at home and has been brought in. She's asked me to ring you, to let you know.'

'Oh no.' I stood up quickly, my free hand flying to my throat. 'Is she OK? When did this happen?'

Jo looked up from typing up Bryony's valuation report.

'It happened at lunchtime,' Di continued. 'We think she's badly bruised her shinbone. It's painful and nasty and she's quite shaken, but apart from that, she's fine. She'll mend.'

'Is she at home now?'

'She's still here, at A&E.'

When I came off the call, Jo had called Dale and Bryony through from their offices.

'Are you OK, Toni?' Dale asked.

I began to garble out the details. 'Mum's stuck in A&E right now and there's nobody to pick Evie up later, I—'

He held up his hand and I stopped talking.

'Go now,' he said kindly. 'I hope your mum's OK. If you need me to do anything, just shout.'

Bryony walked over to me and placed her hand on my arm.

'Me too.' I looked down at her hand, not quite believing she was offering me comfort. 'I could pick Evie up from school, she knows who I am now.'

'Thanks so much.' I grabbed my jacket and coat. 'I'll text you, Bryony, once I know what's happening. Whatever happens, I'll be in the office tomorrow though, no problems. Thank you.'

'Don't worry about it, Toni, we completely understand.' Bryony smiled and I felt a little shiver run down both my arms.

By the time I got to the hospital and found a parking space, it was nearly three o'clock. I had to be back at school for four thirty at the latest, to pick Evie up from her after-school session.

I dashed into the grubby unisex loo near the entrance. My throat felt like sandpaper and the beginnings of the mother of all headaches began to gather momentum at the base of my skull.

Before I could think better of it, as I sat on the loo, I unzipped the compartment in my handbag and shook out a single tablet, swallowing it dry. Just the one.

Out in the main area, I gave Mum's name and the receptionist pointed me to a second patient waiting room, beyond the initial one. I spotted Mum, huddled over in the far corner of the packed, noisy space. She sat close to the wall, her eyes downcast. The domineering, outspoken woman I knew and regularly fought against was absent. She looked smaller, more vulnerable, somehow.

I negotiated my way around the various injured bodies and wheelchairs. Toddlers ran around aimlessly, brandishing the sticky, chipped toys they'd gathered from the chaotic play corner.

'Toni.' Mum's face lit up when she spotted me. 'You came.'

'What are you talking about?' I looked at her pale face. 'Of course I came.'

'I just thought . . .' Mum lowered her eyes. 'You know, we'd fallen out and—'

'Don't be silly.' I shook my head. 'I'm always here for you, Mum, you know that.'

Her eyes glistened and she reached for my hand. I felt her fingers quivering slightly in mine. 'It really shook me up, love, I just don't know how I could've been so stupid.'

'What happened?'

'I slipped, on the stairs,' she said, shaking her head as if she still couldn't quite believe it. 'And you know how strict I am about keeping the stairs clear.'

I nodded. The memories were still fresh in my mind of coming in from school. Within seconds, Mum would demand I take my shoes, coat and bag up to my bedroom. She'd always had this obsessive thing about clutter being dangerous if it was left around the bottom of the stairs.

'I tripped over my shoes, coming down. I couldn't see a thing because I've somehow mislaid my glasses. I still haven't found them.'

I looked at her. 'You left your *shoes* on the stairs?'

In particular, footwear left on the stairs was a lifelong pet hate of Mum's.

'That's just it. I *didn't* leave them there. Of course I didn't,' she said vehemently. She looked down at her hands and her voice grew quieter. 'There were two pairs of shoes there, Toni. On different steps.'

'What?'

'I can't remember even wearing them, never mind putting them there.' She shook her head at the troubling thoughts obviously swirling inside. 'If I actually did that, I'm scared. I mean, you read about dementia and all that stuff, don't you? And I am getting on a bit, now.'

I raised my elbows briefly to ease the clammy feeling under my arms.

I couldn't think what to say, but I also couldn't stop staring at her. For a few seconds, it seemed as if only a diluted version of

Mum remained, compared to the woman who had so recently stormed out of my house in a self-righteous strop.

I looked at her wide, cloudy blue eyes, her pale, soft skin, the way she kept biting the inside of her lip to keep the tears at bay. Mum was only in her late sixties, but this had unnerved me.

'You probably just forgot to move them,' I mumbled, trying to mask my concern. 'We've both had a lot on our minds with Evie being unhappy at school and everything.'

'It's all swollen.' Mum looked down at her roughly bandaged lower leg. 'I'm waiting to see someone else now, who's going to do a more thorough job.'

'I can sit with you for an hour and then I'll go and pick up Evie,' I said, patting Mum's hand. 'Don't worry, we'll both stay over at yours tonight.' We sat mainly in silence. I tried to make bits of inane conversation but, understandably, Mum wasn't in the mood.

I glanced at my watch; it was three forty-five.

Mum's pale, clammy face looked waxen and her eyes were half closed. I could see she was in a lot of pain, despite the tablets they'd given her to take the edge off while she waited for her treatment.

I sighed and stood up. Mum had been waiting for over two hours now; it was time to ask some questions of the staff. At that moment, a male nurse appeared and called her name. We helped her into a wheelchair, which I pushed after the nurse, narrowly missing a scarpering toddler's foot and earning myself a torrent of brusque-sounding words from a large Italian woman.

I smiled graciously and pointed to a sign which informed parents they must supervise their children appropriately.

'Let's get her in here,' the nurse said, indicating a large side room off the main space. He closed the door behind us and a quiet calm instantly settled the charged air. I let out a long breath.

'I know, crazy out there, isn't it?' He grinned. 'Believe it or not, this isn't busy. Compared to last week, anyway.'

He sat in front of a computer and tapped at the keyboard. After a couple of seconds, he swivelled round in his chair to face Mum.

'OK. Anita, isn't it? I'm Tom. Don't worry, we're going to get you sorted out, love.'

Mum looked up forlornly and nodded. I felt a rush of emotion; I wanted to cuddle her close, like I'd do with Evie. 'Can you tell me what happened to your leg?'

Mum was weary but I let her tell Tom in her own words. She didn't mention her memory concerns.

Tom began to open various pieces of sterilised equipment. I glanced at the clock on the wall and saw it was a couple of minutes before four o'clock. I had to say something.

'I'm so sorry,' I said to Tom. 'I have to go and pick my daughter up from school.'

'I see.' He looked at Mum and I followed his stare. She looked as if she was about to burst into tears.

'That's OK, isn't it, Mum?' I said, alarmed. 'I've got to pick up Evie, remember?'

Mum nodded but didn't reply. She seemed totally out of it.

'Is there no way you can stay with your mum?' Tom pulled a wad of cotton wool out from a packet. 'I think she really needs you to be here for her.'

I swallowed down a lump in my throat and tugged at the top buttons of my work blouse to let some air in. For a second I felt like bursting into tears myself. I hadn't got anyone I could call on to help me with Evie, yet I really wanted to be there for Mum. But Evie's safety was paramount.

And then I remembered.

'Give me a sec,' I said, pulling out my phone. 'I might be able to sort something out.'

CHAPTER 52

Three Years Earlier

Toni

I walked outside and called Bryony's number. Her phone rang but went to voicemail. I tried again and left a message.

'Hi, Bryony, it's Toni here. I know it's ridiculously short notice, but I was calling to see if you could pick Evie up at four thirty? I'm still at A&E with Mum. She's a bit shaky and I'd rather not leave her unless I have to.' I glanced at my watch. 'If you can let me know in the next five minutes, that would be great, otherwise I'll go and get her, no problem.'

I ended the call and rang the school office at St Saviour's Primary.

The answerphone picked up right away. 'The office is now closed . . .'

I thought about leaving a message but decided to end the call. My mind felt fuzzy, clouded by worry about Mum and concern over Evie. It wouldn't hurt to wait for a few minutes outside, get a few breaths of fresh air and see if Bryony rang back.

The air was fresh and still damp from a recent shower. I looked down at the ill-maintained layer of concrete outside reception that was long overdue for replacement. A cooling breeze fanned my hot face and neck and for a moment I felt like sitting down there and then to gather my thoughts.

I imagined Bryony picking up my phone message and rushing out to her car. I'd been astounded this afternoon that she'd seemed so understanding and, more than that, genuinely helpful. Maybe she was beginning to thaw at long last. Daft as it sounded, sometimes it took a crisis to give people the impetus to get along.

I waited a minute longer and then went back inside. I tapped on the door of the treatment room and walked in.

Tom was talking to Mum in reassuring tones.

'There you are. Your mum's been telling me she's worried about her memory.' He looked up at me. 'She's been forgetting she's done things and mislaying things.'

'She hasn't.' I shook my head. 'Only today. She didn't remember putting her shoes on the stairs, the ones she tripped over. That's right, isn't it, Mum?'

'There are other things,' Mum said, twisting her fingers around each other. 'Things that I've forgotten but I didn't want to worry you about.'

'Like what?' I glanced at the clock. Five minutes past four and Bryony hadn't returned my call. I was going to have to leave. 'Look, I've got to go and pick up Evie now. Let's talk when I come back.'

My breathing had become rapid and shallow.

Tom frowned. I wished Mum hadn't said anything about her concerns in front of him; he'd only worry her further if he delved into things.

'I thought I could get someone to pick my daughter up,' I explained to him. 'But I can't get hold of her so I've no choice but to go.'

'I'll be fine,' Mum said, but her voice shook and she bit down on her lip.

'Oh, Mum.' I knelt at her side and took her hand. 'I'm sorry I've got to go. I'll bring Evie back here and then we can all go home and spend the evening together. OK?'

Mum nodded, her eyes shining.

'I'm sorry,' I said to Tom. 'I'll be back as soon as I can.'

I walked for what seemed like miles, cursing Mum's court shoes, which cramped and pinched at my feet. When I'd paid the parking and got through the barrier, I queued at the exit of the hospital campus behind a long line of other vehicles that were waiting to leave.

It was twelve minutes past four by the time I hit the main road.

It was going to be tight to get there for four thirty, but I'd left a message on the school answerphone so they knew I'd be coming.

I felt a little dazed – but pleasantly so, as if the sharp gnaw of anxiety had been curbed. I concentrated extra hard on my driving. I knew that technically I shouldn't be on the road but I felt fine and it was a while since I'd taken a pill. I felt sure it would be virtually out of my system by now.

Both Mum and Evie needed me and I wouldn't let them down.

I took a shortcut through the back streets to avoid the busiest parts of town, passing a newsagent where older boys gathered on bikes, eating sweets and shouting to other kids across the road. A group of workmen lingered further along, resplendent in high-vis jackets and hard hats, leaning on their red and white barriers, displaying their paunches to any pedestrian or driver that cared to look.

The tablet I'd taken earlier had afforded me a little welcome separation from reality and I felt I could focus better, instead of being distracted by the million-and-one worries swirling around in my head.

I listened to Smooth Radio, sang along to some old songs that weren't cool anymore but lifted my spirits. For ten minutes

I didn't have a problem. I drove without hindrance, the traffic moving along slowly but making progress. And then, as I approached Moor Bridge, it ground to a halt.

Two lanes of traffic, trailing all the way back to the bypass.

'Shit.' I had eight minutes to get to Evie's school.

Heart hammering, I pressed my phone screen until I reached the BBC's traffic updates. There had been an accident near the City hospital, so I had no choice but to sit in the glut of vehicles until I could get to the roundabout and head for Bulwell.

I swung the car into the outside lane to try and get ahead, but soon realised everyone else had had the same idea. This was my only chance of getting to school on time.

It was twenty-five minutes past four and here I was, stuck in gridlocked traffic that showed no sign of moving.

CHAPTER 53

Three Years Earlier

DIARY ENTRY

9th September

TIMELINE
Arrival at watch point: 11.00 a.m.

11.05 a.m.	Toni Cotter's mother leaves for regular shopping trip to Sainsbury's.
11.10 a.m.	Enter house through unlocked bathroom window.
11.20 a.m.	Complete planned obstacles to facilitate accidental injury.
11.25 a.m.	Leave property.

Departure from watch point: 11.30 a.m.

GENERAL OBSERVATIONS
- House is tidy and in good order.
- Bonus – old woman had left behind her spectacles. These were taken and should assist with objective of causing accidental injury.
- Awaiting further instruction.

CHAPTER 54

Three Years Earlier

The Teacher

'Come away from the window please, Evie,' Harriet Watson said. 'I told you, it isn't time to go yet.'

'The big hand is pointing down to the number six and you said that's the time I can go home,' Evie replied.

'Well, as you can see, it's not quite there yet,' Harriet said, sharply. 'There are at least two more minutes to go.'

There was no doubt about it, this one was a smart little cookie. In Harriet's opinion, she was far too smart for her own good.

Evie's face darkened. 'Where's Miss Akhtar? She's my proper teacher.'

Harriet took a step towards her and the child sat down, shrinking back into her chair. '*I* am in charge of these after-school sessions.' Harriet spoke slowly and precisely. 'They have nothing at all to do with Miss Akhtar.'

Evie folded her arms and looked away. Harriet moved in front of her and perched on the edge of the desk. 'You know your mummy's worried about you, don't you?'

The child looked up at her and frowned. 'No,' she said.

'No, *Miss Watson*,' Harriet corrected her. 'Your mummy told me she's very worried about you and so is your nanny. They're both concerned that you're being a naughty girl at St Saviour's.'

'I'm not!' Evie's eyes grew wide and her bottom lip wobbled. 'I'm not being a naughty girl.'

'You know that and I know that, too, Evie,' Harriet said smoothly. 'But others do not. I want to tell your mummy you're being a good girl, I really do. But . . .'

The child looked at her with shining eyes.

'Between you and me, it's Miss Akhtar who thinks you're a bad girl.'

'I'm not.' A tear rolled down Evie's ruddy cheek. 'I'm not bad.'

'I know that, Evie,' Harriet said, appropriating a kind tone. 'And I've told her that when you're with me, you're very well behaved. Which you are, aren't you?'

Evie gave a faint nod but didn't seem entirely convinced of it herself. The child wiped away the tears defiantly with the cuff of her school sweatshirt.

Evie had complained, this session, about every single thing she'd been asked to do. She'd refused to draw and had snapped two wax crayons on purpose. She had constantly yawned and counted her fingers while Harriet tried to read with her. And for the last ten minutes she'd barely interacted at all. Her eyes had been glued to the clock.

'You see, if Miss Akhtar reports you to the head teacher, you won't be able to come here anymore, Evie. They'll send you to the place for naughty children.'

Evie's eyes grew wide and fearful. 'Where is it, the naughty place?'

'It's miles away,' Harriet told her. 'You might even have to live there, away from your mummy and nanny, away from me.'

The child burst into tears.

'Come on now, wipe your eyes.' Harriet handed her a tissue, looking with distaste at the child's tear-streaked cheeks and snotty nose. 'I'll tell them you're not to be sent to the naughty school. If you want me to, that is? If you would rather stay here with me?'

Evie sniffed, wiped her nose and nodded, never taking her eyes from Harriet's.

'At least, that's what I want to tell them. But first, you have to make me a promise that you mustn't tell Mummy or Nanny about our little chat. Can you do that?'

Evie nodded.

'You mustn't tell them anything about the school for naughty children. Do you promise me?'

'Yes,' the child said in a silly, mardy voice. 'Is it like the one Matilda went to, with Miss Trunchbull?'

Harriet sighed. This was the trouble with children today. Too much television and cinema nonsense, instead of useful lessons that would prepare them for the harsh realities of the outside world.

'Matilda is just a silly story, it isn't real.' Harriet gingerly nipped the corner of Evie's tissue with her fingertips and threw it into the bin. 'I expect your mummy gets rather annoyed with you sometimes, doesn't she?'

Evie nodded and her eyes glittered.

'You mustn't cry again, is that clear?'

Evie nodded. 'Yes.'

'What does Mummy say to you, when she's angry?'

Evie thought for a moment. 'She says I have to come to school.'

Harriet nodded. 'And she's right. It's the law that you have to come to school. If you don't, a policeman might visit the house.'

Evie's chin wrinkled as she chewed on her bottom lip. She knew this was true because her mummy had said as much.

'And tell me, when Mummy gets angry, does she take her tablets?'

Evie frowned and shook her head.

'I mean the tablets that make her go to sleep.'

'Oh, yes,' Evie said brightly, understanding. 'They're in the bathroom cabinet, up where I can't reach without a chair. She goes to sleep for *ages*. Sometimes I get hungry and bored.'

'I expect you do.' Harriet smiled. 'And it's hard to wake Mummy, isn't it, when she falls fast asleep in the daytime?'

Evie nodded. 'I have to do this.' The child mimed shaking something aggressively. 'And I have to shout "MUMMMMYYY".'

Her yell ricocheted around the empty library space.

'Hush,' Harriet hissed, glancing around her. The last thing she wanted was to attract the attention of Mr Bryce, the bumbling, interfering old caretaker who refused to retire. 'There's no need for that racket.'

Evie looked at the floor.

'As I was saying, the only other school around here is the place the bad children go. There are big boys there who will kick your shins in class,' Harriet said. 'So you must stop saying you don't want to come to St Saviour's. Do you understand, Evie?'

'Yes,' Evie said meekly. 'I won't say it anymore.'

'That's good. And you mustn't tell anyone what we've talked about. You won't have to go there, if you do what I say. Am I making myself clear?'

'Yes.'

'Yes, *Miss Watson*,' Harriet directed her.

'Yes, Miss Watson.'

'Very well.' Harriet smiled. 'So, I want you to tell Mummy you've had a good day at school and that Miss Watson is very pleased with you. Which I am.'

Evie nodded and the ghost of a smile skittered across her lips.

'Heavens!' Harriet glanced at the clock. It was a full ten minutes after finishing time. 'Your mummy is rather late. Stay here while I go and check to see if she's waiting out in reception.'

CHAPTER 55

Three Years Earlier

Toni

I called the school at least six times, hoping that someone would be passing the office and might pick up, but each time it went straight to the answerphone.

I'd left one message earlier, saying I might be a little late . . . At least, I thought I had, but now I wasn't entirely sure.

Scenes slid through my mind like a super-fast slideshow: Mum sitting alone in the waiting room; Nurse Tom's disapproving face; Mum falling down the stairs; me calling the school and leaving a message.

Some bits of it didn't feel right, all mixed up and in the wrong order.

I squeezed my eyes shut against the line of stationary traffic in front of me and tried to think. I'd called Bryony's mobile a couple more times but now it just went straight to answerphone. I didn't have Dale's mobile number in my phone contacts. I'd called the shop but nobody had picked up, which meant Jo was probably busy with customers.

Then I remembered Jo had sent me a text last week. She'd asked me for my number so she could share a silly joke that was currently doing the rounds. I found the text and called her. It rang but went to voicemail. I fired off a text and swallowed down the cloying lump in my throat.

> *Jo, it's Toni. Got an emergency. Stuck in traffic can't get to Evie. Could you pick her up ASAP? St Saviour's Primary. Sorry to ask x*

I couldn't work out why Harriet Watson hadn't called me; I was now nearly twenty minutes late. Then I realised, with a sinking feeling, that I hadn't yet completed the parental contact details form that had been in Evie's admission pack.

She had brought home a second one too; I'd found it tucked inside her book bag on her first day at school with a note from the administrator asking me to fill it in as soon as I could. The school didn't have my mobile telephone number.

I opened the window a little but the breeze was choked with exhaust fumes. The car had inched forward maybe five metres in the last five minutes. Five minutes seems an inordinately long amount of time when your daughter has nobody to pick her up and your mother is more vulnerable than you've ever seen her in your life.

I swallowed hard to try to relieve the dryness in my throat, cursing that I'd left my bottle of water at work.

A ball of heat uncurled itself in the pit of my stomach and began to work its way up to my head, where I knew from experience it would explode and give me a beetroot face and add fuel to my already raging headache.

I picked my phone up and stared at the blank screen, devoid of texts or missed calls.

Tapping my fingernails on the steering wheel, I willed the traffic in front of me to move.

I got to school at ten past five. Forty minutes late.

I parked up on double yellow lines directly outside the entrance to the school office, ripping off my seatbelt and jumping out of the car, running full pelt through the main gates. It was like a ghost town without the throng of children and parents to battle through.

The doors were locked and the blinds pulled down. The back of my neck prickled, my throat suddenly parched.

I hammered on the doors and all the windows. I ran around the whole building, banging and yelling. When I got to Evie's classroom window, a man in his early sixties, wearing navy dungarees, appeared from around the corner.

'My daughter,' I gasped, rushing up to him. 'I'm late picking her up.'

'There's nobody here, love,' he answered. 'They've all gone home.'

'No, you don't under—' I swallowed down the taste of vomit, squeezing my eyes shut to try to ward off the feeling of nausea. When I opened them, he was watching me curiously. 'You don't understand. My daughter, Evie, she was here with Miss Watson for an after-school session.'

'But everybody's gone now,' he repeated, shuffling back a few steps. 'I'm the caretaker and I've done a sweep of all the classrooms. There's nobody here. Nobody at all.'

CHAPTER 56

Three Years Earlier

Toni

I ran past the caretaker and back out to the car.

The school building, the road, the passing traffic – everything blurred into one big, messy swirl, spinning around in front of my eyes slowly and then faster, faster.

I stumbled and fell against the school gate, the iron railings cool and unforgiving against my skin.

'Whoa, hold up, miss.' The caretaker appeared at my side. 'You're going to hurt yourself if you carry on like that. Why don't you come inside and sit down for a minute or two?'

'No.' I shook my head, feeling even dizzier. 'I have – I have to find her. My daughter.'

I stood up straight and took a deep breath. He stepped towards me and held out his arms as if I might topple over any second.

'I'm fine, thanks,' I said, wishing he'd just go away. And then I had a thought. 'Have you got Harriet Watson's phone number?'

'Sorry, love.' He shrugged. 'I don't have access to information like that. It's all on a computer in the office, you see. You still look a bit unsteady on your feet.'

'I have to go,' I muttered, stepping out onto the pavement. 'I have to find Evie.'

The caretaker watched me as I walked unsteadily to the car.

'I don't think you should be driving,' he called, but I ignored him and climbed awkwardly into the driver's seat.

I pulled the door to, leaned back against the headrest and closed my eyes. My thoughts were bouncing around like manic ping-pong balls. I couldn't seem to catch them and put them in any semblance of order.

My phone started ringing and my heart leapt. I grabbed my handbag and rooted around in it, pulling out my phone. A mobile number flashed up but no name. I answered it, a sickly dread clogging my throat.

'Hello?' I croaked.

'Toni? It's Jo, I just got your text. Is everything OK?'

'It's Evie.' My voice broke into a sob. 'She's gone.'

I sat and waited like Jo told me to until she arrived. It nearly killed me, doing nothing, but Jo was insistent. I opened the window in an effort to try to clear my head, help me think straight.

'Are you going to be alright, love?'

I jumped, my eyes springing open, to find the caretaker leaning close to the glass.

'Yes, I'm fine, my friend is on her way over,' I said. 'Thanks, but there's nothing more you can do now.'

'I'll go and check the classrooms again,' he said. 'Just in case. You know what little girls can be like.'

I looked at his wrinkled face and thin lips and shuddered. I didn't want to think about him and Evie alone in the building together.

'Thanks,' I mumbled, and closed the window.

Ten minutes later, a small white Fiat pulled up in front of me and Jo jumped out. She ran towards my car, but before she reached me, the caretaker intercepted her, holding up his hand.

The caretaker had his back to me but I could see him shaking his head and speaking. Jo listened and then turned her head slightly so I couldn't see her mouth. She said a few words to him and they both turned and looked at me.

'What?' I shouted from inside the car. Evie was missing and those two were chatting like we had all the time in the world.

Jo rushed over to the car and slid into the passenger seat. 'Oh my God, Toni, you look terrible.' She grasped my hand and her fingers felt cool and damp. 'What's happened?'

'What did he say?' I snapped.' What were you talking about?'

'Mr Bryce is just concerned about you,' she said evenly. 'He said everyone has gone home. You poor thing, you must be out of your mind.'

Dissolving into tears at her concern, I just about managed to tell her the gist of what had happened.

'I don't know who to contact, what to do,' I sobbed, and then a moment of clarity broke through the fog. 'I think I should call the police.'

Jo stared at me for a second and then shook her head. 'There are things to check first. The police will ask what you've done to find her,' she reasoned.

'Like what?' I sniffed. 'There's nobody around to ask and I haven't got Harriet Watson's number.'

'Well, Evie obviously isn't here at school, but you were late, right?' I nodded.

'So maybe Harriet took her home. Have you been back to your house?'

My eyes widened. How could I have been so stupid?

'She might be waiting for me at home,' I whispered.

I reached towards the keys in the ignition.

'No, we'll go in my car,' Jo said, narrowing her eyes. 'You seem so upset and unfocused. Mr Bryce thinks you shouldn't be driving.'

* * *

As we turned into Muriel Crescent, I undid my seatbelt and reached for the door handle.

'Don't open the car door yet,' Jo said quickly.

My whole body shook as my eyes searched out our house at the end of the row of mews-style new properties.

'She's not there,' I cried. And then, louder, 'I can see she's not there.'

I pulled on the handle and the door swung open, narrowly missing a parked car as we moved by it.

'Toni, for fuck's sake!' Jo screamed, slamming on the brakes. 'Close the fucking door!'

I stared at her, mouth open wide. It was like someone had just flicked a switch inside her. I'd never heard her so much as swear in the office, never mind lose her temper. I jumped out of the car and started to run towards the house, the strains of Jo shouting my name growing fainter as I went.

It was clear there was nobody standing outside the house. No Harriet and no Evie. I reached the front door, panting and gulping in air. I dashed down the side of the house into the back yard.

'Evie,' I called frantically. 'Evie!'

A head appeared over the hedge.

'Lost your daughter again, have you?' Colin smirked.

'Fuck off,' I snarled, and ran back to the front of the house. Jo had parked up and was walking towards me.

'Toni, for God's sake, you have to calm down.' She grabbed my arm. 'You have to think logically. Let's go inside.'

CHAPTER 57

Three Years Earlier

Toni

'Is there anywhere Evie liked to go? A local park, perhaps?'

The detective and a police officer, DI Manvers and PC Holt, stood opposite me as I sat on the sofa, next to Jo.

'She doesn't know the area,' I blurted out tearfully. 'We only just moved here. Surely there are other things we can be doing apart from just sitting here?'

'I can assure you there's plenty happening behind the scenes, Mrs Cotter,' DI Manvers replied. 'Our team is currently in the process of contacting the head teacher and the chair of governors. We'll be hearing back from them very soon.'

'Could a neighbour have taken her in?' PC Holt suggested.

Colin. I jumped up.

'Sal's son, next door. He's been in prison.' I moved towards the kitchen. 'He's in the garden now, he's taken Evie before.'

DI Manvers stepped forward with a sense of urgency. 'He's taken her before?'

'He said she could feed the puppy,' I said, faintly aware my words were taut and high-pitched. I couldn't stop shivering.

DI Manvers muttered something to his colleague and walked to the front door, reaching down to his radio. PC Holt put her arm around my shoulders and pressed me back down into my seat.

'I don't want to sit down,' I snapped, standing up again. 'You should be out there, looking for her. Colin could have her next door, he could've snatched her—'

'Toni.' The officer's voice was firm but kind. 'It's important we remain calm. More than likely there's simply been a misunderstanding. Perhaps a friend's mum has taken Evie home.'

'I keep trying to tell you' – I pressed my face into my hands, distorting the words – 'we don't know anyone, we just moved to the area. I can't just sit here, we need to do something.'

'OK. There are things being done, Toni. We're getting school staff, and DI Manvers is next door now, speaking to your neighbour.'

Colin's smirking face flashed into my mind.

'If he's touched her, I'll kill him, I'll—'

'Toni, have you been drinking?' PC Holt stared at me and I turned my face away. 'You seem a little vague.'

'I'm just tired,' I said quickly, the words feeling awkward on my tongue. 'It's been a terrible day.' And then I remembered and I felt colder still. 'Oh my God, I forgot about my mum. She's stuck in A&E.'

'Leave your mum to me,' Jo said, standing up. I gave her the details and she left the house.

The doorbell rang and PC Holt went to the door. I heard voices and then Harriet Watson walked into the room.

'Where is she?' I shouted, dashing towards her. 'Where's Evie?'

PC Holt caught my arm before I could reach Harriet.

'I thought you'd collected her, Toni,' she said quietly. 'I went to check where you were, and when I came back, Evie had gone. I thought you'd taken her without telling me.'

'What? How could you do that? That's negligence.' I looked wildly at the police officers. Everyone looked back at me steadily.

Harriet coughed. 'You've been late so often collecting Evie and you've taken her before without telling anyone, I just thought—'

'I've never taken her before, you're lying!' My eyes darted around the room, trying to remember if I had been late or taken Evie out of school. 'I left a message on the school answerphone. I said I was on my way.'

'I checked the answerphone.' Harriet shook her head. 'There were no messages and no contact sheet in Evie's file, so I couldn't even call you.'

I thought about the incomplete pupil contact form on the kitchen worktop, perched on top of a stack of unpaid bills.

'I left a message, I'm sure I did,' I said faintly, but I couldn't quite recall if I had, or what I might have said.

'Mrs Cotter,' said DI Manvers, who had just re-entered the room. 'Your memory seems a little patchy, have you—'

'No, I haven't been drinking,' I snarled. 'She's already asked me that.' I narrowed my eyes at PC Holt. 'It's the shock, I feel all panicky inside.'

The officers glanced at each other.

'You've been late for Evie before,' PC Holt stated, looking at her notebook.

'I haven't, not that I know of. Anyway, that's not a crime, is it? The traffic can be really bad sometimes.'

'Of course,' she agreed. 'But Miss Watson has also said you've been a little mixed up about which days Evie has her after-school sessions, too.'

I glared at Harriet and she looked away.

'She had a session today, I know that. And she' – I pointed a shaking finger at Harriet – 'she let someone take Evie.'

'I thought *you* had taken her,' Harriet said. 'You were forty minutes late. I asked Evie to stay in the classroom and I went to reception to see if you were there. We couldn't just sit there all night, waiting for you, when everyone else had gone home.'

'We've got officers out looking for your daughter now,' DI Manvers said. 'She may well have wondered off, looking for you, when Miss Watson went to the office.'

'My mum had a fall, she was at the hospital,' I said softly. 'And then I got snarled up in traffic from an accident. There was nothing I could do.' I looked at DI Manvers. 'Did you go next door?'

'Yes, I spoke to your neighbour and his mother. He's been at home all day with her. They were very helpful actually.'

I bet they were. I pushed thoughts of Colin being upstairs in my bedroom swiftly away.

Harriet Watson took a breath, her eyes owl-like behind her glasses. 'If only we'd had a contact number for you, we would have known what was happening.'

Four pairs of eyes turned to me then and I saw a conclusion had been reached; it was plainly etched on their faces.

They had made their minds up. This was all my fault.

CHAPTER 58

Present Day

Queen's Medical Centre

The nice nurse comes into the room and closes the door behind her. I can smell her subtle perfume and listen as she mutters to herself under her breath as she verbally ticks off her jobs.

'So, how are we today?' she asks me as always. 'Did you miss me? I had a couple of days off.'

I did. I did miss you.

'My son, he lives down in Devon with his wife and my grandson, Riley. They came up to see me and we had the loveliest time. Have you got children or grandchildren?' She comes close to the bed. A big smudge of white and blue, right at the corner of my eye. 'Sorry, I should talk to you here, so you can see me.'

Her face appears above me. She has dark hair and blue eyes. She smiles and I see that her front teeth are very slightly crossed. Her eyebrows need waxing and her temples are flecked with grey. Her breath smells faintly of coffee and maybe smoke.

She looks slightly familiar, but this is the first time I've seen her properly. Usually she says hello and her face pops fleetingly in front of me, barely looking at me before she's gone again, busying around the equipment, taking her readings and making her evaluations.

'I'm Nancy. They've put me on this ward permanently now, so you'll be seeing quite a bit of me. Hope that's OK.'

I try to widen my eyes, to make her see I am there, behind them.

She frowns down at me. 'They tell me your sister visited just the once. The names and details she left for herself and for you don't match up with anything. It's like the two of you don't exist.'

I stare back at her. She's looking intently at me, as if she's really puzzling over something.

'Let's see now.' She moves away. I hear her shuffling around in the cabinet next to me, where they put my handbag. 'What have we got here? Maybe something that can show us who you are? Has anyone gone through your things with you?'

No. Most of them have written me off.

She rattles some keys and I hear paper crinkling. I love this woman for trying, for even considering I might be present. I feel the tiniest burst of hope inside.

'A photograph,' she murmurs, and a second later her face is in front of me again. 'So, who's this?'

She holds the small portrait directly in front of my eyes.

It's the photograph of Evie that *she* had taunted me with. She must have dropped it when Dr Chance came into the room unexpectedly. Someone, probably the cleaner, has put it in my handbag, thinking it belongs to me.

Evie had obviously refused to smile for the camera, but that doesn't matter. Her hair is a beautiful chestnut-brown colour and she's wearing a dress I've never seen before, a fancy affair that looks as if it cost a fortune. A soft cream fabric, patterned with red swirls and dots, like winter berries on snow.

I wait for the adrenaline rush to my head, that electrical charge that powered me to blink before. But it doesn't come. As the nurse stares down at me, I am completely and utterly unresponsive.

Something inside me shrivels and it feels like I have just stepped a little closer to letting go of the thread that tethers me to the real world. The world I no longer exist in but haven't fully left.

Soon, it will be time for me to let go, to fade away. If only I can do this one last thing for Evie first, to put right all my terrible mistakes. Then my job will be done.

Yet despite everything, my heartbeat remains steady, pumping life around what used to be my body but is now a strange land filled only with loss and regret. I am bursting with pure disdain for myself, and especially for *her*, my recent visitor.

'Is this your daughter?' The nurse's voice sounds strange and her forehead wrinkles above me. 'She's beautiful and she – she reminds me of someone.' She twists the photograph this way and that, studying it. I watch as her brow furrows, her jaw sets. I am willing her to join up the dots.

'Oh my God,' she whispers, her features contorting. Her eyes slide to my face again and narrow slightly, as if she is trying to focus, to understand the impossible. 'Oh my God.'

She grips the photograph tightly and runs from the room. Relief washes through me like a cleansing balm.

At last, someone has realised the truth.

Someone knows who I am.

CHAPTER 59

Present Day

The Nurse

Nancy sits in the back of the police car and watches as the familiar houses and shops whizz by in a washed-out blur. She sees them every day, but this afternoon they look strange to her. She registers the shapes and colours through the myriad raindrops that stream relentlessly onto the window and it feels like she has never seen them before.

This is the day that the world has turned upside down and inside out.

As soon as Nancy had alerted the powers that be, the hospital management contacted the police, and they had asked her to accompany them. All in the space of a couple of hours. It was an unusual step for them to take, DI Manvers had explained, but this was an extraordinary situation and it would help, they felt, Nancy being there.

The car slows to turn the corner and the memories rush back into Nancy's mind. She squeezes her eyes closed against them, for all the good it does.

'You OK, love?' DI Manvers glances at the uniformed officer driving the car and turns in his seat to look at her. 'We're almost there. We can pull over if you want to take a minute?'

'No,' she whispers, her voice catching in her throat. 'This is not about me.'

But even as she utters the words, Nancy knows it is very much about her. What she knows is about to make someone's agony even more unbearable.

If that were even possible.

The police car travels over the big roundabout, swinging onto Cinderhill Road and finally turning into Muriel Crescent. A delivery man hesitates in getting back into his van, watching the police vehicle approach.

Nancy closes her eyes and feels the car slow to a stop. DI Manvers opens the door and she opens her eyes and climbs out of the car. The air outside is damp and hangs heavy, almost sticky, around her face. She feels a sudden rush of nausea and steadies herself by holding on to the car door.

'Nancy, are you OK?' DI Manvers asks again.

She nods.

But she is not OK, not really.

Nancy bends forward, trying to catch her breath. She sees the cracked, damp pavement and suddenly she is back there, back to that awful day when Evie stood sobbing in the street, covered in wasp stings.

Nancy had given just a few minutes of advice that day. After that, she'd seen the Cotters on the odd occasion when she'd either been on her way out or coming back home from work. It had only happened now and again. She'd wave hello and they'd wave back. It had never been anything more than that.

Six months after the wasp sting day, Nancy had started her new job at the QMC, and moved from Muriel Crescent to take a rented apartment on the outskirts of the city. She hadn't known the Cotters well enough to say goodbye and, she readily admitted, she had never given them another thought.

Until she'd seen those horrific newspaper headlines.

Police appeal for help to find missing five-year-old girl
Girl vanishes from classroom after mother is late to collect her

That had made her sit up and take notice alright. Nancy had thought, at the time, how eager the press had been to criticise Mrs Cotter right from the off.

Now nobody knows if Evie is even alive anymore.

Nancy takes a few more breaths in, the cold air sticking to her nostrils. She is painfully aware they are watching her. Waiting for her.

Of course, Nancy had sent a card at the time and followed it up with a couple of short letters to Toni Cotter, saying she was a good listener and if there was anything she could do and so on . . .

She'd heard nothing back, hadn't really expected to.

DI Manvers waits until Nancy stands up straighter and gets her bearings again. 'Sure you're OK with doing this?'

She nods and he turns, walking towards the house. Nancy follows, strands of pure dread writhing in her stomach like a nest of vipers.

The door is the only one on the street that has been obviously repainted; cheap white gloss on top of the original pale blue PVC. The faint shadow of spray-painted words are still evident; daubed accusations that have not been thoroughly masked by the repaint.

DI Manvers raps on the door and they wait for what seems to Nancy like forever.

The sound of someone unlocking the door on the other side forces Nancy's fingernails into the soft flesh of her palms. Her breathing grows even more erratic and her heartbeat thunders against her breastbone.

The door opens and, with the help of a stick, an old lady stands there. Nancy doesn't recall her face but she thinks it may well be Evie's grandma. If she remembers correctly, she had been there, a far sprightlier woman then, on the day of the stinging incident.

'Oh!' The lady's hand flies to her throat when she takes in the uniformed officer and DI Manver's ID. She staggers and leans awkwardly against the doorframe.

'Come on, PC Holt,' the DI hisses at the younger officer. 'Quicker on your feet now.'

PC Holt coughs and steps quickly inside, allowing the old lady to lean heavily on her and move back a step.

Nancy remains standing outside the front door. DI Manvers is speaking to the elderly lady in low tones, but she cannot decipher anything that is being said because her head is full of white noise.

After a few moments, the group at the door begin to move inside the house. PC Holt helps the old lady through and DI Manvers silently beckons Nancy inside, closing the door quietly behind her.

The group shuffles into the sitting room, where the husk of another woman sits, slumped in the corner of the couch.

Her brown hair is shot through with grey and her lips and skin look parched, as if something has sucked the very lifeblood out of her. For a moment, Nancy doubts she has ever seen her before and then she sees a glimmer of who this person used to be when hope stirs in her face at the sight of DI Manvers.

The small room is gloomy, the blinds pulled low and curtains pulled to, shutting out as much natural light as possible without plunging the room into full darkness. Piles of neatly folded newspapers line the floor against two of the free walls and Nancy catches sight of Evie's photograph and dramatic headlines on numerous editions.

DI Manvers introduces everyone.

'I'm Anita,' the old lady murmurs. 'And you know my daughter, of course.'

'We're here because we think we have some news, Mrs Cotter,' he says softly. 'About Evie.'

'Have you found her?' the woman croaks, sitting up with difficulty. A luminous quality temporarily lights up the dullness of her eyes and she fixes them on Nancy. 'Is Evie coming home?'

'Do you know where she is?' Anita asks. 'Is Evie alive?'

'I'm afraid, as yet, we can't say if that's the case.' DI Manvers looks at his feet.

'Then do you think Evie is . . .'

'At this point, we don't know.'

'Then why are you here?'

'We're unable to verify the facts at the present time for reasons we'll explain later,' DI Manvers continues. 'But it has been brought to our attention that there is a stroke victim, a female patient, in Queen's Medical Centre—'

'What's that got to do with Evie?' the younger woman cries out, jabbing a finger at him. 'Just spit it out. Please.'

'The person I am referring to has in her possession a photograph of Evie with a digital date stamp from after she went missing. In the picture, Evie looks a little older and her hair has been dyed brown,' DI Manvers explains.

'I – I don't understand.'

'Mrs Cotter, we think this woman could be the person who abducted your daughter three years ago.'

CHAPTER 60

Present Day

The Nurse

A strangled gasp escapes from Toni Cotter's mouth. Her hand claws at her throat as if something invisible is squeezing the very life out of her.

Nancy rushes over, sits next to her and gently pulls away her hand. Deep welts rise on Toni's skin, like someone has scribbled all over it with a dark red crayon.

PC Holt stares.

'Can you get Toni a glass of water?' Nancy asks her and she scuttles, almost thankfully, out of the room.

Anita sits down heavily in a chair, staring at the floor.

'Who is this person?' Toni Cotter whispers. 'Has she told you where Evie is?'

Nancy watches as DI Manvers takes a breath, steeling himself to explain the worst. That they know now who took Evie but the woman is as good as dead.

'This woman is paralysed following a stroke,' he says gently. 'She can't speak or move. She is currently on a respirator as she cannot breathe unassisted.'

Both Toni and her mother stare at him. Uncomprehending.

'We don't know if she'll survive.' He glances at Nancy.

'But she has Evie's picture; she must know where she is,' Toni says, her voice raspy. 'I want to see it, I want to see my daughter's face.'

'We have the photograph, Mrs Cotter,' says DI Manvers. 'We also have a photograph of the stroke patient in question. When you feel able, we'd like you to look at both pieces of evidence.'

'I'm ready now.' Toni Cotter sits up straighter, looks at Nancy and nods. 'I'm ready right now.'

PC Holt appears with a glass of water.

'We're ready,' Anita confirms quietly.

'Let's take it nice and slowly,' DI Manvers says, glancing at both women in turn. 'Please, drink your water, Mrs Cotter, we're in no rush. I appreciate this is a very traumatic time for you both.'

'I've lived in hell, 24/7, for the last three years,' Toni says. 'Believe me, I'm more than ready.'

Anita watches her daughter and then turns to DI Manvers. 'We both are.'

'Very well,' he says, looking round the room. 'Would it be possible to let a little more natural light in?'

Toni Cotter shrinks back into her seat, like she's worried she might turn to dust when the curtains are opened.

'It's just that your initial reaction is quite important,' he explains. 'You need to be able to see the photographs as clearly as possible first time.'

'She hasn't been out for months, you see.' With difficulty, Anita gets to her feet. 'We have the curtains shut all the time because she's paranoid someone will see her and it'll all start again.'

'Sorry, all what?' Nancy asks.

'The abuse screamed at her in the street, the broken windows, the filthy messages daubed on the door.'

Nancy glances across at Toni. She seems to have shrunk even smaller, disappearing bit by bit into the corner of the sofa.

'Everybody blamed her, you see.' Anita hobbles across the room on her stick. 'Said she'd neglected Evie, hadn't been there to pick her up. A drug addict, the newspapers said, when the most she'd ever taken was a couple of sedatives to try and cope.'

She stops and regards her daughter, her heavily lined face creasing further with concern. 'My girl was already destroyed, but those bastards, the press, they all but finished the job.'

Anita tugs at the curtains and PC Holt helps her draw the blinds up halfway.

'That's better,' the old woman murmurs, peering through the dusty glass as if she'd forgotten there was a world out there.

DI Manvers moves across the room; Toni pulls herself up a little straighter and shuffles nearer to Nancy. The DI extracts two photographs from his inside jacket pocket and hands Toni the first one.

Nancy sees it is the photograph of Evie she found in the patient's handbag.

'Can you please tell us,' DI Manvers says gently. 'If this is your daughter, Evie?'

Toni stares at it for a few seconds. Everything – her expression, her body, her eyes – seems completely frozen. Everyone in the room holds their breath. A car passes on the road outside; a man walks by chatting animatedly on his phone. The sun ducks behind the clouds and the room darkens slightly.

And then it begins.

Toni's hands begin to shake and a low, primal growl starts from deep inside her, climbing up through her body and exiting her mouth as a tortured howl that makes Nancy want to sob and run from its source.

Instead, she reaches over to Toni to hold her, but the younger woman shrugs her off.

'Where is she?' Toni howls, swaying back and forth in her seat. 'Where is my baby?'

Anita sits on the arm of the sofa, crying and stroking Toni's hair. 'They'll find her, love. Isn't that right, DI Manvers?' She looks up, her eyes filled with mourning, longing for him to say the words. 'Tell us you'll find Evie.'

DI Manvers opens his mouth and then presses his lips together. His face has turned a shade paler. He walks over to Toni and crouches down on his haunches in front of her.

'Toni, can you tell me if this is Evie? Is this your daughter?'

Toni closes her eyes and nods, her whole body rocking in time with her head.

DI Manvers reaches for her hand. 'Toni, I can't, I won't, make any rash promises to you today. But I give you my absolute word that I'll do everything, *everything*, in my power to find Evie. Do you believe that?'

Toni opens her wet, red eyes and stares into his face, leaning slightly forward and squinting, as though she is trying desperately to see the future.

'I believe you,' she whispers. 'I really do.'

He stands up and looks at the remaining photograph in his hand. Nancy sees him take a long breath in, as if he is bracing himself for Toni's reaction.

'And this is a photograph taken of the female patient,' DI Manvers says. 'The doctor removed the respirator for only a few seconds while we took the photograph, so it's a little rushed.'

'Why are you helping her to breathe when she might have abducted Evie?' Anita asks in a cold voice.

'We only *suspect* this at the moment,' DI Manvers says, and turns again to Toni. 'Mrs Cotter, do you recognise this person?'

Toni takes the photograph from him with shaking hands. Her eyes widen as they settle on the face in the picture. Her face instantly drains of colour. She stands up quickly, staring at the door. The photograph flutters to the floor and Toni follows it, her body crumpling like a discarded puppet.

Nancy kneels at her side, gently laying her hand on Toni's cheek. 'She's fainted. She'll come round in a minute.'

Soon, Toni opens her eyes and looks straight at Nancy.

'It was her,' she whispers, spluttering as the cracked and broken words emerge from her dry, parched throat. 'All along, it was *her*. What has she done with my daughter?'

PART II
PRESENT DAY

CHAPTER 61

Present Day

Queen's Medical Centre

I wait and I wait and the clock keeps ticking and I wait and listen and wait . . .

Still, when the door opens it is a surprise.

I hear lots of feet shuffling into the room. I can smell them. Warm, sweaty bodies, desperate minds wanting to know just who I am and why I did what I did.

I hear sniffing and snuffling and a man's voice whispers, makes comforting noises, and two sets of feet shuffle forward, nearer to my bed. And they're whispering to each other – too low for me to hear the words – and then the whispering and shuffling stops and then, all at once, Toni Cotter's face is above mine.

I might not have recognised her, had I not been expecting visitors. But it's her alright. She looks terrible, a shadow of her former self. A ghost.

I did that. I sucked the life right from her, the day I took Evie away.

We stare into each other's eyes. She doesn't know if I can see her or not.

But I know she sees me.

'I trusted you,' she whispers, a tear falling from her eye and splattering on my cheek. Now a man's voice. 'You recognise this person, Mrs Cotter?'

She says nothing for a moment or two, and more tears explode onto my face.

'Her name is Jo Deacon,' Toni whispers. 'I worked with her. I thought she was my friend.'

She squeezes her eyes shut and tears cascade down onto my face – and I blink.

I blink again and then I freeze.

She doesn't see me.

Nobody sees me blink.

CHAPTER 62

Present Day

Toni

The thing about nightmares is this.

While you are asleep, while you can barely function within the terror, there is nothing you can do but ride the awfulness. Once you wake up, the nightmare is still there. But you can begin to fight it. There's the slightest possibility that you can start to do something about it.

Two days ago, I learned about Jo Deacon's involvement in Evie's disappearance, and the existence of a photograph of an older Evie, and I feel as if I have awoken from my nightmare.

I actually feel as if there might still be something I can do.

I decide to start by giving nurse Nancy Johnson a call.

CHAPTER 63

Present Day

The Nurse

'So, what's the story, Joanne Deacon?' Nancy's face looms in close to the patient.

There is no obvious clue whether Jo, as she is apparently known, sees her or not, but Nancy knows that she does. She saw her blink yesterday when everyone crowded into the room. She opened her mouth to tell them, but something stopped her saying anything. What good would it have done? It would have given false hope to Toni Cotter for one thing, a woman who is a mere shadow of her former self and has suffered enough.

And then, last night, Nancy received a call from Toni, begging for her help.

'You have to find a way,' Toni had sobbed. 'Only you can help Evie now.'

Nancy had responded kindly to Toni and asked her to give her a little time to think about the situation, but she had her own ideas of how she might be able to help this broken, desperate woman. These were unconventional ideas – the kind of thing that would certainly be frowned upon by her supervisors. Nancy made her mind up right there and then to keep quiet and try a little experiment with Joanne Deacon.

'I'll pop over and see you in the next couple of days,' Nancy had reassured Toni. 'In the meantime, don't mention anything about this to DI Manvers.' She knew he'd be speaking regularly to the doctors and hospital management team and she didn't want anything slipping out in conversation.

Nancy stares down now at Jo's unresponsive face and imagines that her own blurred features are sharpening in front of the patient's eyes as she begins to come into focus.

Nancy is in uniform, tiny beads of perspiration dotting her top lip. She knows from the bathroom mirror this morning that her mascara is clogged in the corner of her left eye. The concealer under both eyes is badly blended and there's a spot forming on her chin that threatens to be a quite a whopper.

Jo Deacon will see all this in close-up. She will see that Nancy is just an ordinary person. And if she plays the right game, she will start to believe Nancy wants to help her.

'The police are speaking to your mother, your colleagues, Jo,' she says. DI Manvers had told them that Jo Deacon had been living under a new identity for the last six years after serving time for fraud. They'd managed to trace her mother after discovering the truth. 'There's nobody here in the room but you and I.' Nancy stares down at her. 'I don't believe you're an evil person. I'd have *felt* it before now.'

She means it. Nancy has always had the measure of people.

A couple of years ago, a man called Cameron Tandy had been admitted to the ward Nancy worked on. He'd been recovering from a road traffic accident in which both his legs had been badly crushed. He'd told all the nurses he was an eminent barrister, defending the innocent and the good. He was a good-looking chap, with his chiselled jawbone and broad shoulders. The younger nurses swooned and Nancy could understand why.

But she had seen something else. *Felt* it, in fact. A strange sensation, whenever she was physically near Tandy, that literally caused the hairs on the back of her neck to stand up on end.

The next day, two detectives turned up at the hospital unannounced, demanding they be allowed to question him over the disappearance of an eight-year-old boy. Turned out Tandy had been struck off as a barrister four years earlier and now appeared as an entry on the child sex offender register.

Nancy had known Tandy was evil when everyone else had been fooled, just like she now knows that Joanne Deacon is not. Whatever the evidence is pointing to at the moment, Nancy is convinced that there's more to it all.

Three years ago, Nancy tried to help little Evie Cotter when she'd been covered in wasp stings. Now she's going to try and help her again.

Nobody knows if Evie is alive or dead, but Nancy feels strongly that, whichever one it is, the most important thing is to get her back to her mother.

And Joanne Deacon is the key. She is the only key they have.

CHAPTER 64

Present Day

The Teacher

Harriet sits by the window, using her fingertips to lift the net away from the glass, just a touch. She doesn't want anyone to know she's here. Watching. She doesn't want to draw any attention from any of the surrounding properties.

She has good reason.

The street is quiet today, and what a blessing that is. Late last night, Harriet had peered out of the window into the small front garden to find two drunken young men urinating on her hydrangea shrub. Once they'd had a little shake and put themselves away, they staggered off down the street, no doubt heading for one of the overcrowded bedsits at the bottom end.

It's a relief to note there's nothing much to see out there today.

Harriet glances down at her hand and watches as her fingers tremble, the movement transferring itself to the fine net curtain, setting it quivering.

It's definitely getting worse, the shaking. And not only in her hands – sometimes her arms and legs begin to tremor, too. It's most unsettling and can be altogether embarrassing, for example if she's at the supermarket checkout or the post office counter.

She can't bring herself to make an appointment with her GP though. Not with them all knowing what happened.

A figure appears at the gate and Harriet instinctively lets go of the net, allowing it to fall into its loose folds, no longer needing to be razor sharp and perfectly equidistant now that her mother is gone.

Part of her stiffens at the prospect of a visitor, but the other part of her sinks when she sees it is not. She shrinks back behind the curtain, though still upright and flexed in the armchair. A rattle at the door and then the thud of the newspaper hitting the mat allows her to relax again.

Harriet hasn't ventured up to the top floor of the house for many weeks now. She can't face it. She tried to be prepared and to do her best according to her mother's instructions and it has all gone horribly wrong.

She blames herself. She should never have listened to her mother and allowed her to erode her innate feeling of what was right and decent. But of course she did, and now she is left with the consequences.

None of her mistakes can be reversed.

It's easier to see things clearly now her mother has gone, although it's far too late to redeem herself. She can't put things right, can never turn back the clock. Her only option is to lock the room and stay out of it. Pretend the mistake never happened. Which is far easier said than done.

Harriet always thought she'd move out of the house when her mother passed, move to a smaller, newer property – perhaps one of those eco houses on the other side of the river.

All hopes of that crumbled when her mother's plans failed. She can't move forward, can't go back. Harriet is trapped. Trapped by the grisly contents of the locked room on the third floor.

CHAPTER 65

Present Day

The Nurse

A number of years back, Nancy read a couple of fascinating medical academic articles detailing a procedure whereby a paralysed patient, unable to move apart from a single blinking action, could begin to communicate with medical staff via the use of a letter board.

Nancy can't ask whether the hospital owns such a letter board, for fear of drawing attention to herself. She can't discuss her idea with any of the doctors either, because they're all convinced that Joanne Deacon is brain dead and it suits Nancy for their opinion to remain as such, just for a couple more days.

Firstly, Nancy needs time to coax Jo into relearning the action of blinking so that she can perform it at will. Nancy had witnessed that single blink and this is proof enough that Jo has the capability to repeat the action.

When she gets home after her shift, Nancy feeds Samson, makes herself two slices of buttered toast and a coffee and sits down with her laptop. Samson purrs and rubs against the bottom of her legs. She reaches down and scratches his ears, his warmth and loyal affection slowly easing the tension of the day from her bones.

'Sorry, buddy, you'll have to wait for your fuss tonight,' she says regretfully, booting up the laptop.

She googles 'letter boards' and finds a simple and suitable idea that will serve her purpose – at least to begin with.

She has brought home a small sheet of white card she found on the ward desk and now she proceeds to draw a clear, neat grid with the use of a black marker pen and a ruler.

Row 1: A E I O U Y
Row 2: B C D F G H J
Row 3: K L M N P Q R
Row 4: S T V W X Z

She holds the grid at arm's length and studies it.
This is it for now.
This is all she can do.

The next day, when she gets up to the ward, DI Manvers and two uniformed officers are already in Jo Deacon's room. She hovers outside the door.

'Dr Chance is in there with them,' another nurse tells her, with only mild interest. 'They want to question a patient in a vegetative state, how crazy is that?'

'I suppose they have to at least try,' Nancy says. 'There's a lot at stake.'

'Well, in my opinion, the sooner they turn her off the better,' her colleague whispers. 'As far as I'm concerned, that so-called *woman* in there is a waste of a good respirator.'

Presently, the door opens and the officers come out. Nancy nods to them and stands aside.

'Regretfully, there's very little prospect of anything changing,' Dr Chance explains. 'It's more a case of how long we leave things the way we are.'

'Do keep us informed.' DI Manvers shakes his hand. 'We'll try and track her sister down, as you suggested.'

'She only came to visit once, as far as I'm aware,' Dr Chance replies. 'There must have been some kind of mix-up when her details were taken. We've been unable to contact her since.'

They walk away down the corridor and Nancy slips into Jo's room.

'It's just me,' she says, closing the door softly behind her. 'It's Nancy.'

She walks over to the bed and leans over Jo Deacon's face.

'I'm going to be honest with you, Jo, I think you're more than just a reactive blink. I think you're still in there, that you understand everything that's being said to you.' She studies the patient's glassy eyes, the pale, slightly clammy skin. 'I want to try something. It's just between you and me. I promise I won't mention it to anyone else for now.'

Nancy wonders what, if anything, is happening inside Jo Deacon's head. Are her thought processes the same as before she had the stroke? Does she speak out loud inside her head and answer Nancy's questions? All she can do is assume that this is the case, assume Jo can hear everything she tells her.

'OK, I'm going to be straight with you, Jo. They've all written you off. You probably know that, right? If you can hear everything that's being said around you, you'll already know that things are pretty serious.'

Nancy pauses. It's important she says exactly the right thing.

'But I'm not judging you. Not yet. It's important you understand that.' Nancy glances over at the door and moves her face a little closer to Jo's. 'But I need to know the facts. I'll let you into a little secret, Jo. I've worked out a way we can communicate, you and I.'

She watches the patient's face for the slightest flicker of a reaction.

Nothing.

'I don't know if you know what happened to Evie Cotter. You had a photograph in your bag showing Evie at least a couple of years older than when she was taken from her family, so you must know something.'

Nancy pauses, watching Jo's face for a short time before she begins speaking again.

'I need you to tell me where she is, Jo,' Nancy says softly. 'Whether she is alive or dead, you have to give Toni Cotter some peace. Can you do that?'

There is no reaction.

'I've found a way for you to do it. In order for it to be able to work, you have to be able to blink. Just blink, that's all.' Nancy gives an exaggerated blink over Jo's face. 'It doesn't even have to be that big. Just a flicker will do. If you can blink, we can have a conversation. Try now, try to blink.'

Jo's face remains completely still.

No twitch, no blink, nothing.

'I want you to take all your energy to your eyes,' Nancy whispers. 'Imagine it just like lightning, channelling up from your toes, from your fingers, collecting behind your eyes. Think about your eyelids coming down like shutters. The energy is forcing them closed.'

Nancy glances at the door again.

It's just before ten and soon the cleaner will be doing the morning ward rounds, mopping the floor with disinfectant to fight the dreaded norovirus that has swept through so many hospitals in the UK in recent months.

'Just keep practising, Jo,' Nancy urges. 'Keep imagining that energy sweeping up behind your eyes. I know you've blinked before – you can do it again. You can.'

Nancy waits, talking Jo through the process again and again.

Then suddenly, it happens.

Jo blinks. Just the once.

'Brilliant, you did it!' Nancy swallows down her euphoria and tries to keep her voice level. 'You blinked, Jo! You really did it. Now try again. Try again and again until it happens.'

She watches and waits.

By the time Nancy leaves the room, Jo Deacon has blinked three times.

CHAPTER 66

Present Day

The Nurse

The following day when Nancy arrives at the ward, there are pressing staffing issues due to a stomach bug outbreak. Everyone has to accommodate additional duties, so it's nearly midday before she manages to get to Jo Deacon's room.

'OK, let's try something,' Nancy says. 'Can you blink, Jo? Just once.'

She can almost feel the intense effort emanating from the patient.

Jo blinks.

'Fantastic! Now, can you blink twice, please, Jo? Just two little blinks, if you can.'

Again there is a pause while Jo seems to gather energy, and then she blinks. Just once.

Nancy waits, staring down into the glassy, grey eyes.

A minute later, Jo blinks. Twice.

Nancy reins in her excitement. 'I'm going to ask you a really simple question,' she says evenly. 'If you can, you're going to blink twice to answer "yes" and blink once to answer "no". Here goes. Do you understand, Jo?'

Jo blinks twice. Not clear, neat blinks, more of a frail fluttering, but it's an amazing development and Nancy's heart soars with hope for Toni Cotter.

This patient is nowhere near a vegetative state following a stroke, as several doctors have diagnosed. Jo Deacon is suffering from locked-in syndrome.

Nancy has no personal experience of the condition, but, over the years, she has heard about such cases. Locked-in syndrome can completely paralyse the patient. Sometimes, the only action they're able to perform of their own accord is to blink. It's extremely rare, but Nancy is convinced that Joanne Deacon is locked in, and aware of everything happening around her.

She knows she has an ethical responsibility to inform the doctors immediately and she has every intention of doing that. Very soon.

But, ethical or not, Nancy's priority is not Joanne Deacon.

It is Evie Cotter and her family.

Nancy spends the following days dashing around the ward, fulfilling her general duties to the patients on Ward B. She keeps a close eye on Joanne Deacon's room, monitoring when the doctors visit so she can return to the patient and be assured of a little time undisturbed with her.

Jo tires very easily. After a relatively short period, she stops blinking altogether and returns to her previous unresponsive state. But over a period of two full days, Nancy had been able to establish answers to several initial questions.

'Did you abduct Evie?'

Yes.

As soon as Jo had blinked in the affirmative, Nancy was desperate to ask how and why, but of course none of these answers could be satisfied by a mere yes or no blink.

To alleviate Jo's tiredness a little, Nancy graduated to asking Jo to blink just once if Nancy said the right answer. It worked well for some questions, and this afternoon she had one particular question in mind. Nancy waits until the doctors have seen Jo and then, near the end of her shift, she takes her chance to sneak into her room once again.

'Is Evie still alive?'

Jo ignores the words 'yes' and 'no' and blinks once when Nancy gives the option 'I don't know'.

Nancy tries not to let her frustration show. How can she not know? If Jo is the person who abducted Evie, then surely she *must* know.

She picks up her homemade letter board.

'You can spell out words,' she explains. 'I will read the lines of letters very slowly and you can blink once when I say the correct one. Let's have a go.'

The process is long and laborious. Jo manages to blink a few times but the letters spell nothing. Nancy quickly realises the letter board is too much, too soon.

She feels her heart clench as Evie's innocent face floats before her mind's eye. Heat floods through her and the urge to physically shake Jo Deacon forces her to turn around and take some deep breaths until she feels calm again.

'Let's go back to yes and no answers,' she says evenly. 'Do you know where Evie is?'

No.

It's all she has time for before the end of her shift, and she doesn't want to overtire Jo. These initial questions are of the utmost importance and she has to keep Jo onside.

If she asks the right ones, then surely, even without the help of the letter board, she can help Toni Cotter begin to unlock the mystery of her missing child.

On the way home from work, Nancy makes a detour to Muriel Crescent. She knocks on the door of Toni Cotter's house and her mother, Anita, answers.

'How is she?' Nancy asks in a low voice. Anita shakes her head sadly.

Toni sits, a crumpled wreck, in the same corner of the couch as when Nancy visited three days earlier with DI Manvers.

When Nancy enters the room, Toni looks up sharply, desperate hope glimmering briefly in her eyes. Within seconds, it has fizzled out and evaporated, leaving her eyes dull and listless once more.

'I thought it might be DI Manvers with news,' she says quietly, looking down at her hands.

'I wanted to call and see how you are.' Nancy smiles. Have you heard anything from the police?'

'They're questioning people that knew Jo Deacon,' Toni says, suddenly animated. 'But she was such a loner, Nancy. No family or friends to speak of and they questioned all my work colleagues last time and didn't come up with anything.'

'You said the two of you were friendly. Didn't she tell you anything about herself?'

Toni shakes her head. 'She was always really guarded when it came to speaking about the past or about herself generally. She was more interested in me and Evie, for obvious reasons, we can see now.'

'I suppose they have to go over it all again in case anything was missed the first time,' says Nancy. 'But surely, if Jo Deacon took Evie, there should be signs of that in her home.'

'They've sent hairs and other bits off for analysis,' Toni says. 'What I want to know is, where is Evie now? What has Jo done with her if she isn't at her house?'

Nancy shivers.

She knows then what her next question to Jo Deacon must be.

The next morning, Cheryl Tong, the ward manager, stops Nancy at the desk.

'You're back on Ward C,' Cheryl says, handing her some wrongly directed mail for the other ward. 'You can go there right away.'

Nancy doesn't move. 'But why?'

Cheryl looks up sharply. 'Why what?'

'I mean, I've only just come onto Ward B. Why am I being moved already?'

Unconsciously, Nancy feels her eyes drift towards Jo Deacon's private room and she sees her manager register this.

'There's no specific reason, Nancy, just staffing logistics.' Cheryl hesitates. 'Although I have noticed you're spending a lot of time in the stroke patient's room.'

'I do what I need to do in there,' Nancy replies tersely. 'Sometimes it takes a little longer because the patient is unresponsive.'

'Well, they're moving her later today, anyway,' Cheryl says in an offhand manner. 'Can't say I'm sorry, if it's true what she did to that Cotter girl.'

'Evie,' Nancy says. 'Her name is Evie. Where are they moving her to?'

'No idea.' Cheryl busies herself with a pile of paperwork. 'You'd have to ask Dr Chance.'

'I just remembered I left my fob watch in there yesterday,' Nancy says, feeling grateful she placed it in her handbag this morning instead of pinning it to her uniform. 'I'll just get it now and then I'll get off to Ward C.'

Cheryl gives her a vague nod and moves to the other side of the admin station to take a telephone call.

Nancy enters the room. It's quiet, save for the hiss of the respirator and the particularly loud tick of the wall clock. She pads over to the bed and leans forward so Jo can see her.

'They're moving me today, Jo. They're short-staffed on another ward,' Nancy says, leaning in closer. 'I wanted to tell you that I saw Toni Cotter last night.' Nancy pauses for a moment to observe her but there is no reaction at the mention of Toni's name. 'And I have one last question for you before I go.'

Nancy takes a breath.

'Jo, do this for Toni. Was there someone else involved in the abduction of Evie? Yes? No?'

No reaction.

'Jo, please. This is so important. Does someone else know what happened to Evie? Yes? No?'

No blink.

Nancy asks the last question again and adds in 'I don't know' as an option, but still nothing.

Nancy looks over at the door. She doesn't have an excuse if Cheryl Tong comes into the room right now. She'll want to know what Nancy is saying to Jo and why she's acting strangely with a patient.

'Jo, *please*. For Toni's sake, and for little Evie, tell me. Is there someone else involved, who knows what happened to Evie, knows where she is? Yes . . .'

And Jo Deacon blinks.

'Does Toni know this person, like she knew you?'

Jo blinks.

The answer is, categorically, undeniably, *yes*.

CHAPTER 67

Present Day

The Nurse

Nancy leaves Jo Deacon's room and reports directly to her ward manager, Cheryl, who has just finished her call.

'The patient blinked,' Nancy says. 'Jo Deacon blinked.'

Cheryl's eyes widen. 'Are you sure? There's been no sign of life at all.'

'I'm certain,' Nancy says. 'She just blinked.' She can't reveal her experimental communications with Jo because it would be very dimly looked upon. A nurse taking it upon herself to use unconventional techniques on a patient when she should be busy with other duties? Trying to save a grieving mother's sanity by getting information from the patient who broke her world in two?

That wouldn't do at all.

Fortunately, on this occasion, Nancy doesn't give a toss about their ethics.

This time, when Nancy is shown into the sitting room by Anita, she is greeted by a very different Toni Cotter. She stands up as soon as Nancy appears and walks across the room to envelop her into a hug.

'Thank you,' she whispers. 'Thank you for helping me.'

'But you don't know what I'm here to tell you, yet,' Nancy says, struggling with how to break the information she'd managed to extract from a now-blinking Joanne Deacon. 'I don't even know if she's telling the truth.'

This had occurred to Nancy after she had relocated to Ward C. When she'd asked if someone else was involved in Evie's abduction, Jo hadn't responded at first. What if she was playing games? She would probably never make a full recovery, even though the blinking was a sure sign that movement was returning. Though Nancy has no intention of spelling it out for Toni, she knows that Jo Deacon will probably never face justice. She can lead Nancy to believe anything she likes. She has nothing to lose.

Anita brings steaming mugs of tea through and the three women sit, bound only by their desperation to find Evie. Nancy feels selfish even thinking what she was about to say next, but she is going to say it anyway. Just so there is no ambiguity.

'I have some news for you but I have to ask you not to repeat what I've told you or tell anyone where you got this information.' Both Toni and Anita nod solemnly. 'I could lose my job, you see. What I've done is totally unethical and talking to you about it now is breaching patient confidentiality and data protection.'

It's too late for Anita – she's so frail, like a burned-out shell – but Toni Cotter leans forward in anticipation, reminding Nancy of a small, hungry bird, quick in her movements.

Nancy hopes that what she's about to say won't disappoint her.

She outlines the communication method she has used and also gives them a short explanation of what locked-in syndrome is.

'Are you saying that she is fully compos mentis behind that dead face and body?' Toni looks horrified. 'That she's actually alive and probably laughing at us for what she's done?'

'I doubt she's laughing,' Nancy says. 'I would imagine it feels like being buried alive or locked into a transparent prison where no one can reach you.'

'Good,' Anita mutters, twisting her fingers together. 'I do hope so.'

'Through the use of blinking, Jo answered a few of my questions.'

'Go on,' Toni urges, although Nancy notices her face has drained of all colour.

'She did take Evie that day—'

Toni jumps up out of her seat. 'Why? Why would she do that? What has she done with her, where's Evie?' She begins pacing up and down the room, grasping and rubbing at her own throat. 'Where's my baby?' She releases a wail of pure grief – one that Nancy has inadvertently unleashed without the correct environment or supporting professionals to help. A knot of panic twists in her stomach. She has made a terrible mistake in thinking Toni can deal with this.

'I'm so sorry.' Nancy shakes her head and stands up. 'I should never have burdened you with this. I'll go now.'

'No, please!' Toni lurches towards her, grabbing her arm. 'Please, Nancy, don't go. It's just a shock. I want to know everything. I have to know.'

Nancy looks over at Anita and the old woman nods sadly, bowing her head. Nancy remembered how, the day she first met Anita, her hair was brown and set in soft curls. Now it is flat and dull, the colour of ashes.

'We have to deal with it,' Anita says softly, looking to her daughter and back at Nancy. 'Whatever you have to tell us, it's better than this living hell, where we've known nothing for years.'

'That's right.' Toni's grip tightens on Nancy's arm. 'Mum's right. I'll deal with it, Nancy. Whatever you tell me, I'll cope with it. I promise.'

And so Nancy tells her.

She tells her that Jo Deacon has indicated that there was another person involved in Evie's abduction, and more than that, Toni also knows this other person.

Toni sits down heavily next to her mother and Anita puts a shaking arm around her. Nancy falls quiet then, watching them entwined in a terrible shared silence.

Finally, Toni looks up and stares, not at Nancy, but through her.

Nancy can hear the hum of the refrigerator in the kitchen and the shrieks of nearby children playing outside. The ticking of a large clock on the mantelpiece reminds her of the wall clock in Jo Deacon's room. She wonders briefly if the two timepieces tick in sequence or are out of kilter.

Then, unexpectedly, Toni speaks. Nancy is surprised to hear that her voice sounds clear and calm, the panic and grief reburied for now.

'I want to thank you again, Nancy, for doing this,' she says slowly, reaching for Anita's hand. 'It means so much to me and Mum, to know we have a real friend in you. Someone who knew Evie, who is firmly on our side.'

'It's the least I could do,' Nancy says, her eyes fixed on Toni, wondering what it is about her that suddenly seems different. More focused.

They sit in silence for a few seconds.

'Has DI Manvers been in touch?' Nancy asks.

'Yes,' Toni says, trancelike. 'Nothing to report, apparently. It's like Evie was never here in the first place.'

'I'm sure he's doing everything he—'

'I don't need the detective, not now,' Toni says, a smile playing on the edges of her mouth. 'Thanks to you, I can take it from here.'

'Sorry?' Nancy frowns. Had this new information tipped her over the edge?

'I don't need DI Manvers, at least not yet.' Toni smiles, squeezing her mother's hand as though she's just discovered something she's known all along.

Nancy stares, not quite knowing what to say. Toni looks at her, her features soft and relaxed for the first time.

'You see, Nancy, I know what I have to do now.' She stands up and stares out of the window. The light is fading, but it's still bright enough to shine through Toni's sparse hair. 'It's so obvious to me.'

Nancy shakes her head, not understanding.

'I *know*.' Toni speaks slowly, emphasising the words. 'I know who the other person is that helped steal my daughter away from me. I'm going to make that person tell me where she is or I'm going to kill them.' Toni smiles. 'It's that simple.'

CHAPTER 68

Present Day

Toni

As soon as Nancy leaves the house, I ring DI Manvers.

When I move, my bones crack, my muscles strain and ache. I feel like I'm unfurling, like a seedling coming up for spring.

Evie needs me. I believe she's alive now more than ever.

The first call rings and rings and then clicks through to voicemail. I dial again. DI Manvers picks up on my third attempt.

'I need to know what's happening,' I say.

My throat feels choked by the sharpness of my words. I haven't heard from him since yesterday.

'Toni, I can assure you the investigation is ongoing,' he says smoothly, his tone implying he feels mistrusted by me. 'We're currently looking into Ms Deacon's affairs.'

Her affairs? What does that phrase actually mean? Are they dissecting her bank account? Analysing her telephone records? Investigating any recent purchases?

'This is not a fucking traffic incident, DI Manvers. When will you be trying to find my daughter?' I spit. 'When will *that* be your priority?'

'Mrs Cotter. *Toni*,' DI Manvers stammers. 'I do understand your concerns, I really do, but please trust us. We're doing everything we possibly can.'

I'm supposed to feel placated. He is prepared to say anything to calm me down and get me off the phone. I *have* to do something to make him listen.

'There's someone else involved,' I blurt out. I'm met by silence on the other end of the line.

'How do you know this?' DI Manvers's voice takes on an official tone.

I think about Nancy, the way she's helped me and Mum, placed her trust in us. I think about her job, the years she's worked to build up her career.

'What I mean to say is that there *must* be someone else involved,' I correct myself. The last thing I want to happen is for him to become distracted with Nancy's interventions at the hospital. 'Otherwise Evie would be there, at her house, wouldn't she?'

'Toni.' He sighed again. 'We have yet to be convinced that Jo Deacon actually did take Evie. These cases are rarely so clear cut, and it would be extremely unusual for a middle-aged female like Joanne Deacon to successfully abduct a child and evade detection for the last three years.'

'What about the photograph?' I press. 'She had a photograph of Evie looking much older.'

'I know that. But it could have just been a coincidence. She could have found it or been given it. I shouldn't even tell you this much, but we have forensics crawling all over Ms Deacon's flat. If there is anything to find there, you can be sure we will recover it.'

'So what are you going to do now?' I ask, my voice cracking despite my best efforts to stay calm. 'Evie could be out there, still alive. What are you doing to look for her?'

'I can't answer any more of your questions I'm afraid,' DI Manvers says, his tone regretful. 'Until Ms Deacon recovers sufficiently to be properly questioned, we can't begin a full-scale enquiry. We're in touch constantly with the hospital and they will contact us the second she shows any signs of improvement.'

'Well maybe you should check your messages,' I snap. 'Because Jo Deacon blinked this morning.'

I end the call, blood boiling in my veins and my heart splitting open. I have no hard, fast evidence, but I just feel the police have given up on us.

I think they are going through the motions of what is expected, but deep down, they truly believe that Evie is already dead.

CHAPTER 69

Present Day

The Teacher

Harriet sits in her armchair, staring at the front page of the newspaper. Specifically, she is staring at the *photograph* on the front page of the newspaper, because she knows the woman's face.

Granted, it has been a long time, but Harriet is good with faces. Her sharp memory was one of the reasons she was so good at her job. She rarely forgot the face of a parent or child once she'd had a conversation with them. People like it when you remember them. It doesn't matter what age they are, the neediness is there. From young children right along the line to very old people, everyone likes to think they're memorable, interesting enough for you to remember their name or ask how they enjoyed their birthday party, weeks after they told you the date.

So Harriet has no problem recalling the conversation she had with the woman who is now plastered all over the front page of the local newspaper. She'd had several conversations with her, in fact.

The woman had told Harriet back then that her name was Mary Short, but the tagline under the photograph quotes another name: Joanne Deacon.

It's a demeaning photograph, snapped in a hospital bed. In order to get a clear shot of her face, it looks as if someone removed her respirator, which lies discarded on the pillow next to her. No doctor would have allowed the invasion; the press must have found an underhanded way to get hold of the image.

Her grey skin tone and sightless, glassy stare remind Harriet of a dead carp she'd seen as a child on the banks of the River Trent. It had been clutched in the hands of a fat, grinning fisherman with ruddy cheeks and a wispy comb-over and, for some inexplicable reason, it had made Harriet feel desperately sad.

She scans the printed columns.

As she suspected, the article states that the photograph was leaked anonymously, that the image and details of what the woman had done were posted on social media, just before midnight yesterday. The full report is inside.

Harriet turns to page two and her breath catches in her throat. All the words, pictures and headlines scream at her, but do not make an ounce of sense. For a few moments she can neither breathe in nor out, staring at the quarter-page image in front of her.

She coughs and splutters, gulping in air. The page begins to tremble as her hands buckle beneath the tremor.

She is looking at a picture of Evie.

Harriet tries to tear her eyes away but can't. Through blurred eyes she registers the odd shocking word but is still unable to put it into context in a sentence.

Abducted . . . missing . . . alive . . . dead . . .

It says that Joanne Deacon worked with Toni Cotter at a Hucknall-based property agency. *A property agency!*

Harriet closes the newspaper and casts it aside, where it slips from the arm of her chair and onto the floor. She sits in the armchair and stares into space.

None of it makes any sense.

Mary Short – no, Joanne Deacon – had struck up a conversation with Harriet outside the school one day. Ms Deacon had flattered her, told Harriet that she had a wonderful way with the children in her care.

She said she worked as a school improvement officer with the local education authority and had been tasked with recommending outstanding staff at St Saviour's Primary.

She'd worn her ID on a lanyard, displayed around her neck. Of course, Harriet hadn't inspected it properly, that would have appeared rude.

Joanne Deacon told Harriet that her work was confidential. She'd asked Harriet not to mention her involvement to any of the other staff and Harriet had readily agreed, privately hoping her name might appear on the list of exemplary members of school staff that Joanne had explained would form part of her forthcoming report to the regional educational committee.

That had been their first conversation.

Over the next week and a half, Harriet had bumped into her in the supermarket, at the bus stop and in the chemist, where she waited patiently at the same time every Friday afternoon whilst her mother's prescription was made up.

On each occasion, they had conversed.

Harriet hadn't thought anything of it at the time, she'd been too busy revelling in someone official taking an interest in her opinions and educational ethos. Joanne Deacon had a good command of language. Harriet remembered she had this way of bringing someone around to her way of thinking, making them feel special. The woman had been so easy to trust.

One day, the two of them had begun talking about some of the children in Harriet's small library group, including Evie Cotter. Then, somehow, they had gravitated to just talking about Evie – and Joanne Deacon began to ask all sorts of questions about Evie's mother and her home life. Harriet had been frank and unguarded in her responses. After all, Miss Deacon was a professional woman herself, a highly regarded employee of Nottinghamshire County Council.

Harriet's eyes blur as she considers her naivety. She leans her head back, the tweedy firmness of the chair cushioning her skull. When she lifts her face up to the ceiling and thinks about the room on the third floor and what it holds, her heart begins to race and she grapples for a few moments with a sudden and powerful wave of nausea.

When it recedes, she tries to consolidate what has happened as simply as possible, so it is straight in her own mind.

Harriet had allowed herself to be persuaded to do something that went directly against her better judgement.

As far as she can tell, there is only one way to put it right.

CHAPTER 70

Present Day

The Teacher

Harriet has already called the hospital and established the visiting hours. She'd confidently asked which ward Joanne Deacon was on and, rather worryingly, the receptionist had happily furnished her with the details.

It has been a number of days since she had left the house, despite running low on various provisions, and it takes her a while to locate her shoes, coat and hairbrush. She opens her handbag and checks that her purse is in there, then lets herself out of the back door, ensuring it is locked behind her. A chill brushes her cheeks, but it feels fresh and clean on her skin after nearly a week stuck inside, breathing in the still air of rooms filled with dust motes that reveal themselves in the rare arrows of November sun that somehow manage to creep through the thick nets.

Harriet has found that the less she ventures out, the less she actually wants to leave the house, but in this case, it is important. She has a very good reason for making the effort.

She walks down the overgrown path at the side of the house and opens the squeaky wooden gate, automatically bracing herself, even now, for her mother's sharp instruction to 'get those hinges greased'.

But, of course, the voice doesn't come. The squeak will get worse and the wood will dampen and rot without its annual stinking preservation treatment and Harriet will enjoy watching its descent into ruin.

She pulls the gate closed behind her until it catches on the latch and turns left, to walk up to the top of the street and the bus stop. In just over a week it will be Bonfire Night. The smell of burning will carry on the air and groups of students will let off isolated bangers and rockets, scattering in the street in clouds of smoke and laughter that will chip into the stillness of Harriet's front room.

When you are a bystander to life, rather than an active player, the rota of events can be disturbing to witness. Halloween, Bonfire Night, then Christmas. New Year brings talk of holidays, spring brings Easter and then there are the long summer months before autumn once again draws near and the whole cycle begins again.

When she'd still been teaching, Harriet had liked the autumn term the best – the start of a new school year with new pupils to guide and support in her own inimitable way. After so many successful years, her career had ended very badly. She doesn't want to think about that at the moment, though. It is more important to keep focused on the task in hand.

The digitised display at the bus stop tells her the next bus will be arriving in just three minutes. This particular one will take her into the heart of the hospital's vast complex, which she knows very well due to frequent visits over the years to address her mother's countless ailments.

There is nobody else waiting. Indeed, the street is even quieter than usual.

Harriet stares across the road at the familiar Victorian villas that, on the one hand, seem very similar to her own, but on the other have been changed beyond all recognition.

The small, walled front gardens invariably contain torn, rotting bin bags that bulge with dissolving cardboard packets of cereal and empty beer cans and wine bottles. Single light bulbs illuminate sparsely furnished rooms, all of them inadequately screened behind draped sheets or paper-thin curtains that fail to meet in the middle. The student properties look cold and isolated, forgotten by the bustling lives around them. Hiding their grubby secrets like weeping sores under flimsy, inadequate dressings. No more families, huddled in front of their log burners and soft pools of elegant light, like in the old days.

Harriet turns away and watches the digital update, the glowing amber numbers ticking down to the arrival of her bus.

CHAPTER 71

Present Day

Toni

I feel so twisted up inside myself. How could I have failed to suspect her? I'd thought through the possibilities of it being a thousand people, but most of them had been strangers.

Harriet Watson had left Evie alone in the classroom that night, neglecting her for a length of time that was long enough for my daughter to be abducted. At least, that was what I'd believed, and it was what everyone else had believed, too. Most theories – and everyone was an expert – had run along similar lines.

All alone, Evie must have wandered outside, looking for me, and been whisked away into oblivion by an Eastern European trafficking gang, or a paedophile living nearby.

I haven't emerged from the tragedy as an innocent party, not by a long shot.

I am the 'uncaring bitch' who arrived late to school.

I am the 'drugged-up excuse for a mother' who relied on sedatives to get through her crippling grief.

I am the 'inadequate failure' of a woman who must not be trusted or believed under any circumstances.

But it seems so obvious, now.

Since Evie had gone, Harriet Watson has attempted to contact me many times. The police warned her off at first. For a couple of weeks she was actually a suspect in Evie's abduction. But in the end, the police were satisfied that she was merely negligent.

Everyone agreed she should never have left a five-year-old child unattended in a classroom, no matter how late a parent was to collect her.

Mr Bryce, the school caretaker, gave evidence stating that when he checked the classroom doors, Rowan Class was unlocked, including the French doors leading directly out into the unsecured grounds.

To all intents and purposes, it looked like my Evie had just walked outside looking for me and was picked up by an opportunist.

The struggling school budget did not support a CCTV system and a local football match had ensured that most people living nearby were away from the surrounding homes, supporting their local team.

The local media – which quickly gravitated to national media, and then back again, when the big newspapers lost interest – condemned Harriet Watson and specifically St Saviour's School.

But they saved their real vitriol for me. The single mother who'd been unacceptably late that day.

After the 'Find Evie' publicity had started to die down, surprisingly quickly, Harriet Watson began writing me letters. Crazy, rambling, handwritten letters where she would start by condemning my parenting skills, or lack of them, and then graduate, over a few pages, to offering me her friendship and her self-proclaimed counselling skills.

In one letter, she told me she had already begun to counsel Evie on the loss of her father, encouraging her to discuss her feelings in the group. This was apparently going to 'prepare her for her future' and 'help her grow a thick skin for when she moved up to the local comprehensive school'.

By this time, Watson had been sacked from her job by the school governors, but through DI Manvers I expressed my utmost concern at the regular and widely accepted practice of teaching assistants working with isolated groups of children.

Of course, most teaching assistants are not like Harriet Watson, but still, the opportunity was afforded to her and she gladly took it.

After I received that letter I vomited for a full day. I couldn't eat for a week. I hated myself, loathed myself. I wanted to die. I couldn't stop thinking about all those times Evie had told me how she hated school, how Miss Watson made her talk in the group when she didn't want to. She had felt uncomfortable and came to the person she trusted most in the world. Me. And I doubted her, swept her concerns aside.

Mum's gut feelings about Harriet Watson had been right all along.

I ignored all Harriet's letters from that point forward. I read them, I couldn't help myself, but I never replied and eventually they came less frequently and finally they stopped altogether.

'She's harmless enough but mad as a box of frogs.' This had been DI Manver's expert but unofficial opinion. 'And after meeting her mother, I'd say I know exactly where she gets it from.'

But she wasn't harmless.

She hurt Evie, knocked her confidence. Humiliated her in front of her peers, forced her to speak about the most personal things, such as her daddy's death. St Saviour's gave her the opportunity and power to wield over very young children who were not equipped to fight back. And for that reason, I can never forgive the school.

I hated Harriet Watson for what she did. She let Evie down.

But I'd seen a counsellor for eighteen months after Evie's abduction and she helped me see that I was accountable too. I learned how to forgive myself and to forgive Harriet Watson, too.

But I was naïve. New evidence has now come to light that someone else was involved and I am completely convinced it was Harriet Watson. It could only be her.

My rage and hatred has been born anew.

I am certain that, between them, Harriet Watson and Joanne Deacon know what happened to Evie.

I just don't know how or why they did it, yet.

I decided from the outset that I would not be involving DI Manvers in any of my planned actions. He and his team have already let Harriet Watson off the hook and have obviously completely failed to properly investigate Joanne Deacon.

I wait until it's dark outside. I dress in jeans and a charcoal-grey duffle coat with hat, scarf and gloves. I pull the hat down low over my forehead and leave the house. I turn back to the window to see Mum peering out, her face etched with concern.

It's going to kill her, what happened to Evie. If we can't find her, she will just continue to get frailer and then she'll just let go of life. We have never discussed what happened; it's odd. You don't always know how you're going to react to a sudden tragedy breaking your life into little pieces.

Mum and I will discuss whether to have egg or beans on toast for tea, or occasionally what is happening in politics, but we never talk about Evie and whether she is alive or dead. It's how we get through the horror of each long, drawn-out day.

I tell Mum, 'I need a walk to clear my head.'

But when I leave the house, I can tell she doesn't believe a word of it.

It has been a lonely three years but that's the way I wanted it. I couldn't handle people. After Evie disappeared, both Dale and Bryony sent cards and letters, and Dale had turned up with flowers on more than one occasion, but I had Mum send him away. I just couldn't do it.

I couldn't see him.

The only person I kept in touch with, and who has been a true support to me, is Tara. We never get together or meet up, we just chat on the phone. Tara, for all her own problems – her MS has grown steadily worse over the years – understands my need to withdraw and be alone. She has retreated herself since Rob died and because of her illness.

Apparently, Joanne Deacon was so upset by what happened that she immediately resigned from Gregory's and moved out of the area. And now she is lying in a hospital bed, just a shell, a husk. We have no way of accessing further information about what she did with Evie or why she did it.

But Harriet Watson knows. I just feel it.

It takes me half an hour to walk to a bus stop far enough away that I feel a little more anonymous. Frost covers the pavement like a dusting of shimmering icing sugar. Evie used to love it when it was like this. She'd wake up and look out of her bedroom curtains, declaring, 'Mummy, Jack Frost has been!'

For a few blissful seconds I can almost imagine she's with me right now. The warmth of her little hand in mine, the constant chatter and curiosity for the world around her.

My eyes prickle and the feeling quickly crumbles, leaving behind only icy fingers of grief that claw at my heart.

I've always felt . . . known . . . that Evie is still alive.

But what have they done with her?

And what possible reason could two women, both of whom knew me, have for taking my daughter?

After working through a hundred scenarios and what-ifs in my head during the short bus journey, it is all so unexpectedly simple.

I knock on the door of the house and Harriet Watson answers.

I barely recognise her. She doesn't stand but stoops, bent over like the letter C, her shoulders rounded, as if something on the inside has pulled tighter and tighter until she has given in.

Her brown, curly hair has turned white. She still wears spectacles but seems almost blind, peering closely in order to see my features.

'Toni?' she whispers.

I don't answer and she stands aside, watching me, in awe that I am actually here, in front of her, after all this time.

When I get inside the house, I screw up my nose. The air is fetid.

'It's the drains,' she says slowly. 'I'm used to it now.'

Nobody could get used to that smell, it's impossible. She must have dead rats blocking the sewers, waste must be backing up. It can't be healthy, breathing it in, but that's the least of my concerns. I'm certainly not here to advise her on hygiene.

'Please, come through,' she says, like I've arrived for a tea party.

We move into the lounge. The room is dark and smells fusty. The carpet looks as if it hasn't been vacuumed for months.

She offers me tea and I decline.

'I came to tell you that I know,' I say, watching her. 'I know everything.'

'You know everything about what, Toni?'

'I know you helped Joanne Deacon. You helped her take Evie away from me.'

'I – I didn't know who she was,' she stammers. 'Until I saw the newspaper, I didn't know she'd lied to me all that time. She asked me lots of questions, but I swear, I didn't know the reason why.'

'I just want to know where she is. Harriet, where is Evie?'

'You don't understand,' she says. 'I didn't help her take Evie, I just told her things, provided answers to questions she asked.'

'Questions like what?'

'I can't remember. I'm so sorry about what happened but I didn't do anything on purpose. I want to be your friend, I want your forgiveness.'

She's babbling, confused. Her eyes dart around as she speaks to me and she keeps looking at the ceiling. It's unnerving, but I have to remind myself I am here to find Evie and that I have to play a clever game.

And I have to remember that Harriet Watson has managed to fool the police once before. The worst thing I can do is underestimate her.

'Could I use your bathroom?' I say, standing up.

She jumps out of her own seat. 'No, I'm afraid you can't because of the drains, you see.'

'Is it OK if I just get a glass of water, then?' I change tack.

'Of course, I'll get you one.'

I follow her into the kitchen. We pass the steep, dark stairs on the right and I swear the smell is worse. I hold a tissue up to my face.

The kitchen is tidy but old and the cupboards are falling to pieces. There is a faint smell of damp. She runs the tap and fills a glass. While her back is turned, I slip a key that is hanging from a hook by the table into my pocket. It looks like a back-door key.

She turns and hands me the glass.

'I'm sorry for your loss, Toni, I am. I don't know—'

I don't answer, I just walk out of the kitchen. She rushes in front of me, shepherding me past the stinking stairs.

'Do you think we could talk?' she says, her eyes glistening. 'I'm so sorry for everything. I liked Evie, she was my favourite.'

I look at her and I think about the kitchen knife I slipped into my bag as insurance. But it's too soon. If I find out the worst about Evie, then someone is going to pay. I don't care what they do to me after that, I'll only want to die myself if I find out she's gone.

The only thing keeping me going is the feeling I am getting closer to finding Evie. The police seem to be retracing their steps, regurgitating old investigations that haven't led anywhere.

But maybe, just maybe, a different tack could work . . .

'I'll give you some time to think about things, write down what Joanne Deacon asked you. Try to remember everything you can. And I'll be back tomorrow evening to talk. It's the only way we can ever become friends again.'

'Thank you, Toni,' she says in the horribly vacant manner she now has. 'I will have a good think.'

I leave the house and walk up the street. When she can no longer see me from the window, I stand for a moment, leaning on a gate for support, gasping in fresh air.

She's hiding something.

Something terrible has happened in that house and I am going to find out what.

CHAPTER 72

Present Day

Toni

The next morning, I am up early, before Mum is even downstairs. Overnight, I'd been thinking about that smell in Harriet Watson's house. What if it turned out to be . . . I can't even think the words. Would I be strong enough to face the worst?

I close my eyes against the horror of my wild imagination.

I ring DI Manvers. To my surprise he picks up right away. I quickly tell him about visiting Harriet Watson and about the smell.

'Toni, please, I need you to listen to me very carefully,' he says firmly. 'Leave it to us. Do you understand me?'

'That's easy for you to say.' My stomach twists. 'You haven't done anything to find Evie for the last three years.'

It was unfair, I know that.

'We're doing everything we can, Toni,' he says. 'I promise you.'

'Like what?'

'I can't divulge every single action, but I will let you know if our lines of inquiry lead to new information.'

That stupid fucking jargon again.

'Is Harriet Watson a suspect?'

'Again, I'm not able to say, Toni. I'll pop over and see you tomorrow. How's that?'

I put the phone down without answering. He's taking me for a fool; underneath, he blames me, just like the media. They'll never find Evie, they're moving too slowly and they think she's already dead.

I'm not going to wait for them to help me anymore. From this moment forward, I will only rely on my own gut instincts.

'What are you playing at?' Mum demands when she comes downstairs. 'What's happening?'

'Nothing for you to worry about, Mum.'

I feel energised for the first time in years. I feel close . . . close to finding out the truth about Evie. Good or bad, I have to know.

Thirty minutes later, I am waiting at the end of Harriet Watson's street, the opposite end to the bus stop. At nine o'clock, she comes out of her gate and walks down to the bottom end of the road.

I don't wait until she's out of sight, I don't have time. Evie could be upstairs, being held prisoner in that house – or, judging by that smell, even worse.

The police haven't been round here in years. They'd believed all the lies Harriet had fed them, dismissed her as some kind of harmless loon.

I hurry through the gate and walk quickly around to the back of the house. There's quite a large garden at the back and the house itself is tall – three stories high. I slip the key I took yesterday into the back door. The lock is greased and turns easily. I open the door and step inside the kitchen.

I gag when I reach the stairs and get the first strong waft of the smell, but I have one of Mum's scented hankies in my hand

and I hold it up to my nose and breathe through my mouth. I climb the stairs up to the second floor. The smell grows stronger.

I take a quick look in the two bedrooms. The bed is unmade in the double room overlooking the road, obviously where Harriet slept last night. The other bedroom is unused; the bed has a fitted sheet on it but no quilt.

I come out of the second bedroom and look at the second set of steep stairs, which lead up to the third floor.

I press the hankie closer to my nostrils and climb the stairs quickly.

There is a small bookcase on the square landing at the top and just one other door. I try the handle and find it is locked.

The smell is unbearable. I think about going downstairs and ringing the police. But they'll only tell me to leave and wait for them outside, and I have to know.

I have to know right now if my daughter is in there.

I refuse to be apart from her for another second.

CHAPTER 73

Present Day

The Teacher

Harriet waits in the hospital reception area until five minutes before the start of visiting time. Then she joins the droves of people swarming towards the lifts and stairs. Thanks to her 'dry run' visit the day before, she knows exactly where she is going. Joanne Deacon has been moved, apparently, to a stroke recovery ward. Less intense monitoring and more accessible for visits.

When Harriet arrives at the entrance of the ward, there is already a small group of people waiting to be allowed through the secure doors. Harriet tucks in behind an old lady and her grandson. The buzzer sounds and someone pulls open the doors. Harriet looks up just as a woman strides out of the ward, busy tapping on her phone. Too busy to notice Harriet's mouth drop open as she stares at her.

It's her. The woman she'd seen Joanne Deacon talking to several times outside the school.

Harriet had completely forgotten about it until now.

There had been another woman.

As Harriet had hoped, the ward station is chaos, the nurses running to and fro or caught up talking to relatives and giving progress reports. Harriet spots a young nurse looking nervous and inexperienced, standing back from everyone else.

'I wonder if you could help me, dear.' Harriet smiles, affecting a harmless façade. 'I'm looking for my cousin, Joanne Deacon. She's just been moved here, apparently.'

The nurse smiles and glances at the clipboard in her hand, apparently pleased to be asked something she can actually help with.

'She's in her own room at the end here. It says here access is strictly for family or the police.' The nurse glances at Harriet, seemingly taking in her benign appearance and pleasant smile. Satisfied, she nods. 'I'll take you to her.'

Harriet takes full advantage of the short journey across the main ward.

'I understand she can't move. Paralysed, they told me,' Harriet says, remembering what the newspaper article had relayed.

'Oh, haven't they told you? Your cousin blinked at a nurse. It's the first sign that her movement is returning.' She smiles at Harriet. 'The doctors have moved her here for recovery now they know she isn't in a vegetative state as they first assumed.'

The young woman seems completely unaware of the controversy surrounding Joanne Deacon or the recent newspaper coverage. Harriet can't believe her luck, the ease of access she's been given to such a high-profile patient.

How long such access might last is another matter, though, thinks Harriet. She can reasonably expect intervention from a senior member of staff very soon, once they realise the young nurse's mistake.

She enters the room. It's quiet, away from the busy drag of the main ward.

Harriet walks over to the bed and hovers above Joanne Deacon's face. The patient is pasty, marked by red welts left here and there by the respirator's different positions. Puffy and slightly swollen, her features look different to how Harriet remembers.

'Remember me?' Harriet says, staring down at the staring, unmoving eyes.

Joanne Deacon blinks. Twice.

'They say you're beginning to recover. Even though you did the most terrible thing, you're getting better.'

The eyes stare up at her. Harriet glances at the door and looks back down.

'You lied to me. You made a fool of me. I lost my job and my reputation.' Harriet picks up a pillow from the chair at the side of the bed. Joanne Deacon blinks again. 'It's time to pay for what you did.'

Harriet reaches for the respirator mask and pulls hard.

CHAPTER 74

Present Day

Toni

The door at the top of Harriet's third-floor stairs might be locked but it seems quite flimsy. If I kick hard at it, I might be able to break it down. I'm just about to try that when I hear a noise downstairs. I freeze and listen.

Is Harriet back already?

I hear a banging, then a crashing noise as something is knocked over. I creep back down the stairs and wait on the second-floor landing. I think I hear a whispered voice but I'm not sure. I thought I'd locked the back door behind me . . . but now I can't remember.

'Hello, Toni,' a woman's voice says clearly. It sounds familiar.

I move to the top of the stairs. My eyes widen. I begin to descend the stairs, unable to process who I'm seeing, how this makes sense.

'Tara?'

There is a man with her. 'What are you doing here, I mean . . .'

She looks strong, healthy. Her fair hair is long and dark now. The expression on her face is . . . strange.

'Come downstairs, Toni,' she says. 'We've something important to tell you.'

I begin the descent. 'How did you get in here? How did you know where to find me?'

'We've been watching you,' says the man, smiling. 'For weeks.'

I follow them down to the ground floor, too confused to ask anything. When I finally reach the bottom of the stairs, my heart thudding so hard it makes me feel faint, he steamrollers me into the living room and closes the door behind the three of us. He stands, arms folded, blocking my exit.

'What are you doing?' I turn to my friend. 'Tara, what's happening here?'

'They've found her, Toni. They've found Evie.'

I stagger back and hold on to the edge of the rough, worn wing of one of Harriet's armchairs.

'They've found her?' I say faintly. 'Is she . . .'

'I suppose I should say that we let them find her. I've had my fun, but yes, she's fine. She's a delightful girl and you don't deserve her, you never have. She needs a decent family who'll take care of her.'

I feel dizzy. Sick.

'I don't understand . . .'

'I've had Evie, all this time,' Tara says lightly. 'We've kept her in a little cottage in the remote Highlands. She's a delight. You neglected her, and you made it so easy for me to take her.'

I rub my forehead, trying to understand. '*You've* had Evie all this time? But why?'

Our telephone conversations echo in my mind. All the tears we'd shed together about our husbands, about Evie.

'Why should you get to make a fresh start in life when it was *your* husband who killed mine? I lost my baby too, you know.'

'Yes, I know that, Tara. I'm so sorry for your loss, but—'

'But nothing. I didn't hear from you for months and months. God, this place stinks.'

'I was grieving, just like you! I sent you a card and—'

'A card? A fucking *card* for the loss of my husband and un-born child?' Her eyes grow wild. The man touches her arm and she takes a deep breath. 'I got to thinking, how can you get revenge on a dead man who ruined your life?' She smiles to herself. 'And the answer came to me. By taking his only child. Phil and I can't have children so I got to thinking it's like beautiful poetic justice, almost.'

She has a manic, crazed look about her.

I turn to the man. He's tall and broad, athletic looking, but his eyes are cold.

'I worked with Andrew, I was there that night he led us off the cliff.' He holds up a mangled hand. 'Some of us challenged his directions, but he was a stubborn bastard, wasn't having it. Fortunately, I came off fairly unscathed. Apart from losing my career, that is.'

'But Tara, your health, you said—'

'You're so gullible. I was never ill, never had MS. I just needed a reason not to visit you. I loved our telephone calls, when you'd tell me how awful your life was. And then to listen to your suffering after I took her, well, that was pure heaven. You were so selfish, all you wanted to talk about was your own pain.'

'You're sick, I mean really sick in the head.'

'Maybe. But I'm clever. I've been watching you for a long time. We watched you and followed you here.' She turns to Phil. 'Can't you open a window or something? It's making me retch in here.'

He doesn't respond.

'Watching me?' I repeat.

'You're clueless. I watched you from across the road in a house I rented in Muriel Crescent. I even followed you to work. We followed you here. Watching you, watching Evie. Phil took all your photo albums and Evie's birth certificate from your bedroom so we had evidence she was ours if we needed it. You were so out of it, you never even realised anything was missing.'

I think about that day I'd entered my bedroom and just felt inexplicably that something was wrong. The bin bags full of stuff had been open but I thought it was just my imagination.

'Phil's a military man, an expert. He documents every detail so there are no mistakes.' She turns to him and smiles, in her stride now. 'He even planned your mother's demise. That was a stroke of genius, as it turned out.'

I think about Mum's distress about her accident on the stairs. How she thought she was losing her mind.

'I was waiting for my chance, I just didn't know how I'd do it. You getting the Gregory's job was perfect, Joanne Deacon was a gift. On the verge of bankruptcy and desperate for cash, she gave me a way in. In time, I knew your routines better than you did. We wanted your interfering mother off the scene and that's why Phil planned the accident, but, as it happened, you made such a mess of everything that the incident led to our chance to take Evie.'

'I thought Jo was my friend.' I have to say it out loud, to make it count for something.

'You're a bad judge of character then,' Tara sniggers. 'Although she did start to get cold feet once she'd taken her. I think she actually believed us when we said we were just teaching you a temporary lesson, that we'd return Evie to you. We had to snatch her back from Jo pretty quickly, she seemed to think Evie belonged to her.'

'Evie,' I whisper. 'I want to see her.'

'She's safe. I'll tell you that as my parting gift. But you can't see her; you'll never see her again. Just like I never got to see my baby. You see, Phil here is quite the expert at making death look like a beautiful accident.'

'Tara, why? Why do all this now?'

'Because this ending is just perfect. They've got Evie back, so the heat is off us, but I've got you. So, you see, you'll never get to see each other. Two lives ruined for the price of one.'

'You'll never get away with it, not now you've come back.'

'I wouldn't be so sure. They haven't found us so far. We had to practically deliver little Evie right into their hands, they're so incompetent.'

'So why did you bring her back?'

'Things were hotting up. Haven't you seen the national newspapers this morning? That stupid bitch Jo Deacon, getting herself a nice little paralysing syndrome instead of just dying when she had the stroke.' Her face contorted. 'They're interested again, the police will be stepping up their inquiries. I've got my revenge, now I'm ready to start a new life and there's just one last thing to do.'

Phil takes a step towards me.

'Joanne Deacon will never make a full recovery, even if she has blinked. I've been to the hospital, spoken to the doctors. We always used fake names with Evie, told her we were her aunt and uncle. She loves us, won't betray us, because she knows nothing. Police resources won't stretch to a national manhunt for a child that's returned unharmed.'

She hands Phil a bottle.

'Make her a nice cup of tea, Phil, and put plenty of this in.' She smiles at me. 'It's time to end it all, Toni.'

'I don't understand why you—'

'That's just it. You never tried to understand my pain, you were so involved in your own suffering.'

'Tara, I couldn't function, *please*. Let's just talk about what happened, about Evie.'

'None of your clever tricks,' she snaps, as Phil comes back into the room. 'We're not here to talk. You can either drink this or I'll force you. It'll only take a few sips.'

She takes the mug from him and he holds my arms behind my back in a lock. My back arches, my face tips back. She pours the tea and I seal my mouth shut as the burning fluid scorches my skin.

Her fingernails dig into my lips, trying to prise them open. I knock my head from side to side so she can't get the mug near me. I'm vaguely aware of a shadow coming from behind her when suddenly her face explodes forward, blood and bits of flesh everywhere.

My arms are released and I stagger forward, tripping over Tara's body and falling to the floor. I look up to see Harriet Watson smashing a hammer into Phil's arm, then his already mangled hand, crushing it completely.

He throws his head back and screams and Harriet smashes the hammer into his face. He falls to the floor. She hits him again on the skull as he falls and then she turns to me, the hammer raised.

I cower, holding up my hand uselessly as protection.

'Shall we have a cup of tea now the unpleasantness is out of the way, Toni?' she asks, calmly. 'Then I'll show you where the smell is coming from.'

CHAPTER 75

Present Day

Toni

I sit, dazed, on the couch, staring at the bodies of Tara and Phil. In films, people who look dead suddenly jump up and start throttling people again. But these two don't look like they're getting up any time soon.

Was Tara telling the truth? Is Evie still alive?

I breathe in and out. Harriet's right, you get used to the smell.

I can hear Harriet pottering around in the kitchen. She really is making tea. Everything seems so ordinary, but I can't move.

I hear the back kitchen door smash open, hear yelling, shouting. Suddenly, the room is flooded with uniforms and I feel myself being led away, outside into the fresh air.

I look up into the face of DI Manvers.

'Toni, are you OK? Did she hurt you?'

'You were right,' I say quietly. 'She's harmless. Just mad as a box of frogs.'

'I was wrong.' He shakes his head. 'She's murdered Joanne Deacon. Suffocated her in her hospital bed.'

I receive the news, understand it. I don't feel anything.

'Toni, look at me.'

I do.

'We have her. We have Evie.'

The world stops turning.

'She's fine,' he says softly. 'She's not hurt, she knows she's coming home.'

I begin to softly sob. 'Have they hurt her, is she hurt?'

'Evie has been well cared for.'

'It's true,' I say faintly, feeling woozy.

'We're going to take you home now to pack an overnight bag and then you're going to see your daughter.'

'Thank you,' I hear myself say. 'I'll be fine.'

'Wait, please!' Harriet Watson shouts, breaking away from the police officers trying to restrain her and rushing into the room. 'I want to show Toni the smell. I want you to see it's not Evie. I would never hurt Evie.'

DI Manvers gives his grudging permission for Harriet to lead us upstairs. As we move upwards, the smell grows stronger.

'Jeez, I'm gonna throw up,' I hear one of the officers say. 'I know this smell, it's not going to be pretty.'

We wait at the bottom of the second flight of stairs while Harriet and DI Manvers climbed to the top.

'I want her to see,' Harriet says.

DI Manvers nods and I follow them up.

Harriet produces a key from her pocket and inserts it into the door. She pushes it open and we stagger back from the stench. Bluebottles buzz frantically at the window, more than I've ever seen in my life. The officers at the bottom of the stairs clutch their noses.

'It's Mother,' Harriet says softly. 'You see, she refuses to come downstairs when she's nursing Darcy.'

Much later, on the way to the unit, DI Manvers explains a few things.

'Darcy was Harriet's sister, born before Harriet. She died from cot death when she was just six months old. The old woman kept the baby swaddled and wrapped in a bottom drawer all those years. Even when they moved, Darcy went with them.'

I shudder. Harriet's rotting mother had been sitting in a rocking chair, nursing the skeleton of a baby. It's a sight I'll never forget.

'She'd lost her mind, plagued Harriet to get the room prepared so she could nurse her baby. Then she refused to come out. One morning, Harriet found her dead in the chair and . . .' He shakes his head. 'Inexplicably, she just left her there.'

He also tells me that Dale Gregory has been in touch. He'd seen the newspaper reports about Jo Deacon. When she'd resigned and they cleared her filing cabinet, Dale had discovered my 'lost' purse buried in there.

'Apparently he'd called at your house with flowers and to tell you about the purse because they'd all blamed you at the time, for being careless. But when you weren't able to speak to him, he decided not to burden you with the knowledge, with everything else you were dealing with. It didn't seem that important back then.'

I don't know what to say. I remember Mum turning Dale away at the door during the weeks, even months, when I just felt incapable of facing anyone.

Jo must have taken the purse for the cash in there but also to make me look scatty and disorganised. As if that would count against me when Evie went missing.

But I swiftly push all thoughts of that from my mind. I can only think about one thing, and that's the little girl I lost, who is inside the low concrete building in front of us.

'I know all this is hard to take in. And I know Harriet Watson left Evie unattended and allowed her to be abducted, but I just wanted you to know something – she's the reason Evie is back with us today.'

I look at him.

'She recognised Tara Bowen at the hospital. Said she'd seen her in a photograph in your lounge and you'd said it was your friend, Tara. But when Harriet asked, a nurse said the woman was Joanne Deacon's sister so Harriet told her she thought it was an imposter. The hospital panicked and contacted us.'

I let his words sink in.

'Unfortunately, in the process of doing so, taking their attention off Harriet Watson. We began making inquiries as to Tara Bowen's whereabouts and suddenly Evie is left outside a doctor's surgery.'

The realisation that Tara had been discovered just by chance made me shiver.

'Please thank her for me,' I say, realising how crazy things have become that I am actually thanking Harriet Watson.

CHAPTER 76

Present Day

Toni

She sits in a cream-painted room on a beanbag. The carpet is azure, like the sea, and her hair is brown. She is big, bigger than before, and her face has changed, though the essence of her shines through. She is assembling some kind of building with Lego bricks.

The bricks aren't large and brightly coloured anymore. They are small and technical and the building looks like something you might see in an architect's office.

She looks up as we enter the room and our eyes meet.

I smile and she stares back.

The psychologist, Sarah, pulls out two chairs and we sit down. I remember my conversation with Sarah, about how important it is not to rush things. Not to approach her or touch her. Everything must come from Evie. She must not feel overwhelmed.

'It's going to be a very long road for her,' Sarah said before we came in here. 'We don't know how she'll react or if she's formed emotional bonds with her abductors.'

After a few minutes of silence, Sarah nods at me.

'Hello, Evie,' I say.

'Hello,' she replies.

We look at each other.

'What are you making there? It looks complicated.'

She looks at the building and then back at me. She stands up and walks over to me, but stays a step or two back.

'I used to dream about you, sometimes,' she says. 'Your hair has changed. And your eyes. Your eyes are different now.'

'You've changed too, you're even more beautiful,' I say.

She turns without replying and walks back to the beanbag.

We sit in silence a while longer, watching Evie click together the bricks. Then she turns to me again and sighs.

'When can we go home?' she asks.

A LETTER FROM K.L. SLATER

Thank you so much for reading *Blink*, my second psychological thriller.

The story was inspired by several different news stories I've seen over the years about missing or abducted children. I became fascinated by how the public and press are almost more interested in how parental error may have contributed to events than in debating the actual issue of by whom the child has been taken.

I got to thinking about how easy it might be for someone, if they were so inclined, to take advantage of a parent in a bad place. Perhaps a single, grieving parent, someone who is struggling with everyday life.

At times, we all make decisions that we later regret. But what if those decisions lead to a nightmarish outcome that can't be reversed? How do you cope with tragedy but also the crippling guilt accompanying it? *Blink* is the story that grew from there.

The book is set in Nottinghamshire, the place I was born and have lived in all my life. Local readers should be aware I sometimes take the liberty of changing street names or geographical details to suit the story.

I know you hear this a lot, but reviews are so massively important to authors. If you've enjoyed *Blink* and could spare just a few minutes to write a short review to say so, I would so appreciate that.

You can also connect with me via my website, on Facebook or on Twitter. And If you'd like to be kept up-to-date with news of my next book, please sign up to my newsletter (see below). We promise we won't bombard you with anything else

I am now writing my third psychological thriller. It's troubling and tense with a creeping sense of dread . . . I think you're going to like it!!

Best wishes,

Kim x

www.bookouture.com/category/k-l-slater/

 KimLSlaterAuthor/

 KimLSlater

www.KLSlaterAuthor.com

ACKNOWLEDGMENTS

Firstly, huge thanks to Lydia Vassar-Smith, my editor, for her expertise and guidance during the editing process. Thanks to ALL the Bookouture team for everything they do, especially Lauren Finger and Kim Nash.

Enormous thanks as always to my agent, Clare Wallace, who continues to be such a valuable support to me, even on her maternity leave!

Thanks also to the rest of the hardworking team at Darley Anderson Literary, TV and Film Agency, especially Mary Darby and Emma Winter, who work so hard to get my books out into the big, wide world, and to Naomi Perry, Kristina Egan and Rosanna Bellingham.

Massive thanks as always go to my husband, Mac, for his love and support and for taking care of everything so I have the time to write. To my daughter, Francesca, and to Mama, who are always there to support and encourage me in my writing. To my stepsons, Nathan and Jake, and to our daughter-in-law, Helen, who loyally reads everything I write. To Dad, who always asks how things are going.

Special thanks must also go to Henry Steadman who has managed to do it yet again, designing a mind-blowing cover for *Blink*.

Thank you to the bloggers and reviewers who did so much to help make my debut thriller, *Safe With Me*, a success. Thank you to everyone who has taken the time to post a positive review online or taken part in my blog tour. It is noticed and much appreciated.